Acclaim for

ELITE

"*The Matrix* meets *Divergent* in this sensational dystopian novel! Every suspense-filled chapter kept me on the edge of my seat wondering if Flick would survive or be caught. I barely ate or slept for two days as I consumed this book and the end left me yearning for the next installment. Easily the best young adult novel I have read this year!"

— MORGAN L. BUSSE, award-winning author of
the Ravenwood Saga and Skyworld series

"A gripping, unpredictable journey that keeps you guessing, never knowing who to trust. *Elite* unravels the eerie world of the Love Collective and delivers the perfect heroine you can't help but root for. In this second installment of the Collective Underground series, Young paints a beautiful allegory of hope and love persevering through tangled darkness."

— SANDRA FERNANDEZ RHOADS, author of
the Colliding Line series

"Another strong, compelling narrative from Young with great characters and just enough tension to keep the pages turning even though I really needed to sleep. Apprentice Flick must figure out who to trust... and who not to, as she navigates through her world which has been completely turned upside down. A great next installment in the Collective Underground series."

— CECILY ANNE PATERSON, author of *Invisible*

ELITE

ELITE

COLLECTIVE UNDERGROUND | BOOK TWO

KRISTEN YOUNG

Elite
Copyright © 2021 by Kristen Young

Published by Enclave Publishing, an imprint of Oasis Family Media.

Phoenix, Arizona, USA.
www.enclavepublishing.com

All rights reserved. No part of this publication may be reproduced, digitally stored, or transmitted in any form without written permission from Oasis Family Media.

This is a work of fiction. Names, characters, places, and incidents are products of the author's imagination or are used fictitiously. Any similarity to actual people, organizations, and/or events is purely coincidental.

ISBN: 978-1-62184-191-3 (hardback)
ISBN: 978-1-62184-193-7 (printed softcover)
ISBN: 978-1-62184-192-0 (ebook)

Cover design by Kirk DouPonce, www.DogEaredDesign.com
Typesetting by Jamie Foley, www.JamieFoley.com

Printed in the United States of America.

For J, S & C.
Love you lots.

1

By the river waters
We sat down and wept
Yearning for Lyric's country.
—Song of the Exodus, Fragment 1.1

MY NAME IS KERR FLICK. OR CADENCE. OR . . . something. I don't know. A month ago, if anyone told me that my Dorm Leader would be offering to break the law for me, I would have laughed. No—worse than that. I probably would have reported them for losing their minds.

But that was before.

Before the Filtering exam.

Before my best friend became an alien.

Before I discovered that I'm not actually Kerr Flick at all.

On all the infotab entertainment streams, you always get some kind of warning about bad things ahead. Ominous music builds. The shadows lengthen onscreen. The hero walks down the darkening street while the camera flicks to the nightmare waiting around the corner.

All I got was a cold, grey concrete bunker and a rush of unwanted memory.

"My mother was a Hater . . ."

Like a starving waif I snatched at Akela's solution before

I could think. Would I have jumped so quickly to retrieve my memory if I'd known what I would find? Would it have made a difference if I knew what was going to happen next?

"DON'T DO THIS IF YOU'RE NOT READY," Hodge says.

I straighten, and my back makes squeaking noises against the ancient vinyl. "I have to."

He moves closer to the treatment chair, hovering near my feet. "Everything is going to change."

"Then change it."

The halo fits around my head like a snug helmet. A smell of dust and damp concrete tickles at my nose. I lift my hand up against my nostrils to stop the sneeze from erupting, and Dorm Leader Akela's face comes into view.

"You okay?" she says, brows furrowed.

"I'm . . . ah, ahhh . . . fine." I wrinkle my nose and gulp back the reflex. "Dust. Makes me . . . ah . . . ACHOO!"

"We'll get the cleaners in next week." Wil's deadpan expression glows from the light of the console at the other end of the room.

Everything here looks like someone went for a coffee fifty years ago and never came back. The battered old filing cabinet sits in one corner, a single drawer hanging out. Posters peel away from the walls. Old plastic instruments line shelves, discolored and forgotten. It's way different to the sterile infirmary of Elite Academy that lies somewhere above our heads. This forgotten bunker, a relic of the old wars against hate, has hidden under Elite Academy for years. For the hundredth time, I wonder how I got myself into this predicament.

"The Hater is me."

Oh yeah. That's how. My best friend was Realigned and reported me as a Hater like it meant nothing to her. Then, just when I thought I was headed for discipline, it turned out that Elite Academy's Dorm Leader was part of some underground resistance, and instead of arresting me, she gave me the chance to fix my memory.

Now I'm lying in a defunct bunker with a halo around my head, ready to be solved like a math problem.

"All set to go," Wil says, his hands falling away from the keyboard. His grin is wide and handsome, and when his eyes rest on mine, I feel an unwelcome flush of heat along my cheeks. I force my glance away, not wanting to let him see that he affected me. But I catch his smirk from the corner of my eye. He knows.

"Last chance, Cadence. Are you sure this is what you want?" Akela asks. When it finally sinks in that Cadence is me, I blink. Turn my head around to get a better view of Dorm Leader's face.

"I need to know who I was." The echoes of my single recovered memory float back into my mind: Screaming. Boots running down the hall. Terror as they ripped me out of my mother's arms. There is something important just beyond my reach, memories just waiting for me if I could only get access to them.

Dorm Leader swivels in her chair. The rusting wheels squeak against the concrete until she comes to stop beside my head. Her face has that "don't mess with me" look that makes so many Apprentices quake in their boots.

"I'm not sure you understand exactly how much this will change things," she says.

"It will change everything. I know. I want to see my parents."

"What if you learn things that you didn't want to know?"

"At least I'll know the truth."

She regards me. "You may begin to doubt everything you've been taught."

"Only Haters doubt the Love Collective." I grin, reciting the Hater Recognition Signs I'd known for years. But it doesn't have the effect I was hoping for. Dorm Leader's frown deepens, and she shoots a look at Hodge.

"You're not ready." Dorm Leader reaches up toward my head as if to remove the halo. I jerk my head away, reaching up to clamp the small plastic headset in place.

"I'm ready. Do it." I grit my teeth.

Dorm Leader pats my elbow. "I don't think so. We'll try in a few weeks when—"

"No. Let her do it," Wil urges. "We'll just keep her down here until she's okay to go back up. Teach her how to handle the memories. She'll be great. You'll see."

"Wil, I've been doing this for longer than you've been alive. I've learned the hard way that it's better to be cautious than to rush this step." She reaches up to my head again, but I just clamp the halo down harder.

"I promise I won't say anything," I beg. "Please."

She stares at me, an invisible war being fought behind her expression. I put all my pleading into my eyes.

"Please."

For the longest time I'm sure she is going to take me out of there. But then she nods to Wil. He lets out a whoop of joy.

"Whoo! Okay, Cadence. Get ready to meet your family again!" With a few taps on his console keyboard, the halo begins to hum over my forehead. I only have a split second to feel nervous before my world fades to black.

THE FIRST THING I FEEL IS PAIN. THEN COMES wave upon wave of nausea bubbling up through my stomach. I fight back the urge to vomit, and a rush of memory flies at me like a thousand infotab streams playing all at once: Sounds. Smells. Lights. Faces. Rooms and places that were completely new and totally familiar all at once.

I try to concentrate on one thing at a time: The feel of warm fabric against my skin. The smile at the corner of Mumma's mouth. The smell of food cooking over the stove, warm and inviting. But the onslaught is too great. I am drowning in a flood of history, leaving me gasping for breath.

—

MEMORY DATE: UNKNOWN

Memory location: My bedroom. Home.

My fingers are chubby and small. They reach up eagerly for the soft toy bear that Dadda holds out, snatching it away from him. Ted feels soft and warm against my face. I breathe in his fur, and the smell fills me with joy. When I laugh, the sound is small and childish.

"Lyric loves you, Cadence. Do you know that?" Dadda's smile spreads across his face, and his deep brown eyes twinkle at me. "He loves you even more than Ted."

"Where is Lyric, Dadda?"

"In his country. One day we'll get to see him, Composer will it."

I snuggle closer to Ted, wondering if Lyric's country will smell like home too.

MEMORY DATE: UNKNOWN

Memory location: Kitchen. Home.

Mumma stands beside the stove. The wooden spoon in her hand turns slow circles in the pot. She stares into the distance, her eyes red with spent tears. I run in to the kitchen toward her, holding my little paper bird.

"Mumma! Mumma! See? I made something for you!"

Mumma's face changes as she snaps out of her reverie. A sad smile creases her face, and she quickly wipes at her eyes.

"That's beautiful, sweetie." Her voice cracks.

She wraps me in a hug. Her arms tighten around my shoulders, and soon her whole body is shaking with sobs. Her tears dampen my T-shirt.

—

MEMORY DATE: UNKNOWN

Memory location: Lounge room. Home.

The lounge room is warm, thanks to the fireplace crackling away in the corner. I sit on a cushion near the fire, watching the Sirens slowly filter into the room. Their smiles are wide. Nobody speaks.

After half an hour, the room is full. Mumma enters and nods to everyone that the doors are safely locked. On Dadda's signal, two of the men begin humming a low bass note. Other women and men begin to sing, and sweet harmonies flow over the bass like a river over the bedrock. The voices swell, and then Dadda begins the Song.

"In the beginning was the Lyric . . ." he sings in a voice that is strong and warm.

The whole group repeats each line after Dadda. Their tune is so sweet it makes me want to cry. As the song continues, harmonies weave around the melody like an intricate tapestry. I am caught in a wave of song, carried out of the room into an infinite reality, to the Composer's own presence. I listen and smile. I am home, here with the Sirens and Lyric's good news. No matter what happens outside our house, inside we are safe and loved.

"And the Lyric was with the Composer,
"And the Lyric was the Composer.
"He was with the Composer in the beginning . . ."
A warm, secure sense of peace falls over us all.

—

MEMORY DATE: UNKNOWN

Memory location: Kitchen. Home.

Dadda sits across the table from me, his face smiling and earnest.

"You are doing so well, sweetie. You remember all the words already! Let's try the tune to that one again."

"Lyric and the sad man?"

"That's the one."

"I know how it goes, Dadda. Up here." *I tap my forehead.* "So why can't I get the notes right?"

"It takes time, Cadence. Your head knows the words, which is the most important thing. But your mouth and your throat need to practice how to make the proper notes. Watch me again, okay?"

"Okay, Dadda."

He begins to hum, using his hand to show me the pitch. I eagerly copy his sounds, letting the words flow from my mouth. Dadda nods encouragement as I go.

"That's it, Cadence. You're going to be the most amazing Songbook one day."

—

MEMORY DATE: CE 2273.247 (8 YEARS AGO)
Memory location: Nursery Dorm 492, assembly hall.

Up on the giant screen, a Love Squad soldier raises his baton and brings it down with deadly force on the back of Hater One. She falls to the ground, and the crowd lets out a wild whoop and cheer. A small drip of blood splatters on the ground beside her head.

The wild and raucous cheer echoes around the concrete walls of our assembly room. I raise my hands in the air with my friends and yell along with them. Then the cheer stutters into confused silence. Against all expectations, Hater One raises herself from the ground with slow, pained determination. The Apprentices around me begin to boo and hiss.

Hater One stands and faces the Love Squad soldier. Her Hater mask has broken, and my mother's face swings into view, marred by blood and bruises. She mouths words that cannot be heard above the jeering audience. A trickle of blood runs down her neck as the jeering resolves into an unrelenting chant:

"Vote her off! Vote her off!"

My fingers flutter to the infotab sitting in my lap.

EVERY MEMORY IS A STRING OF BARBED wire, lacerating my emotions. Unable to stop the flow of my forgotten years I cry out. The pressure builds until my head feels like it is exploding in unbearable light, then as quickly as it comes, everything dissolves into black nothingness.

VOICES FILTER INTO MY HEARING BEFORE I can open my eyes. A soft, tinny tune plays somewhere in the distance.

"Will she live?" I recognize that deep, gentle voice from somewhere. It's someone tall, with olive skin and a scar on their face like . . .

"You've seen this before, Hodge. You know she'll get through it." Another guy speaks. His voice is more playful and confident, and not as deep. He's the guy with piercing green eyes and a face that could easily be an infotab stream idol.

"It's perfectly normal. Maybe a little long, but that's to be expected from someone with Cadence's . . . gift." Whoever is speaking now has a calm, gentle voice. It's a voice I've heard before, if only I could get through this mind fog to find the memory. I try to open my eyes, but they're welded shut for some reason. The tinny music keeps on playing, a soft, crackling soundtrack behind the chaos. I feel as if I should know the tune, but my brain's normal recall system seems to be broken.

"She's been out for three days. That's longer than anyone I've seen before," says the deep voice. Hodge, that's his name. My bunk room leader. Scar down his left cheek. He sounds like he's standing a few feet away.

"Stop bothering Akela, Hodge. If she says this is normal, then it's normal."

"No problem, Wil. Oh wait. How many three-day recoveries have you seen again?" Hodge sounds sarcastic now.

"What does it matter? Everyone upstairs thinks she's in

Watcher isolation anyway. This just helps our cover story." Wil keeps that bright, confident tone in his voice.

"The girl is unconscious, and all you can think about is the revolution."

"One of us has to."

"Boys, let her rest." The woman's calm voice has a note of exasperation in it this time.

"Fine." The response is in unison.

I try to cut into the conversation again, but my mouth won't move. Footsteps shuffle around me, and then there's a gentle pressure across my forehead. The plastic halo shifts a little, and there's an answering beep from somewhere across the room. Inside my head, the music hiccups, then continues its winding song.

"Anything yet?" Akela's fingers brush across my forehead as she asks.

"There's an uptick in the waveform, so she should be coming back up soon."

"Good."

A soft groan escapes from my lips. The tinny music stutters. My mother's face is there, her sad smile replaced with a horrific, bloody mask. I try to run away from the memory, but all I manage to do is turn my head slightly to the left. Her death mask remains, mocking me.

"Cadence?" Akela asks outside my head somewhere.

"Mmm," I mumble, still trying to flee from the unwanted mental image.

"Can you speak?"

"Mm-yah." My mouth feels like it's full of cotton. Dry and stuck together.

"See, Hodge? Nothing to worry about." Wil's bright, chirpy voice lifts my spirits a little.

Hodge sounds unconvinced. "I'll relax later," he says. "When she can say actual words."

With a huge effort, I blink away the sleepy haze from my

eyes. The bunker treatment room slowly comes into focus. Three concerned faces watch me from various spots in the room. Akela is closest, hovering over my head. Near the door, Wil peers at me from behind the ancient console. Hodge is leaning against the rusty filing cabinet, his arms folded and a stern scowl on his face. His expression softens when he catches me looking at him.

"You took your time."

I try to sit up, feeling a dozy kind of ache around my temple. My cheeks are wet and my eyes feel as dry as sandpaper. But that memory of my mother refuses to fade. Every time I blink, she's there again.

"Don't move just yet," Akela warns. "We need to make sure you're stable before we get you out of there."

Ignoring her, I continue to struggle to sit. The ache in my head grows and throbs with a persistent, uncomfortable rhythm. I go to put my head in my hands, but the plastic halo presses uncomfortably against my skull.

I moan.

"Lie down, idiot," Wil says. I ignore him.

"I must look awful," I finally speak, lifting my head back up with effort. "Sorry."

"Don't be sorry." Hodge is looking straight into my eyes.

"This isn't your fault," Akela assures me.

Wil crosses his arms and leans back in his chair. "None of us looked like model material when we were in your place. Believe me." I know he is lying. I'm willing to bet my infotab he's never had a bad hair day in his life.

Akela presses a cup into my fingers, and I drink. The water tastes metallic and stale, but it quenches my thirst. My lips are cracked and dry. I look up into Akela's face, and the image of my mother finally disappears. In its place, a long-forgotten memory floats gracefully back into my mind.

"Hello, Lyra," I say.

Akela's eyes fill with tears.

Remember your Composer in the days of your youth,
   before the days of trouble come . . .
   —Song of the Exodus, Fragment 2.5

A SMALL DRAFT OF COLD, STALE AIR SIGHS around my ankles, and I wrap my hands around my shoulders to try and keep warm. It's like a fridge in this dining hall. The Elite Academy Dorm Leader now sits across the table from me, her eyes fixed on my face with wary patience. I rest my elbows on the steel surface in front of me and let the goosebumps prickle along my arms. Cold seeps up into my uniform from the hard steel chair under my legs.

"Lyra," I say again. My voice is hoarse.

"I haven't used that name in . . ." Akela's eyes are moist. She leans across the table. How much do you remember?"

"All of it."

MEMORY DATE: UNKNOWN
   Memory location: Home

Long after my bedtime, Mumma lets someone into our lounge room with lots of shushing. I want to know why they were shushing so much. So I tiptoe to the edge of the stairs and lean my head around the banister. Mumma is talking to the someone who has come to visit.

"We can't just leave everyone. Not when you all need us," Mumma says.

"An . . ." The other lady's quiet voice.

"I know what you're going to say, Lyra. But my mind is made up."

"An, please. You need to listen. Octavo is . . . is beyond my help now. I have tried, but I can't do anything to get him back. But I can help you." The lady sounds insistent.

"You've already helped. We have this safe house because of you."

"It's only temporary, An. The Collective will find this place eventually, and then what?"

"Lyra, I am not going to desert you."

"If you head for Lyric's country, you're not deserting us. You're saving us. It's only a matter of time before Octavo crumbles under his Embracement, and they'll be pounding down this door in the middle of the night. And mine. And everyone else in our group."

"That's why we moved the meeting space. I can't tell them what I don't know."

"You know enough, An."

"They can't make me say anything."

There's a shuffling sound. "You have no idea what they can do, An. What they will do."

"The Composer will protect us." Mumma's voice is firm.

"Yes. Your eternal home is safe in the Composer's care. But presently the Love Squads are arresting people. They are disappearing. It's too dangerous to stay. Our safest option is to get you out of the Collective altogether. The Exodus—"

"Lyra, you risk your life every day in that place. I won't leave you. I won't be a coward."

"Then think of Cadence."

Mumma's voice goes super quiet then. At the bottom of the steps, I peek around the corner. Mumma and the other woman sit on our lounge. The lady has short dark hair. She wears the same clothes as the scary Collective people.

Fearful, I gasp and step backward. The bottom stair catches my ankle, and I fall with a thumping noise. The talking stops. As fast as I can, I bound back up the stairs to my hiding place. I'm scared that I'm in trouble. But Mumma just comes and puts me back to bed. She holds me for a long time. She sings Lyric's songs until I fall asleep.

Next morning, I ask about Lyra, but Mumma just shakes her head.

"You were having a dream, sweetie," is all she says.

I know the difference between a dream and a memory. I just don't know why she won't tell me.

AKELA'S FACE PALES. "I'M SORRY. I TRIED—"

"Why didn't you tell me?" I ask.

There is a slight pause. "It's complicated."

Anger rises like heat to my face. "No. No, it's not complicated at all. All you had to say was, 'Kerr, I knew you before.' Nothing more than that. I would have understood."

"I didn't lie. Cadence, you don't understand—"

"That's Kerr Flick. Elite Apprentice."

Akela looks at me silently for a moment. "All the more reason why it's not safe to tell you anything."

"But it's perfectly safe to make me remember how I killed my own mother." My voice cracks.

Akela's lips press into a firm line. "You didn't kill her."

"My finger pressed that vote button. How did she go from our house to being executed on a Collective broadcast, anyway?" My voice is rising. "Did you report her?"

Akela seems shocked. "Of course not."

"Someone did." My head slumps down onto my arms. Akela sighs.

"It's natural to feel overwhelmed at first Cadence." She touches my arm. "Receiving your old memories is always a shock."

"Octavo is . . . is beyond my help now."

Mumma says we should hide and not make any noise.

"An, please . . ."

"I'm not going to desert you."

"Lyric's country is over the far horizon, sweetie."

"Cadence!"

"This is not . . . overwhelming." I can't find the word. "This is . . . something else. So many . . ."

Memories keep tumbling around in my head, piercing me with their vivid clarity. It's like I have a new set of tattoos now. Invisible tattoos that nobody except me can see.

"I thought knowing would be better." I swallow, staring at the incomplete black bars on my wrist that mark me as an Elite Apprentice.

Akela tilts her head a little. "It won't always be this bad."

"I voted my own mother off the Pavilion Show. I thought I could get rid of all of that, but . . . but now the memories are all there and . . . and . . ." I break off. The words don't leave my mouth, but they still fly around in my head: *I'm a murderer.*

Akela waits patiently for me, letting the silence spread out as I cry. My nose begins to run, and I wipe feebly at it with my sleeve, looking around me for a tissue. All I can see is sterile concrete and steel. With a sudden burst of emotion, I push myself up and away from the table. My chair clatters to the floor with metallic echoes.

"I have to get out of here," I gasp, groping toward the door. Akela stands and moves to block me.

"You will. You'll get back outside soon. But right now you're too—"

"Need air." Panic is like a hand grasping my throat. I snatch at the fabric near my neck, feeling strangled. My legs feel shaky, but I push forward toward the door.

"Sit." The command in Akela's voice is strong, and I'm still accustomed to years of Nursery Dorm training that molded me into an obedient drone. Almost against my will my legs buckle, and I land back down on a metal chair with a thud. In the sternness of Akela's face, I see exactly how she could rise to be the Elite Academy leader. I feel my body become unnaturally still.

"This is normal. The panic is normal." She emphasizes every word. "It will recede in time. But you cannot go anywhere until we make sure you're going to be safe."

"You're going to keep me in this prison?" I squeak. The thought of being stuck here with nothing but my memories sends my heart into panicked thumps again.

"Your gift means this initial step is even harder for you than anyone. It will take time to adjust and be at peace with your life before and after the Nursery Dorm abduction. I can't let you leave here until I know for certain that you're ready."

"But . . . but . . ."

She places firm hands on my shoulders. "Cadence—"

"Don't call me that!" My eruption causes Akela to strengthen her hold.

"Listen. There are lives more than just yours at stake right now. Sending you up there could lead to the deaths of some pretty special people."

I scowl. "As if I would tell anyone."

"In your current state, you wouldn't have to say a word. Someone like Fuschious would sniff you out and have you Realigned before you could blink. Trust me."

I stare at her. "So I just have to stay here."

"It won't be for long. A few days, maybe a week. How long you need to stay here is up to you."

I slump against the icy metal of my chair, arms folded. Breathe in. Breathe out. I know she's right, but it feels awful to have to say it.

I nod.

Akela's grip relaxes a little. "It will be okay."

"How do you know?" The tears begin to prickle at the corner of my eyes again.

"I have every confidence you will survive," Akela tells me. "Others have."

"How many?" I really want to know.

"Enough," she says briskly. "Look, Hodge will be here with some food soon. With a full stomach, you'll start to feel a little better."

I open my mouth to tell her that there's no way I'd keep any food down in my churning stomach right now, but I don't get the chance. Two sets of footsteps pound down the hallway, and shortly after that, my two bodyguards stroll into the room. Hodge is carrying a football-sized package, and Wil holds something small, thin, and black above his head.

"Got it!" he cries triumphantly as the two reach our sitting place.

"Ah, good," Akela says, nodding in my direction. Wil holds his hand out to me, and a thin silicone band falls into my palm.

"My fitness tracker? But what . . ."

"Your new fitness tracker," Wil gives me an exaggerated wink and a knowing tap to the side of his nose.

"This tracker has a few mods to keep you safe," Akela lets me know.

"Mods? But why?"

Wil counts off reasons on his fingers.

"One: when you approach the bunker entrance, this tracker will begin a random loop. On the Watcher system, you'll look like you go for a run around the obstacle course, then back to your room for a shower and sleep. The tracker will sense you coming out of the bunker again, and come out to meet you where the cameras start coverage. Two: the tracker sends distress signals to the right people in case of emergency."

"And three," Hodge adds, "the tracker will let you know when to check your Siren app."

I nod silently, fitting the silicone band around my left wrist, already thinking through ways to ignore all of the alerts. If they ever let me out of this underground nightmare, I'm pretty sure all I'll want to do is put this whole thing behind me and never return. I don't even want to know about the Siren app, whatever that is.

Wil pulls an infotab from his pocket and squeezes it. He places the small white rectangle into my hands, and the screen whirls into life. I flick the globe around, not sure what I'm looking for.

"Here." Wil stretches over me to flick the globe to the entertainment app. He points to a blank space in between the Triumph replay and Elite Lover Force Six reruns. I stare at where he's pointing, confused.

"What?"

"Swipe like this," he says.

As I watch, he draws a spiral with his index finger. The empty space widens, and a picture glows into place that looks suspiciously like the Hater's Pavilion crowd. Wil taps on the picture three times, and a small dialogue box appears.

"This is your Siren message app," Wil explains, entering a passcode. "When your tracker alerts you, find somewhere away from the cameras to check your message here."

"Your bunk is safest," Hodge informs me. "You just need to keep the screen angled away from that bathroom camera."

I nod though my head is in a spin. "This is all so weird."

"You'll get used to it," says Wil. "It's not possible to accidentally open this app, and it always times out if you don't use it for twenty seconds."

"There's a hidden chip built into the infotab's motherboard," Hodge adds. "If you're wearing a modified fitness tracker, the app will install itself during the device boot sequence. The LC App doesn't even know it's there."

"Oh."

"It's still important that you never use Collective names on this, you understand?" Akela's tone carries a load of warning. I nod, though I don't think I'll ever use the messaging app anyway. She continues on, "I've given you access to some of your textbooks. Keep your mind busy while you're down here so it won't be such a shock when you go back upstairs."

Hodge thrusts the football-sized package he'd been holding into my arms; a package of food wrapped in a small cotton towel.

I look up at him, feeling guilty. "I can't eat this."

"It's okay. Save it for later." His smile is encouraging. "Protein cereal lasts forever anyway."

"Uh . . . thanks."

A dull ache begins to throb behind my eyes. I press the heel of my hand against my forehead, trying to stave off yet another headache.

"You need rest," Akela says, concerned.

"But I only just woke up," I protest, even as the room starts to lose focus. I'm dimly aware of Wil being pushed aside as the larger, more solid presence moves to my side.

"Come on," Hodge says gruffly. "Back to barracks for a bit."

I want to argue, but it's suddenly too difficult to move my mouth. All I can manage is a tiny moan as Hodge lifts me into his arms and carries me from the room.

3

The Composer is my father,
Lyric's country is my home.
Every day is one day nearer.
—Song of the Exodus, Fragment 2.1

FOR DAYS I WANDER THE HALLS OF THE underground bunker like a ghost. Akela doesn't appear at all, but Hodge checks in with me every day, bringing packages of food and brief rundowns of life above my head. Wil only arrives once, breezing in to the dining hall with a dazzling smile and promises of fun to come. But even he never offers to let me out.

Memory haunts me. Every waking moment is filled with mental images of my mother. Her smile is warm and loving. Her speech is gentle and kind, which only serves to drive the knife of guilt deeper into my heart.

MEMORY DATE: UNKNOWN
 Memory location: Kitchen
 Mumma hands me a plate of sandwiches, cut into little hearts.
 "Enjoy your lunch, sweetie," she says, cheeks dimpling.

MEMORY DATE: UNKNOWN
Memory location: Bedroom
Mumma's weight sinks into the mattress beside me. She begins to sing softly.
"Composer's light be with you
In the darkest shades of night,
Composer's peace go before you
As you battle hatred's fight,
Composer's love within you
From Lyric's breath to send the Muse,
You are beloved, child of Lyric,
Let him lead where he will choose."

BEFORE LONG, MY EARLIEST MEMORIES become a blazing fire, burning away at my sanity. They battle against my Nursery Dorm education, eating away everything I thought I knew like embers consuming paper. By the end of each day, my head is a spinning whirl of confusion and anxiety.

I am Kerr Flick, Elite Apprentice. But I also used to be a small girl called Cadence. I had a mother and a father. A home. They were arrested as Haters, so I should be glad they're gone. But my memories of them are unlike anything my Hater Recognition Signs taught me to fear. There was no chaos in the way they treated me. No doubt or rebellion. Only quiet, caring words and hugs.

Lots of hugs. Like a starving refugee panting for food, I realize with longing how much I missed the gentle physical touch of my family. The ache gnaws at me every day. But even worse than the longing for connection is the music. Whenever I'm awake it runs through the back of my thoughts, a constant and unsettling soundtrack. It sings to me like an invitation, urging my footsteps toward an unknown destination.

Covering my ears doesn't work. The music just goes on playing, weaving itself through my newfound memories. It feels as if there are answers somewhere in them, but I can never organize the fragments well enough to find anything that makes sense.

"I have loved you," says the Composer.

Composer? Who on earth is that?

"Before you were born, I knew you."

"The Muse speaks our groans to him, when words cannot be found."

"Never ending is Lyric's love for us, never failing, always strong."

Lyric. Composer. Muse. Fragmented mentions in overheard conversations.

When I try to sift through the garbage heap that is my recovered memories, I end up with a sore head. It's as if the Collective built a dam to hold back my early life, and now memories rush at me like a wall of water, drowning me in a torrent of recollections every time I try to think. There's too much.

A week after I first wake up, Akela calls me into the dusty old office decorated to look like her real one. The painted scenery seems to mock me with its fake promises of sunshine.

"How are you feeling?" She is watching me carefully.

I shrug, staring at my hands.

"Have the memories settled down yet?" she asks.

My mouth twists. I bite back a response and shrug again. Akela doesn't speak, and when I look up at her she is evaluating me studiously.

"You're not ready," she declares.

My eyes widen in shock. "What? How can you say that?"

"It's written all over your face, Cadence. You're still an open book. I know you want to get out of here, but you would just walk straight into a Collective trap."

"I wouldn't say anything, I promise. I—"

Akela stands. "Like I said before, you wouldn't have to. And in case you've forgotten, Fuschious is out there looking for a chance to take you down—and all of us with you. I'll get Wil to come and help you out in a day or two, but—"

The protest bursts out of my mouth. "You can't keep me here like a prisoner!"

"I'm sorry you feel like a prisoner. But I can't let you hurt yourself or others."

"It's not fair!"

"It's not forever."

I rage. Akela answers every shout with words of quiet strength. When rage turns to tears, she listens stoically. When tears turn to pleading, her steely resolve never wavers.

"You cannot leave yet," she repeats for what feels like the hundredth time.

I'm so angry, I spit memory-evoked words at my Dorm Leader, not understanding half of what I'm shouting.

Akela's expression hardens. "Are you aware that Executive Crucible wants to personally oversee your education?"

That stops me. My mouth opens and closes like a caught fish. "W-why would he . . . ?"

"He thinks you would make an 'interesting project' as a Watcher. His words, not mine."

All the blood drains from my face. "A . . . a *Watcher*? But I failed the Filtering exam."

"Apparently you didn't." Akela's nod is curt, but her expression softens. "I am not trying to ruin your life, Cadence. The stakes are much higher than you realize." With a graceful sweep of her hand, she walks toward the exit.

AKELA LEAVES ME WITH MY GUILT FOR TWO weeks. Then one day Wil arrives with a smile warm as sunshine. He takes me to Akela's bunker office and sits me down on one of the old vinyl chairs in front of the desk.

"Here," he says, dropping a tiny scrap of paper into my hand. I unroll it carefully, squinting to read the minuscule type:

> Crucible determined to make you a Watcher. Can't hold him off any longer. One more week, then get ready.

Incensed, I screw the paper into a tiny ball and hurl it as far away from me as I can. Wil just watches me from where he's leaning against Akela's desk. I glare at him until my anger subsides.

"What's her deal?"

Wil's face dimples. "You gotta understand, Flick. She's been doing this for longer than you've been alive. She's not going to let some untrained rookie burn her whole enterprise down just because the rookie wants to see trees."

I let out a deep sigh, leaning my elbows forward on my knees. "I wouldn't 'burn her whole enterprise down.' I don't even know what her enterprise is," I mutter.

"Wait. I thought you got your memories back." Wil's eyes narrow in suspicion.

"I did. But there's too much. I'm so busy reliving dinners of ramen and playing with toys that I can't work out what's important. Five years of nearly full recall is a lot to work through, you know."

"You really are amazing." Wil sounds impressed. Something in his voice makes me wish I could impress him more.

"So help me," I plead. "Explain what is going on so I can understand. Because right now, I just want to run away."

He raises a skeptical eyebrow at me.

"I won't tell anyone, Wil." I put my hand to my chest. "Promise."

His dimpled, lopsided smile makes me all too aware of how unkempt I must look in my weeks-old uniform.

"If I tell you, you owe me." He grins.

I roll my eyes. "Fine. Just help me."

"You may regret that later," Wil says, his cheeks dimpling again.

"Whatever." I put on a mask of a bravado I don't feel.

Wil walks back to the floor-to-ceiling bookshelf and pulls out a small leather volume. He brings it toward me, face suddenly serious. "You remember the history lessons on the wars against hate, don't you?"

I nod. "Haters rising against the government to bring down life as we know it. Bombs, all that stuff. Collective swooping in to save us from certain destruction," I say, hundreds of lessons playing through my head.

Wil hands over the book, which turns out to be a photo album. I turn the pages slowly, feeling my heart jump into my throat. As soon as they swing into view, the faded nightmarish images impale themselves into my memory. The low, rolling nausea begins, and I close my eyes. I can't take it anymore.

"The history lessons weren't telling you the whole truth," Wil says. I open my eyes. He nods at the album in my hands.

I stop beside a page containing only two large photographs. On the left, a smiling group of people sit in front of a weird old building. A vaguely familiar sign hangs above their heads. The group standing beneath it look peaceful and happy.

My breath catches. In the right-hand image, the Love Collective–branded bulldozer is caught by the camera in the middle of tearing down the weird-looking building. In the foreground of the building, a line of bodies is neatly arranged beneath white shrouds, their heads still visible.

I gulp. After a steady diet of Haters' Pavilion Shows, I should be used to the sight of blood and damage by now. But I've never seen anything on this scale before.

"It's . . ." My voice trails off into nothingness. No words can describe what I feel right now.

I flick through the album, seeing more "before and after" images of other groups and buildings. In all of them, the familiar tree image lies in various states of disrepair, dragged from rooftops, facades and roadside signs into piles of refuse and rubble.

"I know this," I say suddenly, pointing. "That's . . ."

"Lyric's tree." Wil nods. "The Sirens were branded a Hater Organization, and every member was assigned for immediate Embracement."

"The group my parents were a part of? They must have done something pretty bad."

Wil looks at me quizzically. "Not really."

"How were they dangerous?"

"They wouldn't bow to Supreme Lover Midgate."

I look at the pictures again. "But why wouldn't they? It would have been easier."

Wil doesn't answer straight away, and I catch a conflicted shadow at the corner of his expression.

"Yeah . . . well . . . never mind." His eyes shift. "If you believe Akela, it was a nightmare for everyone at the time. The Sirens stepped up to tell the Collective to stop killing people. The Collective tried to force them to swear oaths of absolute allegiance. When they wouldn't swear the oath, the squads moved in."

"That's horrible!" I exclaim.

"That's why Akela started her mission," Wil says soberly.

I imagine Akela watching while all of this death happened

around her. What must it have been like? How afraid she must have been, watching her friends losing everything. I begin to feel ashamed for the things I've said to her.

"What did she do?" my voice is almost a whisper.

"She was a government official before the Love Squads rolled in, and she used her position to rescue children."

I thought of her with my mother. "What about the adults?"

"The Sirens who survived either disappeared or went underground. Heaps of them left in something called the Exodus. Only a tiny handful stayed to work under the Collective. They created the reversal procedure to help us get our memories back and managed to salvage a bunch of other stuff. But . . ." He trails off.

"What?"

"Caught. All except Akela."

A shudder goes through me. "Oh." I slowly close the photo album, unwilling to let any more nightmares plague my memory. "I guess I can see why she's so cautious, then."

The photo album suddenly feels too heavy, as if I'm carrying the weight of the souls captured in the pictures. I take it back to the shelf. In my head, the ghosts of smiling faces chase me around, morphing into the hideous specters of their final photos.

"Crucible wants me to be a Watcher." I shudder, clasping my upper arms and rubbing them against the cold seeping in to my bones.

"Really?" Wil's voice sounds far too bright and chirpy for such news.

I glare at him. "You're *liking* this?"

He quirks a smile. "You could make the cameras look the other way."

"What good would that do?"

He looks over my head. "The Love Squad won't arrest people they can't see."

"Oh."

"You're finally getting it."

"Well, I still don't like it." I stare at the floor, clutching my hands together. It feels wrong to be so disloyal to Akela when she's just given me my memories back. "But I'll get over it, I guess."

"Don't," Wil says, the word brimming with intensity.

"What?" Startled, I stare straight into Wil's earnest gaze.

"Akela might want you to get over it and move on, but don't," he says, leaning down until his face is only inches away.

My heart begins to race. He drops his voice to a tantalizing whisper. "You're more useful that way."

Confused, I lean back and push my chair a few inches away from him.

"Akela's idea of rescue is to help you remember the Sirens and Lyric and the Composer," he continues. "That's it. She can't see the bigger opportunity we have to make *real* change."

"I don't get it."

"You will. Just remember: you owe me." Wil's smile has a slightly mocking edge to it this time. "One day I will call in that favor."

Against my will, I feel a rush of excitement at his words. "What did you have in mind?"

Instead of replying, he reaches out and places his hand over mine. My body is instantly on fire at the warmth of his touch. It's the physical connection I haven't felt in years. "I can't tell you yet," he says quietly. "Just promise me one thing."

"What?" I say, leaning toward him.

He gives my hand a gentle squeeze. "You can't tell anyone about this. Okay?"

I nod and smile. At this moment, I would happily do anything Wil asks as long as he keeps looking at me the way he's looking now.

The road to becoming a Watcher in Training is notoriously difficult. This is a truth known and accepted by all. It is hard enough to achieve entrance to Elite Academy, and then only the best of the Elite Apprentices pass the Filtering exam. You may therefore be growing smug, living as you are at the peak of Elite success.

Do not flatter yourself.

Few pass into the Watcher training program. But fewer still make it all the way to the hallowed Hall of Love. So do not fall into the deception that you are somehow superior to your fellow Apprentices, or that you are something worthy of adulation. You have merely begun the path of becoming nothing at all.

(Elite Watcher Training Manual, 51st edition, page 3)

MY EYES FLUTTER OPEN. HE IS STANDING before me once more. The darkened sleeping quarters form a stark contrast to his appearance. Where everything around us is drab grey and black, his coat is a color that shines brighter than my eyes can stand. His face is the same as I remember—loving and kind.

Am I dreaming? Last time I saw this man I was on a

train, heading for Elite Academy. Back then I thought I was going crazy.

"Who . . . who are you?" I ask, even though somewhere deep down I already know.

"I am Lyric," he replies. He smiles and holds out his hand toward me, and I feel an overwhelming urge to run toward him. But something holds me back. My clothes feel shabby and soiled. My head is swimming.

"I-I don't . . ." I stammer. "I can't make sense of anything. These memories—"

I clasp my ears, feeling the familiar streak of pain across my temple as memories battle for my attention. They splinter into razor-sharp fragments, piercing me with guilt.

Mumma says we should be quiet. But I want to go out.

"Kill the Hater!"

Dadda hasn't come home. Mumma won't stop crying.

"The Composer will keep us, my darling," Mumma says, wiping at her face. "In the darkest valleys, Lyric sends the Muse to be with us."

Boots echo down the hall. My screams split the night as the Squad drags me out of the closet hiding place. I am kicking and spitting like a cornered animal, scratching at anything I can. But their grip is too strong, and I cannot escape their arms.

I am lying in a sterile treatment room. There are people moving around, strapping things to my arms and feet. I want them to go away, but I cannot move my legs. Not even my mouth will do what I tell it to do. My heart screams but nobody can hear me.

In the distance, a haunting melody swells, off-key and mournful. As the memories continue to jostle through my mind, the melody follows them like a soundtrack. That time when I played with Dadda in the park? Behind the memory, the soundtrack echoes the birds in the trees, the sighing wind and the deeper satisfied laughter from my father. But my tearful tantrum brings brokenness into the symphony, and it veers out of tune. That memory of Mumma stirring food in the kitchen? A solemn and quiet song hums along, the peaceful melody interrupted by my jarring, discordant entrance. Each time, joyful songs are ruined by my presence. My life is a series of dropped notes. I break the melody every time I appear.

Tears begin to flow down my face.

"Cast your cares on me," Lyric says, and I long to reach out for him. But, again, a knife-sharp memory cuts into my thoughts.

The infotab in my lap glows. On the screen, the Haters' Pavilion Show app shines with options. Who am I going to vote for? Who is the worst of the contestants tonight?

It's a no-brainer. Hater One is the worst. Get rid of her.

I smile in satisfaction as Carell Hummer makes the announcement. The crowd roars.

"I can't," I say, squeezing the dream from my head in a wave of guilt and shame.

TO STOP MYSELF FROM THINKING unpleasant thoughts, I begin to replay the memory of Wil in Akela's office over and over. With no one around to stop me I drink in his every expression. His face is imprinted in my mind. The slender but firm set of his shoulders. The way his hair is shaped perfectly around the top of his head. His eyes—pools of green so deep I could sink into them forever. And the touch of his fingers over mine . . .

Each time I sit back to replay the memory, a small voice of warning sings music into my heart: *Cadence, do not do this.*

Each time, I push the small voice away. I know I should be paying more attention to my dream. I know I should be preparing to be a good and obedient Elite Apprentice again, but I can't. Or won't. Nobody has ever paid attention to me the way Wil did in that office. The way he looked at me sent a raging fire through my whole being, burning away any desire other than the deep need to see his face again.

My sleep is fitful and full of strange new dreams that I could never admit in public. The once-strong axiom *Elites don't fraternize* grows weaker than a whisper, thanks to the destructive force of my imagination.

In the morning, I am drawn back to the secret office. Although the secret door through the bookshelf is locked, I hover in the hallway like a stalker. Wil's memory seems more vivid here: the way he leaned toward me. The mystery of his words and the way his eyes danced as he . . .

Cadence, do not . . .

A distant clank sends a shiver of anticipation through me. Muffled through the walls of Akela's room, I hear a metallic sound and determined footsteps.

"Wil's here." A silly grin spreads across my face. My frizzy dark hair is probably sitting up around my face like a halo. With sweaty, slightly trembling palms, I make a feeble attempt to smooth it down.

The muffled footsteps grow louder. I take a few steps back from the door, heart racing. As the door starts to creak open, I step away, wanting to get a little more space between me and the entrance.

"What are you doing here?" Hodge stares at me in bewilderment, another cloth-covered bundle his hands. His bulky figure fills the doorway.

"I was just . . . I mean . . ." I flounder, trying to think of a reasonable excuse. No way would I ever tell him the truth. Elites show no weakness, after all. Between Hodge and Wil, Hodge is the last person I want to speak to right now.

"Never mind," Hodge says. "Come into the dining hall. I've got something for you."

I follow him down the winding corridor toward the room

of steel tables where he invites me to sit. I do so, still mute with disappointment.

Hodge sets his package on the table beside me. "Akela's getting ready for you to get back into the Academy, so she can't come for a few days," he explains. "But you're getting out soon."

"That's a relief." Curiosity nips at me. "What does she need to do?"

He shrugs a shoulder. "Who knows? There are a lot of things she won't tell me. But that's safer. The less we know, the less we can betray if something goes wrong, eh?" His thick fingers struggle with the tight knot of cloth. I bite back an impatient desire to take over for him.

"I brought you something nicer for lunch," he says, loosening the cloth around the bundle. He gives a half smile. "And a present. You must be bored by now. Here."

Hodge pushes a small white rectangle toward me. The device is small enough to fit in my palm and wrapped in a thin white cord with two strangely shaped bulbs at the end.

"What is this?"

"Try to figure it out," Hodge says.

I unwrap the cord and disentangle the bulbs. One end of the cord disappears into a slot on the device. The bulbs dangle and twirl around each other when I hold them up in the air. Seeing my confusion, Hodge reaches forward to grasp the bulbs between his fingers.

"Put them in your ears," he instructs, showing me how they fit. I follow his example, and the little bulbs rest snugly against my head. Hodge taps a small button on the side of the rectangle, and a screen glows into life. He touches a small circle marked "music," and through the bulbs, my ears flood with melody. My eyes widen.

"I remember this tune," I exclaim. I am suddenly choked with emotion.

Hodge's smile widens. "It's the Song. Or a fragment, anyway.

Usually Akela gives this to every new Siren at their induction, but she thought you should have it before then. Do you like it?"

I don't reply, unable to speak.

"We have to learn the music by heart and give the device back," Hodge tells me. "It's more valuable than a hundred Love Cities. If they caught you with this, you'd be dead straight away. So normally you only get to listen to it while we're with you, but Akela decided to make an exception in your case."

Awed, I turn over the tiny device in my hand. Through the tinny earbuds, music continues to dance into my mind.

> In the beginning was the Lyric,
> And the Lyric was with the Composer,
> And the Lyric was the Composer.
> He was with the Composer in the beginning . . .

"Dadda sang this song," I murmur. "And Mumma."

As the music continues, the image of Mumma's face transforms, and she is back to wearing the Haterman mask in the Pavilion, her smile gone and her cheeks lined with blood and dirt. The invasive memory drowns out the recorded music with a new tune: off-key, out of rhythm, so broken and discordant it taints everything.

"Get it away," I cry. I rip the earbuds out of my ears and throw the device across the room. It glides away under the dining tables until I can't see it anymore.

"What did you do that for?" Hodge says, startled as he leaps after the device.

A vise of panic squeezes my chest, and I clutch at my uniform, willing more air into my lungs. Before I can think, I am running out of the dining hall.

"Cadence! Wait!" Hodge calls.

But panicked and guilt-stricken, I sprint to my room and barricade the door behind me. The song from the recording continues to sing in my memory, its gentle invitation biting and puncturing my heart until I feel as if I am bleeding all over the floor.

I sink down against the wall, hands over my ears. I shut my eyes tightly, blocking out the harsh LED light from the ceiling. But nothing stops the music. Nothing can hold back the constant reminder of what I have done. The song can only taunt me with the love and comfort I won't ever experience. Love I am too unworthy to experience ever again.

"Murderer . . . murderer," my voice whispers at me over and over. The words twist themselves into the music, dragging the melody off-key with broken harmonies and lost notes. I only heard a brief snippet of the tune, but that's enough. It replays over and over for hours. All I can do is cry.

5

Invisibility is a necessary function of our privileged position. Were we to be seen by the general community, familiarity would make us contemptible. It is hard to fear something when it is in the same food queues each day. By hiding ourselves from the citizenry, we become something greater than our individual parts. We approach the status of mythical beast, ever-seeing and all-knowing, present in the hidden places and active at all times. That is why they fear us. They fear us because invisibility renders us worthy of fear.
   (Elite Watcher Training Manual, 51st edition, page 18)

ALONE AGAIN, NOT EVEN THE MEMORIES OF Wil help me to avoid the accusing mental barrage. The music player incident has ruined that strategy. Sometimes I hear a musical phrase and I'm instantly back in that long-forgotten house, surrounded by people.

—

MEMORY DATE: UNKNOWN
   Memory location: Lounge room. Home.

Someone arrived with a rare treat tonight, and the smell of coffee now fills the room. Mumma managed to find a batch of sugar and flour at the markets, too, so her sweetcooks add to the delicious scents tickling my nose.

Dadda waits for the conversation to slow and then gives a small nod. A hum swells from the men, answered by a gentle harmony from some of the women in the room. Dadda begins tonight's Song.

When the song finishes, Dadda speaks,

"We will need to move the meeting location," he announces. A few people nod.

"But the Exodus..." a small woman with red hair sitting near me speaks hesitantly.

"Not until we have finished our work here," a man beside her counters. "We can't join the Exodus until we're done."

The memory is so vivid now that I can still feel Mumma's arms wrapped around my chest. But her embrace doesn't comfort me. Instead, her arms become like beams of iron, strangling me with the guilt of what I did to her.

By day, I high-step alone around the dining hall, practicing my loyalty chants and march formations. The echoes of my solo voice and footsteps just add to the black cloud of emotion weighing me down. But I keep going until I am exhausted. Only when I have marched for hours can I get a few hours of fitful sleep each night. But even then strains of broken melody swoop to attack my dreams like Love Squad drones on a riot of Haters.

IT'S IN THE DUSTY OLD CLINIC ROOM WHERE Akela finally gives me my freedom. But not before I endure a few grueling hours of interrogation and drills.

"Name?" queries Akela for the hundredth time.

"Kerr Flick. Elite Apprentice #540/187503."

"Cadence!"

I pretend to look busy, ignoring the instinct to look up at the sound of my old name.

"That was no good. You flinched," Akela says with a shake. "Again," she barks. "Name?"

"Kerr Flick. Elite Apprentice #540/187503."

"Where have you been?"

"Watcher training sector. They accepted me into the program after all."

"So why didn't we see you at meals?"

"Training drills. It's hard work being a Watcher. I'm not allowed out until I pass my assessments."

"Cadence!"

She peppers questions at me with rapid-fire precision, and I battle to answer them until they become so rote I don't have to think about how to answer anymore. After my voice has become weak from the constant speaking, Akela gives a small nod.

"You're ready."

Relief floods through me.

"I know it's been a rough time for you." Akela gives me a look of sympathy. "But I'd much rather be too cautious than dead."

Right now I only want to know one thing. "When can I go?"

"As soon as Hodge arrives to escort you."

"But I answered everything right, and I know the way."

Akela eyes me, then smiles. "It's always good to have some backup. Get yourself washed up, and we'll take it from there."

She hands me some linen, which turns out to be a brand-new uniform. A vivid indigo band is embroidered around the collar, indicating my special status as Watcher in Training. Holding the uniform close, I skip back to the shower rooms and tidy myself up.

When I emerge, hair freshly washed and still damp, Hodge

is waiting in the hall. He gives me an approving nod. "Let's get the show going."

As we march to the exit. Hodge towers above me as always but keeps his steps in time with mine. I take a quick glance at his face and wonder why the scar on his cheek used to intimidate me.

"I can't believe she's sending me to Watcher training," I say. Our footsteps echo on the concrete floor.

Hodge nods. "You've done well."

I glance at the walls of the bunker, feeling a tiny flicker of insecurity. "What if I fail again?"

"You won't."

"I wish I had your confidence."

Hodge stops marching and faces me. "Don't do that to yourself." His brown eyes search my face. "As long as you remember that the Composer is with you, you'll be fine."

The flicker of my insecurity grows insistent. "What if I'm not good enough?"

"You *are* good enough."

I am shocked at the intensity of his little speech.

He must notice the expression on my face and takes a breath. "You know what I mean."

I'm not sure I do, but I manage a halfhearted assent. "Okay."

I feel lighter as we arrive at Akela's office. I feel lighter still when Hodge creaks open the old metal door leading back into the stairwell.

The climb up the spiral staircase makes me dizzy, but I don't care. All I can think about is the trees outside, the cool shade of the obstacle course, and getting back to normal life.

We reach the final landing, and Hodge pauses. "Do you remember the way back?" he asks, eyes searching my face in the yellow light.

"Of course I do," I reply.

He hesitates for a moment, then turns. "I'll take an alternate route."

I reach out toward him, feeling a sudden rush of uncertainty. "Do I just go back to my room?" Cam and Chu and Sif's faces flash in front of my eyes. The last time I saw them, I was being taken away as a Hater. It's been weeks, but I realize I don't feel ready to deal with questions yet.

"Don't sweat it," he tells me. "I'll meet you in the atrium."

He lightly touches my shoulder, then pushes open the door, and we step out into the dim light of an early evening. The dense undergrowth crowds in, all tree limbs and scraggly weeds. I can smell the fresh scent of the leaves in the cool air mixed with the woody scent of the timber beams on the obstacle course.

As I move through undergrowth, memories of the day Hodge first brought me here flood back. Back then, I thought I was being sent to Haters' prison. If it were normal circumstances, Sif's accusations after the Filtering exam should have ended that way.

"That's exactly what I'd expect to hear from a Hater," the Sif I didn't recognize had said. Before Realignment stole her mind, she was my closest friend. My ally. After Realignment, she forgot almost everything and reported me.

"Don't hang around in the cold too long," Hodge's low voice says into my ear. I jump, surprised he is still here. Before I can say anything, he melts away into the shadows. I take a deep breath and head the way I remember through the thick undergrowth toward the obstacle course.

The trees begin to thin out as I walk. Through the treetops I catch glimpses of the Elite Academy rising high above my head, a giant white halo that encircles us all in Elite training. I drink in the fresh air, drawing it into my lungs with a relief I haven't felt in weeks.

Then, in the quiet of the evening, small doubts take root in my mind. How am I going to settle back into normal life when

I don't even know what normal is anymore? Will I ever be able to face Sif again? Will she see right through me and report me to Lover Fuschious? Fuschious has always hated me. I bet he'd snatch any chance to get his revenge.

Skirting around the edge of the heavy timber beams on the obstacle course, I use the trees as cover until I reach the exit. When I step onto the wide avenue leading toward the atrium entrance, a small gust of wind lifts the tips of my hair. There's no one around—not a single soul. Something must be happening back in the building to keep all of the Apprentices indoors.

As I walk up the avenue toward the Academy doors, Hodge materializes beside me. I pretend not to be startled. He silences the question hanging on my lips with a quick shake of his head and then goes through the doors ahead of me. I hang back a few steps, placing a safe distance between us. He drums his thumbs on his thighs and affects a casual march across the polished concrete floor.

"We can recode the CCTV to put you in there," Wil had told me. "But we can't get Fuschious to pretend he's seen you."

The atrium is deserted, but a low hum of conversation drifts up the wide staircase leading down to the dining hall. Everyone must be at dinner. Ahead of me, Hodge turns away toward the lifts at the opposite end of the open space. I act as if I know where I'm going, imitating a purposeful march as I stare at Hodge's retreating figure. A nervous prickle runs down the back of my neck. It makes me twitchy.

A lift at the far end of the atrium dings, and the doors glide open. Hodge becomes incredibly still. A familiar figure steps from the lift, broad shoulders and thick muscles defined by the loose-hanging linen of the Lovers' uniform. At the sight of Fuschious's familiar scowl, my heart sinks. I tense, waiting for the inevitable sneers and insults.

Fuschious sweeps toward me, brushing past Hodge with barely a nod. I stand straighter, pushing my shoulders back, ready to salute. Fuschious's eyes wash over my face, then away, and the instructor continues down toward the dining hall. Stunned, I stand still until he's gone, wondering what I just witnessed.

Hodge jolts forward then, and I follow him to the lift. He lifts his wrist to show that I need to scan my ID on a small panel in the wall. I do as he says, pretending that this is something I've always known how to do. When the door finally closes, I turn toward him.

"What was that?" I ask breathlessly. "Fuschious had the perfect opportunity to go for me then, and he just . . ."

"You're a trainee Watcher now," Hodge says. "That changes everything."

"I don't believe it," I say.

Hodge grunts. "Better get used to it."

I open my mouth to object, but the words die on my lips. With a soft electric *ding*, the lift doors glide open, revealing a room that is like nothing I've ever seen before.

6

Watchers are both the least and greatest of the Love Collective's citizens. We are the least because our work goes unseen by anyone other than the Supreme Executive. We exist only by reputation and shadow. The least of all individuals in this land.

Yet we also hold the very future in our hands. Without us, the Collective will suffocate under the rule of hate and chaos. It is only through our work that other citizens can breathe. Because we are indispensable, we are therefore the greatest.

(Elite Watcher Training Manual, 51st edition, page 32)

THE DARK GREY CARPET BENEATH MY FEET deadens the sound of my steps. The air smells of air freshener and crisp climate-control fans. Dim lights leave pools of shadow across the expansive space.

"How do you like the renovated quarters?" Hodge grins. "Dorm Leader wanted to make sure you had a . . . safe place to learn."

Holding back the urge to skip, I stroll from one part of the room to another, taking in as much as I can. There's a plush lounge area, a series of dark leather couches formed into a hexagon around a large, low black table. Each couch is long enough to fit four people and deep enough that I could stretch my legs out without my feet hanging over the edge.

To the right of the lounge are a series of VR stations decorated in deep indigo and navy blue. Vivid white LED strips outline each console, and shiny black seats hang above the running belt on each floor. In the black-and-grey kitchen area I discover a wide fridge full of bottled water and snack packs. Beside the kitchen is a table large enough to fit twenty people, sleek and black with indigo highlights along the edge of the chairs, and a vidscreen at one end for presentations. A long picture window runs beside the table, giving a perfect view over darkened fields and trees in the center of the Academy.

"So I get all of this to myself?" I ask in amazement.

"Well, strictly speaking, they're designed to handle a whole class of Watchers, but since you're the only one for now . . ."

"You know she's not the only one," chides a familiar voice from one of the doorways. My heart gives a little excited leap. Looking relaxed in his uniform, Wil steps out into the lounge, a towel snug around his neck. "Welcome to the club." He smiles at me.

I look away, hoping my face isn't too red. "You're a Watcher, too." My voice sounds thin and high-pitched. I cough.

Standing between us, Hodge's face is stony. He gives a curt nod to Wil, but Wil doesn't even glance his way.

"You know it." Wil inclines his head to the doorway he's just emerged from. "By the way, that room's off-limits. Yours is over there." He points to one of the other four doors that lead off the central living space.

I go over to the place he indicated and find a tube-like bunk room, not unlike my old dorm room downstairs.

"This is the best thing I've ever seen!" I exclaim as I emerge and go to explore the remaining door. As I open it, any further speech fades away. Unable to move, I lean against the doorframe with heart thumping in my chest. Hodge comes to my side.

"What is it?" Voice quiet, his brows are furrowed in concern.

I shake my head, voiceless. The room in front of me is almost identical to one I've seen before, black and windowless.

A blank vision screen fills the walls from floor to ceiling. Four spherical consoles stand spaced out in the middle of the room, control panels blinking silently. All at once, I'm back in front of a thousand images of Sif's disobedience, listening as Supreme Lover Midgate speaks beside my ear.

"Have you found the Hater?"

The memory of the Filtering exam returns with vivid and dark intensity. It was the exam that I've supposedly passed to get here. Supreme Lover Midgate set me up to report Sif as a Hater. But no matter how much she had changed, I couldn't hand over my friend to be Embraced, so I betrayed myself instead. *"The Hater is me."*

The irony. I should be in Realignment, not staring at my very own Watcher room. I couldn't even pass the most basic Watcher entrance test. What on earth is Crucible thinking?

"I . . . I can't . . ." Backing away from the door, I shake my head violently. My voice is cracked with fear. I look to Hodge for comfort, and his eyes flick a warning at the ceiling. Following his gaze, I spot an array of cameras stationed around the room. In a split second, I understand.

"It's just like the exam." I force my voice to become unnaturally bright. "What a surprise. I can't believe I get to be here for real!"

I put on a show for Crucible, giving my best imitation of delighted joy as I pull the door shut behind me. The act becomes easier as I dance back around the room and throw myself on the nearest couch. A small console opens up, embedded into the arm of the chair. I pretend to be fascinated by the controls. A vision screen rises from the table to face my seat, and the Collective app globe spins into life. I look down at the console beside me, but nothing happens.

"Speak to it," Wil says.

"Entertainment." At my command, the globe whirls around to the Entertainment hub, and a dizzying array of options flick open on the large flat screen. I try out a few more commands, and the screen delivers. Wil flops down into a couch opposite.

"Remind me to avoid asking you to pick," he teases.

"Aren't you going to give it a try?" I ask, turning to look at Hodge.

"I have to go," he replies, face grim. "I'm only here to get you settled, then I have to get back to Squad duties."

"What? You can't just leave me here," I yelp, feeling a small flutter of panic. The thought of being alone with Wil is thrilling but scary at the same time. I jump up from the couch.

Hodge gives a wry nod. "You'll be fine. Meals are downstairs, and you'll still be doing marching drills with your old crew. And"–his voice changes–"Wil's here too."

My eyes flick across the room. Seeing my glance, Wil winks at me.

"From tomorrow, Dorm Leader will personally oversee your training," Hodge adds.

I nod, hearing the message hidden in Hodge's words. "In that case, I'll do my best to be ready." I hope the cameras can't see the lie. I don't feel ready at all. Not even a little bit.

"I've organized for your meal to be brought here tonight. In the morning you can just take the lift down to breakfast." Hodge walks back to the kitchen and slides open a cupboard door, revealing a small tray.

Wil rises from the couch. "Your uniform and personal items are already beside your bed. You can charge your infotab there, too." He comes over as if to guide me away from Hodge and the kitchen, but Hodge somehow manages to put his body between us.

"Dorm Leader has left this week's Watcher lesson on your infotab," Hodge continues. "She asked me to tell you to check your material before you sleep tonight."

I nod again. The bed is the best place to read hidden messages from the Sirens. Obviously Akela will have some extra information for me to read, too.

"I will." I promise.

"It is an honor to be able to speak to a future Watcher." Hodge's gaze flicks to Wil, and his expression hardens once more.

Wil laughs. "Don't worry. I'll be here to help with anything you need now."

"I have to go," Hodge says abruptly. His expression is thunderous.

"Thanks again, Hodge," I say.

We salute, and Hodge turns to leave. The flutter of panic returns, and I rush over to him again, grasping at his arm. He freezes, then looks down to where my hand is clasped on his wrist.

"What are you—?"

"I just . . . I wanted to . . ." I am suddenly acutely aware of the cameras watching. Embarrassed, I let go of his wrist and take a step back. Gather my whirling thoughts. "Thank you. For everything."

"I have to go and watch the evening broadcast," Hodge says, his face expressionless. "Don't forget to check your messages. Love all, be all."

He exits stiffly to the waiting elevator.

EMBARRASSED BY MY SLIP, I AVOID GOING to the Siren messenger app. Instead, I take my tray of food over to the lounge, slumping into the waiting cushions and letting my feet slide up onto the seat. Wil disappears into his room until the Collective broadcast begins. At the sound of the Love Collective anthem, he emerges, hair brushed and a toothbrush hanging from his lips. I try hard to pretend he's not there.

"Good evening, my Lovelies. May you follow your dreams and find yourselves in the universe. I love you all. I mean it. Tonight, we are privileged here in this great Love Collective to be preparing ourselves for the ultimate expression of our togetherness: Triumph of Love. Can you believe that it will be our fiftieth anniversary in three months? I certainly can't. But I hope that you will all join me to make this year's Triumph an unparalleled success. Get ready for the celebration, my Lovelies!"

"Why am I here?" I ask myself aloud for what feels like the thousandth time. I must be the biggest fraud in the history of the Love Collective.

"You know the answer to that." Wil deposits his toothbrush into a glass. "Your test results were off the charts."

I rub my eyes, feeling weary. "Maybe. It's just . . ."

Wil clicks his tongue with impatience. "One: you are here to serve the Love Collective, Apprentice. Two: you were personally selected by a member of the Supreme Executive." He stares at me with an intensity that makes me distinctly uncomfortable. I'd have to be an idiot to miss the warning in his words.

"You're right." I compose myself hurriedly. "I embrace myself in penitence." Although a rebellious part of me wants yell insults about Crucible and his sadistic streak.

"Will you be all right here?" Wil asks. "I have to report back to Dorm Leader's office for the evening."

Nodding, I drop my gaze back to my food.

"Don't forget to check your messages." Wil gives an official salute and disappears. The room seems to expand to gigantic proportions now that he's gone.

Alone and miserable, I manage to slurp down only a few mouthfuls of the protein cereal before putting the tray aside. The night sky beckons through the picture window, and I peer out at the orange haze blocking most of the stars.

Only a few tiny white specks manage to glint weakly in the distance. I stare at them for a while, wondering how long I can possibly keep up this charade. I've already nearly blown my cover just by making physical contact with Hodge. How can I call myself a Watcher if I can't even cope with the very first step?

Elite Axiom: Elites show no weakness.

Down below, the Academy grounds stretch across the great big circle of the Academy. At one side, drill yards form great big green segments, illuminated around the edges and glistening with evening dew. Tree-lined paths meander through the middle of the circle like curving spokes on a wheel. In one sector, a large dark patch indicates the wilderness beside the obstacle course. It looks so obvious compared to the well-lit sections surrounding it. How on earth has Akela managed to keep the Siren hideout secret for so long?

Mind full of doubts and unanswered questions, I drag myself away from the window and go into my sleeping quarters. As Wil promised, the shelves beside my bed are packed with crisp new uniforms. I let my fingers run across the satin thread of the indigo collar. Wil is the only one who will be dressed as I am, but he is always stationed in Akela's office where none of the regular Apprentices see him. Whenever I finally appear back downstairs for drill practice, I will stand out.

"It's for the best," I say to myself, wishing I could mean it. Unopened, I put my infotab on the charger beside my bed and slump down into the bunk. The architecture is almost the same as my old bunk downstairs. But the walls are slightly darker, and there's a more luxurious feel to the blanket now covering my legs.

A year ago, this would have been the answer to my wildest hopes and dreams. No longer tagged as "Memory Freak." No more hiding from the Nursery Dorm bullies who I called the Three Fists. This should have been the happiest night of my entire life.

I just wish I didn't feel this way, as if any moment now the whole world will see me for the fake I really am. Daughter of two Haters. Mother-killer. Failure and fraud. In my head, off-key music whistles a messed-up soundtrack to my inner turmoil.

"I'm never going to be able to keep this up," I sigh, every bone in my body heavy with dread.

7

Vigilance is our hallmark. We are the eyes that survey the Collective. Always alert. Never blinking. Not by choice but by necessity: a single careless moment of inattention can bring down an empire.
(Elite Watcher Training Manual, 51st edition, page 41)

MORNING ARRIVES WITH THE SOFT CHIMING of my alarm. Groggy and disoriented, I'm shocked at first when I don't see Cam and Chu bantering in the walkway. Sif isn't in the bunk over my head, either. As these facts sink in, my brief moment of pre-waking bliss melts away, replaced by a dull emptiness.

After a quick wash and comb through my untamable hair, I emerge back into the Watcher lounge. The tray I left on the table last night is gone, and the room looks pristine and clean.

Feeling a guilty thrill, I tiptoe over to Wil's door. I lift my hand to knock, then think better of it and just put my ear closer to listen. No sounds of life come from inside, so I take a step back.

At that moment, my fitness tracker buzzes. I look down at the display and see a message from Akela: *Timetable on infotab.*

Suddenly reluctant to obey, I meander over to the fridge, grab a bottle of water, and take a swig. I do a lap or two of the living area, walking in a wide arc to avoid the scary surveillance room. Only when I've exercised so much my breath is coming in heavy gasps do I head back to my bunk to get the infotab.

The small white rectangle rests snugly in its charging shelf and feels cool in my hand as I lift it and give it a little squeeze. The screen whirls into life, and, as promised, a message from the Dorm Leader glows in the top corner. I sigh, tap the notification, and my mapped-out life floats into view.

0600 : RISE
0700 : MEAL
0745 : DRILL PRACTICE
0900 : WATCHER TRAINING 1
1230 : LUNCH
1330 : WATCHER TRAINING 2
1500 : COMBAT PRACTICE
1600 : ELITE AXIOMS
1630 : DRILL PRACTICE 2
1700 : WATCHER TRAINING 3
1900 : DINNER
1930 : COLLECTIVE BROADCAST
2000 : WATCHER TRAINING 4

"Never thought I'd be excited about drill practice," I sigh, looking at my mostly lonely day. I give myself a little shake and then drop the infotab on the bed. It lies accusingly on the sheets, reminding me that I haven't checked the secret Siren notifications yet. I turn away. Life is already complicated enough without some secret society to follow around.

I have loved you . . .

The crooning voice is almost too sweet to resist. But I squash it aside. I have to be downstairs. Can't be spending my morning talking to some invisible being who keeps singing in my head.

The lift, sullen and silent as it glides down with a smooth hum. In my mind I go over the routines I've practiced with Akela. We rehearsed the answers I would give when asked about where I've been (training alone), why I'm not in Realignment (they appreciated Sif's enthusiasm, but I'm no Hater), and why I'm now a Watcher (because Executive Lover Crucible).

When the doors slide open, a riot of butterflies flits around my stomach. It seems like an age since I was last here.

"A Watcher in Training is at the top level of the Elites. So act like you're Supreme Lover, not some Love Squad lackey," Wil had said back in the bunker. It was impossible to miss the way Hodge's shoulders had stiffened at the insult.

Here in the atrium, people mostly ignore me. One or two Apprentices whisper to each other behind their hands. But they follow up the whispers with respectful nods, which leaves me feeling a strange mix of pride and shame. Pride, because I'm a Watcher. Shame . . . well . . .

Murderer. Mother-killer. Traitor . . .

The dining hall greets me in a thundering storm of conversation. I join the back of the queue and obediently take my daily morning rations.

"Don't spill it," a warm, deep voice speaks over my shoulder. Cam's words have nearly the opposite effect, as I jolt my tray up in the air in surprise.

"Cam! What are you . . . ?" I splutter. "Hi!"

He smirks at me in amusement at the messy slop now oozing across my tray. "You still talking to us?"

"Of course! Not my fault they kept me in training for so long."

"Come on, then." He smiles and nods toward the seating area, inviting me to follow.

With a faint glimmer of pleasure, I do so, and we weave our way through the dining benches. The butterflies in my stomach go into overdrive as I spot a row of familiar faces. Chu's back is to me, but he's speaking to Lee and Pim with his hands gesticulating wildly. Near them, Farr and Dona are talking with Buff. The bulky twins Rook and Arah have their backs to me, too, but they look completely engrossed in eating. Only Sif and Zin are absent.

"Look who I found!" crows Cam as he reaches the table. All eyes turn toward him, then land on me. Chu's face goes through a range of expressions before shutting down. Farr looks like she's swallowed something unpleasant.

"Watcher girl!" Lee exclaims with glee. He is silenced with a sharp elbow to the ribs from Pim.

"Hi, Flick!" Pim smiles brightly. She pats the empty space beside her, inviting me to sit.

"Shove over." Cam uses his hips to push Chu along the bench before sitting down.

"Hi, everyone." I smile, feeling all sorts of awkward.

Pim gives me a shy look. "How have you been?"

"To be completely honest? I miss you guys." I give a noncommittal shrug.

"Not possible. You're living the high life, Watcher girl," Lee says with a hint of envy.

"If by 'high life' you mean 'hours in a dark room with nothing but vision screens for company,' then, yeah, I guess you're right." I feel relieved that I had a prepared answer to give them.

"Wow," Pim says dryly. "You're really selling it."

"What have you guys been up to, anyway?" I ask, diverting the conversation.

"Eeeeeverything has changed," he says. "We hardly get any time to slack around anymore."

"Poor you," Pim sniffs without a hint of sympathy.

I scoop up another spoonful of cereal. "Where were you guys sorted?"

"I thought you'd know that, being an all-seeing Watcher, and all." Lee's smile is jovial, but I catch a hint of suspicion in his expression.

"Ha. Ha."

He shrugs. "Pim and I are officially Engine Roomers,

along with Buff down there. Chu's been put into the Coders with Cam—"

"What? I thought you wanted to be in the Love Squad?" I ask, surprised.

Cam gives a despondent shrug. "They didn't want me."

"Your brain was too big." Lee smirks.

"Hey! I heard that!" exclaims Dona from further down the table.

"Oops. Don't offend the beef," Lee says in a loud whisper, before ducking further to avoid Dona's death stare.

I look around. "What about the twins? Are they in the squad too?"

Cam lets out a bark of laughter. "You'll never guess where they were Filtered."

"Love Squad?" I say, confused by his demeanor. Seeing my blank expression, he rolls his eyes.

"Nope. Pleasure Tribe!" He laughs.

My mouth drops open slightly, shocked.

"That's how they looked when the results came out." Pim points her spoon in my direction.

Cam looks supremely satisfied by his dorm-mates' misfortune. "Apparently their . . . ah . . . physique is good for the performance stream."

"At least they've got Farr for company," Pim says.

"What about—?" I ask, then stop at the silencing head shake from Pim. She seems to know what I was going to say. Her eyes widen toward Chu, and I get the message.

Chu's scowl deepens as he snaps his spoon down on his tray and pushes up from the table. "Gotta go do something." He stalks off.

"Now you've done it." Cam's gaze follows Chu from the room.

"What?" I ask, flustered.

"We've had to put up with that for weeks." Lee rolls his eyes up to the ceiling and gives a weary shake of his head. "He's been a nightmare, ever since Sif—"

"Ah," I say, suddenly understanding. "He's still not over it?"

"She makes sure he never will be," Pim says, her lips barely moving. "I used to like her. But now . . ."

Cam leans toward me. "She's playing with him," he says, glancing from left to right. "Or at least, that's how it seems. One minute she's almost like the old Sif, then next minute she's a block of ice."

Lee grimaces as he scoops up another spoonful of cereal. "She gives me whiplash with her—"

"With her what?" finishes a cold voice behind me. Lee's face freezes in a contorted mix of shock and embarrassment. I turn to see Sif with Zin beside her. When she sees me, Zin's face clouds with fury and hatred. My stomach lurches.

"Go on," Sif challenges. "What were you saying about me?" She folds her arms, and every hair stands up on the back of my neck.

Lee scrambles for an answer. "You . . . uh . . . you give me whiplash with your dazzling smile," he finishes lamely, attempting a dazzling smile of his own.

It doesn't take a genius to see that Sif doesn't buy it. "You're full of it. Less than five minutes with her, and you're already betraying everyone." Arms folded, she gives an angry jerk of her chin in my direction.

"Well this is awkward," Cam mutters under his breath.

"WHAT A DISASTER." I CLENCH AND UN-clench my fists, leaning back against the cool concrete of the atrium wall. My face is hot, my heart racing. Frustrated, I kick my heel back against the wall, feeling a satisfying jar of pain.

Cam, who had been leaning against the wall beside me with his arms folded, jolts forward in surprise. "She went on at you for a long time. You okay?"

"She still thinks I'm a Hater, doesn't she?"

"I don't know about that . . ." Cam begins.

"How else would you take the phrase, 'You're the same old failure' then?"

Cam lets out a nervous bark of laughter. "Oh, come on. As if she'd report you. You're a freaking Watcher in Training, for Love's sake."

"So what? Telling her that Midgate visited me in the Filtering exam didn't stop her from reporting me. She's a machine."

Cam bites his lip, lost in thought. "True."

I turn toward him. "Has she really been like that the whole time?"

Cam sighs. "Not always. Sometimes it's like she snaps out of it. She'll joke around for a few minutes. One night she even started flirting with Chu again. You should have seen it."

"How did he react?"

He leans back again, lost in the memory. "We were up in the lounge. Pim and Lee were arguing about their latest Engine Room sim. Chu and I were finishing up a Coding assignment when Sif rocked up. She squeezed herself between Chu and me and well . . ."

"What?"

"She did all of these weird things. Like she touched Chu's knee. Complimented him on how good his haircut looked. Said she missed hanging out with him all the time now that she was in Love Squad training. Ruffled his hair." Cam fidgets, not seeming to want to share these details. "It was like watching an Infotab Romance stream. His eyes went really big, and then he said a whole bunch of flirtatious things. You know how he is."

I think back to the suave moves Chu used to make on Sif all the time. The times he leaned in toward her. The sweet words that made her smile. Then I remember the cold, hard way Sif responded to him when she first returned from Realignment.

"What happened?"

"She smiled and flirted back, and they got canoodling like old times. It was disgusting." The look that splashes across Cam's face is so comical I giggle.

"Hey, you didn't have to sit next to it," he protests, face stricken. "I didn't know where to look."

"Sorry. But I'm kinda glad she came back. Chu was a mess for ages."

Cam harrumphs. "Don't get too excited. The next morning she shut him down worse than she's ever done. We were lucky that Chu didn't end up in Realignment the way she was going off at him."

"Oh no."

"Oh yes. Chu's been a nightmare ever since. Barely speaks to any of us and watches Sif like he's not sure whether she's a Triumph gift or a hand grenade. Meanwhile, she flip-flops between the Sif you saw at breakfast and some confused lost person."

"I had no idea." For some weird reason, I feel like I should apologize. But the words won't come.

Cam shrugs and gazes out the atrium windows. "You've been gone a while. Things happen."

"I guess."

In the distance, Sif and Zin march purposefully across the atrium floor, heading away from us with a group of other Apprentices toward the Love Squad wing. She looks the image of a Haters' Pavilion guard, all solid muscle and precise marching movements.

"Machine is right," I mutter, feeling an irrational flash of anger. "Poor Chu."

"What?" Cam asks, turning his head sharply toward me.

"Nothing," I reply. In the distance, another group of Love

Squad Apprentices pass, heading for the drill field. Although their uniform is the standard Elite grey, they've already developed a soldier's swagger in the way they walk. Almost as if they're already carrying a firearm over their shoulders and a utility belt around their waists.

"So, is being a Watcher as hard as it sounds?" Cam interrupts the flow of my thoughts.

"You have no idea," I reply. "What about you?"

"Being a Coder is fine. It may not be weapons training, but at least I get to make stuff happen. The Love Collective know best, don't they?"

I ignore the hint of sarcasm at the end of his words and sigh. "With Coding, you get to create. I just watch things."

"Creepy."

"You wait. Everyone's going to start avoiding me."

He steps in front of me. "I won't."

"How can you be sure?"

When I look up at Cam, his face breaks out in that familiar, goofy grin. "We're friends. Remember?"

His expression reminds me of the day we first met. The memory of Sif and Cam bouncing around the train playing "Catch the Hater" brings a sudden rush of grief and a lump to my throat.

"Things can change," I say under my breath, fighting back the torrent of old memories that riot in the back of my head.

8

You may think that a well-functioning Love Collective would not require correction. But Hate is never inert. At any moment, a spark of dissatisfaction or flickering ember of dissent may flare into hateful flames, consuming citizens in its ceaseless hunger for living flesh. What may seem at first to be innocuous or innocent may turn out to be the very thing that brings down our way of life. So Watchers must never brush off suspicious activity if it is visible. For where there is smoke, there is usually fire.
(Elite Watcher Training Manual, 51st edition, page 54)

DORM LEADER IS WAITING FOR ME WHEN I arrive back in the Watcher lounge. She holds something in her hands.

"I thought we'd begin today's lesson with some quick VR drills," she says after the proper Collective salute and formal greeting.

"Yes, Dorm Leader." Hands clasped behind my back, I keep my face still and solemn.

"Did you check your messages?" Her voice is cool, but I know exactly what she is asking.

I don't look her in the eye. "I found my timetable. Thank you." In my head there's a sudden flicker of horrid music, then a small burst of pain. I snap myself out of it in time to see Dorm Leader frowning at me.

"Do not disappoint me, Apprentice," she warns. She hands me what turns out to be a streamlined version of the VR headset. Sleek, black and lightweight with a small indigo band to match my uniform, the headset fits over my forehead comfortably.

Dorm Leader takes a seat near the kitchen bench and pulls out her infotab while I step up to the nearest VR station. The VR headset is so light I almost don't feel like I'm wearing it, but as I slip it down over my eyes, the sights and sounds of the room around me evaporate completely.

"Welcome to Watcher simulation training," drones a quiet, soothing AI voice in my ear. "Begin Lesson 1. Your goal: find the Haterman."

I'm suddenly standing in the back of the Triumph gala concert, behind a million people who sway to a pounding beat so loud it hurts my ears. I stand on tiptoes, craning my neck to see over the multitude. All I can see is the backs of heads bobbing up and down to an incessant beat. The hypnotic bassline numbs my senses.

In the distance, a tiny figure stands behind a mixing desk. Lights flash and twirl over our heads, interwoven with lasers that split the dark night sky with needle-thin, flickering beams.

Within minutes, the relentless beat bores into my ears, repetitive and mind-numbing. Thoughts become hazy, as if travelling to me through a fog as thick as the billows of artificial smoke pouring from the front of the stage.

My vision clouds. My body begins to sway. I am not me anymore, just an object moving in time to bass and synthetic drum. There is nothing except the moment. Up and down, back and forth like an ocean wave, the crowd undulates in time with me.

I don't know how long I remain trapped in a mind fog, but a sudden buzzer sears across my hearing and an electric shock snaps me out of my reverie. I recoil, emerging out of VR to see Akela staring at me.

"Again," she says.

Dazed, I blink and rub at my temples to try and clear my senses. "Yes, Dorm Leader."

I slip the visor back over my eyes with reluctance, and the VR throws me straight back into the mind-numbing Triumph party. Instant cacophony invades my senses, overwhelming all of my conscious thought in seconds. Red lights wash over me. Dark shapes dance before my eyes. At the same time, the thudding rhythm ensnares me into the same swaying, thoughtless state.

Dance.

Beats.

Thump thump thump.

Movement.

Swaying.

Thump thump . . .

A sudden loud buzz. Painful shock. The VR screen disappears.

"You lost it again," Akela says, looking at me with a blank expression. I can't tell whether she's mad or bored.

"Sorry."

"Again."

I nod obediently, and enter back into the concert for a third time. Fourth time. Fifth time. Every time, I barely get a glimpse of the crowd before the beat takes control of every conscious thought.

After the eighth failed attempt, my patience finally fizzles. "Can we move to something else?" I gasp, feeling slightly dizzy.

Akela pauses for a moment. "No," she says quietly, staring at some point in the distance.

"What? Why? It's not like this is real life, or anything," I protest and then feel my face get hot.

"Elite Principle One." Akela fixes me with her commanding glare. Out of habit, I recite back to her.

"Elites focus on the goal, not the game. But . . ."

"What's the goal, Apprentice?" A hard note enters Akela's voice. I falter.

"I . . . uh . . . to be a Watcher?" I scramble for an answer. When I don't say anything more, she sighs.

"Elite Principle Two."

"Elites put performance ahead of pleasure."

"Three."

"Elites are always on duty."

"Four."

"Elites are never sloppy."

"Five."

"Elites put Collective before concern."

Akela continues to stare at me with an intensity that could probably burn holes through the wall. I shift uncomfortably.

"Do you want to be a Watcher, Apprentice?" she says, voice deceptively calm.

I bite back the answer that immediately springs to mind (*No! Crucible is making me do this!*), and push forth the expected loyalty for the sake of the watching surveillance cameras.

"I live to serve the Collective, Dorm Leader." I bow my head slightly, hoping I look submissive. Inside, I'm feeling mutinous. If it wasn't for those cameras . . .

"Good," Akela acknowledges. "This"—she gestures at the VR stations—"is the course of education determined by the Supreme Executive—by Executive Lover Crucible himself, no less—so this is how you will be trained. Understood?"

I hold myself still, hearing the unspoken message that sends a jolt of fear through me. Crucible is watching me right now. So I'd better be the most loyal, hardworking, perfect Apprentice ever seen.

I suddenly feel weak and small. "Yes, Dorm Leader. I embrace myself in penitence." I seem to be saying that a lot lately.

Dorm Leader lets out a slow breath. "Then get back to it," she commands. "You cannot progress to the next level until you've succeeded in this task."

I nod, and fit the headset back over my head again to enter back into the artificial wall of sound.

WHEN I AM BUZZED ONCE MORE OUT OF THE concert sim, I let out another gasp of frustration.

"Argh!" I rip the headset off. "This is useless!"

"That's not the kind of Approved Lexicon a Watcher should be using," says a deep, raspy voice. The blood drains from my face, and I turn on shaking feet to see that a visitor has arrived while I was busy being hypnotized again.

Akela still sits on the couch, her mouth etched in a deep, disapproving line. Beside her, Dorm Leader Crucible lounges on one of the wide cushions, one leg crossed over the other. Shrewd, beady eyes watch me from the sunken hollows in his finely wrinkled face. Steel-grey hair sits like a snug cap on his head. A shiver passes down my back.

"I . . . uh . . ." I stammer.

"Executive Lover Crucible wanted to see how our newest Watcher was proceeding with her training," Dorm Leader Akela says carefully.

"I embrace myself in penitence, Executive Lover," I say, immediately bowing as low as I can.

Executive Lover is silent for a few moments. "She is below standard so far," he snaps.

"Yes, Executive Lover."

Painful moments stretch out while I stare miserably at the floor.

Finally, Executive Lover Crucible speaks again. "Well, I can see we still have quite some distance to go before we make her."

"Yes, Executive Lover," Akela agrees in a voice that is way too calm for my liking. As if she doesn't even care that Crucible could Realign me without blinking.

"Return to your posture, Apprentice," Crucible commands. I straighten so quickly it makes my head spin.

"Yes, Executive Lover," I say. I stand at attention, but risk a glance at Crucible. His face is leathery and cracked, and his eyes consume me with slow malevolence.

"Tell me why I should allow you to remain in this room for one second longer." Venom and displeasure ooze through his every word.

"I live to serve the Love Collective."

"Unconvincing."

"Being a Watcher is the truest way to follow my dreams and find myself in the universe," I say. "I exist for no other purpose than to do the Love Collective's work."

That's a lie! screams my conscience.

Executive Lover Crucible's eyes narrow at me. "Really?"

"Yes, Executive Lover." I stand pinned to the spot by the force of his glare.

"Show me," he says. I begin to pull the VR headset over my eyes, but he raises his arm. "Not there."

Startled, I pause. His arm moves to point at the open door of the Watcher room, and I feel the blood drain from my face.

"In there."

MEMORY DATE: UNKNOWN

Memory location: Outside

Afternoon sun shines brightly through the city haze. A breeze across the grassy hill cools my hot face, flushed after running around the park. My laughter echoes off apartment buildings.

"Here comes the sky-bird!" Dadda calls in his warm, deep voice. I squeal with delighted fear and run, but he scoops me up in his strong arms and swings me around in a big circle. I thrust my arms out, becoming the sky-bird in his arms.

He lifts me high above his head. I squeal again, and he clasps me in a tight hug, laughing.

"Ah my darling, you are the Composer's gift to me," Dadda says, smiling joyfully.

NOT THIS. NOTTHISNOTTHISNOTTHISNOT—

"You know what to do," Crucible says. A slow, wicked smile spreads across his face.

The door to the Watcher room yawns open, showing me the black hole that is the last place on earth I want to see. I hesitate. Turning back to where the two leaders sit, my eyes are a silent plea for Dorm Leader to intervene.

I would bite off my own hand if it could get me out of this nightmare. My skin is crawling. My heart beats in fearful thumps.

MEMORY DATE: 93 DAYS AGO

Memory location: Filtering exam

Supreme Lover stands beside me in the darkness, waiting. The bank of screens in front of me is frozen. Every single screen shows Sif's face.

"Find the Hater," Supreme Lover says.

"YOU KNOW WHAT TO DO," AKELA REPEATS HIS word to me, pointing at the open door, and all my hope is dashed.

"Yes, Dorm Leader. Executive Lover."

"Have you found the Hater?" Midgate asks again.

"The Hater is me!" I yell.

As I go through the doors, I try my best to look like an obedient Apprentice, but inside, my whole being is clawing for the exit.

Once inside, a thick, suffocating silence falls. The Watcher room has all of the best sound-proofing technology. I try not to shudder. A Hater could be executed in here and nobody would ever hear them scream.

I reach the first spherical control panel, and there is Wil, stepping up beside me. The hairs along my arms rise in a mixture of alarm and nervous excitement. Behind him, the door closes with a soft click.

"When did you—?"

Wil moves to the second control sphere in the room. "Executive Lover Crucible is observing from his infotab," he says, reading my thoughts. I nod, and my anxiety levels increase. "Dorm Leader has sent me in here to assist you on this first official expedition."

I get the message and place my hand on the control panel. The entire room glows into life. I gasp as not just the wall in front of me, but the surrounding walls, ceiling, and floor shine.

Wil and I now stand on the projection of a wide street that leads up a hill toward the gleaming Hall of Love. The late-afternoon sun washes everything in a magnificent yellow-orange glow.

"Love City!" I gasp, awed by the vision. Projected in this way, it somehow feels larger and more impressive than the VR sims I remember.

"You'll get used to it." Wil's tone carries a hidden message: *you'd better get used to it, or else.*

I press forward on the sphere, and the scene shifts forward, as if Wil and I are in an invisible overcar. We head up the hill toward the Hall of Love, and the gates twinkle at us with bright golden gleams.

We fly over the gates and into a sunny garden courtyard. A crowd emerges from the Hall. They are dressed immaculately in ceremonial white linen costumes, their hair and faces colored with vivid Triumph decoration. A band of musicians begins playing strange wooden instruments that I have never seen before.

Revelers mill around, glasses of red and yellow liquid clasped in their hands. A small group of blue-uniformed Engine Roomers wander amongst the group, silver trays bearing small colorful jelly-like blobs in their hands. One passes less than a meter away from us, and a partygoer takes a small blob from the tray, popping it in their mouth.

"What do we do now?" I ask.

"Watcher, show schematic," Wil orders.

At his command, a display screen overlays the party, showing blueprints of the location. Little red circles are dotted around the walls.

"The cameras." Wil points to the red circles. "Mostly you just navigate scenes the way we just did. But if you need to jump to a specific location quickly, this is how."

With a wave of his hand, the diagram disappears, and the party scene returns.

"If you need to zoom in, do this." He makes a gesture on the sphere's surface, and the camera zooms so close that it shows the pores on the nose of a woman wearing a hot pink wig. I swallow, not quite sure where to look. Thankfully, Wil makes the same gesture in reverse, and the screen pans away to a more comfortable viewing angle.

"Your turn."

Feeling a little stupid, I use both my hands to maneuver. I zoom in on a small group of Lovers chatting near a wide circular fountain. A jet of water streams up in curving patterns, sending a fine spray over the small group.

"Watcher, focus," Wil commands, and the microphone begins to play their conversation.

"... so I said to them, I said, 'But why on earth would you put one of those monstrosities in your living room? Of all places!'"

The well-dressed man laughs loudly, and the whole group joins in.

"Honze, you are always the most entertaining at these soirees," chuckles a tall, bony woman. Her face is almost completely hidden beneath swirls of fluorescent yellow and magenta.

The man chuckles again. "I know!" he agrees, placing a chubby hand on his chest to reveal long gold-painted fingernails. "It's never a party until I've been invited."

I flick the controls and the scene shifts sideways toward a different group of conversations. More inane chatter. I scan the crowd for any sign of someone acting suspiciously. A lone figure in the distance bends over the garden beds ringing the side of the walls. I flick my wrist, and the vision zooms in on the lone figure's face. Dressed in the rainbow livery of a menial worker, the man bends down to tend a hedge at the side of the garden bed. His lips are moving softly. I press the focus button, but the footage zooms away suddenly.

"Hey!" I grumble.

"Let's look over here," Wil says, distracted.

"Why?"

"I have a hunch."

"Fine."

I let Wil take control of the vision and concentrate on what's in front of me.

"See that?" Wil leans forward, his eyes pinned.

"What?" I scan the scene, trying to find the thing that's caught Wil's attention. It's hard to find something when you don't know what you're looking for.

"What do you think of that guy?" Wil zooms closer to a well-dressed Lover leaning against one of the ornate columns around the edge of the courtyard.

I scan back through my memories. "He's been in that spot since the beginning."

"Let's take another look," Wil says. Then lets out another command: "Watcher, data check."

As if we're in a time machine, the vision begins to rewind. Partygoers walk backward, their movements stilted by the time-lapse replay. The man we're watching remains almost motionless, staring from his leaning post.

"What's he staring at?" I ask.

"That's what I want to know." Wil grimaces. "Watcher, end data check."

The vision jumps back to the place we were initially watching. While his body appears relaxed, the man's hostile gaze gives an entirely different impression. Whatever he's watching, it's clear he doesn't like it.

"Zoom out and see," I say. Wil moves the screen back, and I follow the lone man's gaze. A group of VIPs mingle near a tall ice sculpture, which appears to be the figure of a Hater just after their beheading. At the center stands a lone figure, his wizened face immediately recognizable.

"Executive Lover Worthing!" I gasp, feeling a sudden strong urge to throw myself on the floor in a low bow.

"So why is our guy staring at him?" Wil asks.

"Go back."

The screen zooms back to the man lounging against the column.

"His mouth is moving," I say.

"What's he saying?"

I flick a switch on my console, and a muffled sound plays into the room.

". . . Thinks he's all . . ." the lone figure mutters. "What would he know? . . . He's just an old. . ."

Wil's voice cuts over the audio. "Flag him."

"But—"

"Do it. Now." His tone is urgent.

"How?"

"Red button."

I flounder about, looking for some kind of button on the screen, then look down. A small red circle sits on top of the sphere like a glowing red eye.

When I press it, a yellow circle appears on the screen. I guide it toward the lurking figure, until his face is ringed by the yellow line. "How do I make this work?"

"Red button."

I press the red button again.

"Target acquired," croons a soft female voice.

"Now what?" I say, turning to Wil.

"Now we leave it to the Love Squad," Wil replies, stepping away from his sphere and giving me a grim smile.

"Wait—this isn't a sim?" My heart sinks. "It was real?"

"That's what you're here for," Wil heads toward the exit with barely a glance in my direction. I start to follow.

"Stay." Wil puts his hand out to stop me and walks on without a backward glance. "Crucible won't let you out before you identify three more targets."

I turn back to the screens, horrified. The party continues its lively course, but I can't focus. Even when the black-uniformed guards haul the lone figure out of sight, and long after he is gone, all I can think is that another person has been added to my guilt file.

Just like my mother.

9

What happens to citizens after flagging is not a Watcher's concern. The Love Collective is a many-limbed creature, requiring a vast array of cooperation to work in harmony. You can be assured that when you pass a citizen to another, they will be trained as you have been to handle their responsibility with the utmost loyalty.

So do not waste your mental prowess on things you will not know. You have only to congratulate yourself on performing your duty as you should have done and allow yourself to move on to the next duty that needs be performed.

(Elite Watcher Training Manual, 51st edition, page 59)

"I AM SO GRATEFUL TO THE COLLECTIVE FOR putting me in the Engine Room. But if I have to look at another spreadsheet, I think I'll scream!" Pim exclaims, dumping her metal tray on the table with a loud clank. The sound makes me jump, dislodging a heap of protein cereal from my spoon. It lands heavily on my uniform, leaving a cold, wet, green blob on my leg.

"I'll take your spreadsheet and swap it for a console screen," Cam replies, mouth full of protein goop. Without looking, he passes me a napkin, which I accept gratefully from his hand. The green blob on my uniform spreads wider and soaks further into the material, leaving an unpleasant damp sensation on my skin.

"You can keep your Coding consoles. At least I get the occasional view of a street camera," Pim retorts. "I mean it's not much, but I'm closer to seeing Love City for real than you are."

"Training can be hard," I say, wishing I could tell everyone exactly how hard it's been.

"What's your problem?" Chu spits out. "Isn't having your own private dorm enough for you? Maybe if you ask nicely, they'll let you stay away from us lowlings. I'm surprised they let us even talk to you now that you're such an important Watcher person."

"Chu! That's not Approved Lexicon!" Pim gasps.

Angry, I open my mouth to defend myself, but a warning look from Cam stops me.

"Give it a rest, Chu," Lee interrupts. "Just because you got shot down again, don't take it out on the rest of us."

"What?" Chu's furious eyes glare at Lee, who wilts visibly.

"Never mind," Lee mumbles, suddenly fascinated by his lunch tray.

Cam holds up a hand. "Chu, just be patient," he says. "I'm pretty sure she's 'old Sif' more often today. Give it time, and you might find that she goes back to normal for good."

"When? One second she's all over me, and the next she's about to report me as a Hater. How long do I wait? It's doing my head in."

"I'm sorry, Chu. If I could do anything to—" I feel a hopeless sense of pity.

"Forget it," Chu mutters. He lifts his head to stare into the distance. I follow the direction of his gaze and see the cause of his foul mood. Sif and Zin are on a table at the other side of the room, surrounded by larger, beefier boys.

"Don't worry about those guys," I try to assure him in a low voice. "They'll never fraternize."

Chu's face remains fixed on the distant table. "For some reason, that doesn't make me feel any better."

"She's with Hodge," I point out, seeing the familiar head seated a few places away from Sif. "If there's anyone you can trust to enforce the no fraternizing rule, it's him."

Chu scowls again. "Even he can't do anything about her right now."

I search around for some way to change the subject. "Pim, do you really think you'll get to see Love City?"

Pim smiles at me and does a little excited jiggle in her seat. "That's what Lover Jenks says. He's given us a Triumph of Love assignment."

My eyes widen. "For real? Does that mean you get to see the Triumph festival for yourselves this year?"

Pim glows. "Yep."

"You'll be too busy standing in loading docks to have time to enjoy yourselves," Cam quips.

"Maybe standing in a loading dock *is* Entertainment for Engine Roomers," adds Farr, leaning in from her position further down the table. Pim begins to respond, but a loud announcement tone plays over the speakers. We stop midmouthful, surprised.

"That's never happened before," Cam says worriedly, looking around at the ceiling.

Lee's expression is tinged with alarm. I can't help feeling a little nervous too.

"Fire alarm?" Pim wonders, staring around at the stunned dining hall crowd.

I scan the room for some kind of clue. No one is running. And the older Apprentices are sharing excited glances at each other.

"No fire," I say.

"Attention, Elites," drones the authoritative announcer voice. "Triumph of Love meeting in the main atrium in twenty minutes. Compulsory attendance."

The loud musical tone plays again, and the dining room is suddenly ablaze with animated voices.

"Triumph season? Does that mean it will be Triumph season soon?"

"So ready."

"Do we actually get to be there this time?"

"How many Triumph gifts did you collect last year?"

"Oh man, I danced so much it took a month before I could walk properly!"

"I just want to know which Pleasure Tribe crew will get main stage!"

I look over at Chu in time to see an enigmatic smile cross his face. He looks like the old Chu.

"What?" I ask.

"Nothing," he says, still smiling. He gives a little laugh, then starts eating with more animation than I've seen in a long time.

I lean into him. "You can't do that to me," I say, delighted by his heightened mood. "What's made you so happy?"

Chu swallows down a mouthful of food, the self-satisfied look still creasing his face. "47b." He looks at me, waiting for me to understand what he's saying.

I frown for a second or two, rummaging through my mind to try and work out what he's talking about. Then the memory clunks into place. "Ohhh," I say slowly.

"What?" splutters Cam, looking from Chu to me and then back again. "What am I missing?"

I wait for Chu to reply, but he's grinning into his food, lost in his own happy thoughts.

I quote from memory, "Elite Regulations, Behavior Standards and Protocol, 47b.iii.: Fraternization rules may be suspended for the duration of Triumph of Love season only."

Cam looks at me, confused. Then recognition dawns on his face, and his eyes go wide. "Ohhh," he breathes, nodding. He glances at Chu, who is now staring off into space and grinning like an idiot. "She's in for a shock, isn't she?"

I grimace. "I don't think Sif is the one we need to worry about."

THAT NIGHT, THE ELITE ACADEMY IS ABUZZ with excitement. The entire Academy turns out in the atrium well before the twenty minutes is up, and a loud rumble of happy conversation echoes off the concrete pillars. Out of habit, I fall into line beside Cam and Pim, facing the high, blank wall that forms the screen for our nightly Midgate lectures.

Pim dances on her toes, craning her neck to see above the hordes standing in front of us. "When Lover Jenks said we were going to have assignments this Triumph season, I was excited. But this . . . this is a whole other level. I have been hanging out to see it for myself for years."

"I've only ever seen it on a vision screen," Cam says, staring over everyone's heads. His cheeks are dimpled with an eager smile. "It doesn't feel real."

"We don't know what's going to happen yet." I fight back my own excitement. "I'm not going to celebrate until I know what they say. We may still end up watching it on a vision screen."

Cam's shoulders slump. "Way to dent my buzz, Flick."

"I'd rather be pleasantly surprised than shattered." I wink at him.

Cam puts his hands on his hips like a petulant child. "Well *I'd* rather enjoy the moments of pleasant self-delusion. So stop ruining it."

Pim pats him condescendingly on the arm. "Cam, Cam, Cam. I've got more chance of fraternizing with Carell Hummer than you have of getting out of the Coding center."

"All the more reason to let me enjoy my mental fantasies," Cam tilts his chin toward the ceiling, eyes closed and a look of desperate bliss on his face. "Besides, Flick lives in a dark room too, from what I've heard."

"With every blessing comes responsibility," I say automatically, echoing the words of the Watcher manual I've been forced to read.

"And my responsibility is to code until my fingers bleed." Cam waggles his fingers at me.

"You poor thing," Pim pouts. "Would you like me to bring you back a souvenir from the party you won't see?"

"Now you're just asking for it," Cam turns to her but Pim squeals and dances away.

Above our heads, the projection screen begins to glow. Titles appear across the proudly waving Collective flag. Everyone stops.

Supreme Lover Midgate appears on the screen.

"Welcome to Triumph of Love season, my children! It is my pleasure to announce the date for our official opening of Triumph festivities. To commemorate the fiftieth anniversary of the Death of Hate, we are producing a celebration on a scale you have never seen before. Prepare to be dazzled. Prepare to live the experience. Prepare to be forever changed as Love Defeats Hate, fifty years on!

"Our Triumph Parade will be bigger than ever before, showcasing the best and brightest of our former years, as well as an exciting new feature on our youth.

"Innovation, inspiration, and imagination will be on show for one and all during this time. Join us in the Triumph Festival Parklands in Love City, where you can enjoy everything your heart desires. Attendance is not an option, but compulsory. You have three months to prepare for the greatest display of Love we have ever seen.

"May we all love all, be all together and find ourselves in this great universe.

"You are all my Lovelies, I mean it."

Supreme Lover Midgate's image fades from the screen, and the lights come back up again.

"A feature on our youth," Pim says. "What does she mean by that?"

"It means we're all going to Triumph this year!" Cam crows.

"I don't know," I reply. "It could mean anything."

"I think it means we're all going to Triumph this year," Cam repeats more forcefully.

"I bet she's talking about the Pleasure Tribe performing, or something," Pim tells him. "There's a reason they keep Coders shut away from the world's eyes." Cam arcs up at Pim's words, but she pokes her tongue out at him, smiling.

Cam shrugs. "Still think I'll get to see Triumph this year."

"You keep thinking that, Mr. Coder-in-the-dark." Pim turns away with a flick of her hair. "The rest of us will just have to wait until the Lovers tell us what we're going to be doing."

"You guys enjoy yourselves," I can't help saying. "I've got a few missions to complete before I can sleep tonight."

They are silent as I leave. Berating myself as I walk to my self-imposed exile, I resist the urge to turn back. I'm pretty sure they'd just be looking at me as if I've suddenly grown fangs and claws. It's best not to know for sure.

So I slink away, feeling like I've just broken something. Off-key music follows me like a mocking band. No matter where I go, I can't win.

10

Attachment brings complications. Regular citizens may blind themselves with relational ties and the concomitant storms. But for Elite Watchers, attachments are only ever a liability. Therefore, it is imperative that we remove ourselves from the pollution of human contact. The emotional bonds wrought by attachment to another human can cloud our vision, reducing our ability to identify suspicious activity. We must not build relationships that would only hamper our ability to see Hate when it is under our noses.
(Elite Watcher Training Manual, 51st edition, page 67)

MEMORY DATE: UNKNOWN
Memory location: Home
Dadda isn't in his normal place on his couch. So I toddle to Mumma and Dadda's bedroom. He isn't there, either. When I get to the kitchen, I see Mumma leaning over the bench, her back to me and her shoulders shaking.
"Where's Dadda?"
Mumma wipes her face and turns back to me. Her face looks wrong. She's smiling, but her eyes are red and puffy.
"I'm sorry, sweetheart," Mumma says and her voice sounds croaky. "Dadda has gone away for a while."

"When is he getting home?" I want to know. It's getting late. Nearly story time.

Mumma's mouth twists. "He's . . . he's not coming back, sweetie. Some people came and—" Her mouth twists again, and she stops talking.

Puzzled, I think hard about this news. It doesn't seem to make sense. "But when he gets back, Dadda said he's going to read me a Lyric story."

Mumma swallows. "How about I tell you a story instead?" she asks, her cheeks dripping wet.

TWO WEEKS PASS FOR ME IN A WEARY FOG. I try everything I can, but I never get through the VR Triumph party test. After a few days I can control myself enough to stand at the back of the concert for a few minutes. But no matter how hard I work, I'm always overtaken by the hypnotic sound.

Failure means long hours in the Watcher room, where Crucible sets me more and more impossible tasks to find increasing numbers of Haters. I am sure I can get some relief if I can just survive the Triumph simulation first. But that seems an impossible fantasy.

"Why don't you ask Wil? He's ahead of you in training, so he must have passed it somehow," Cam says one night at dinner, and I immediately wonder why I hadn't thought of it before.

I finally work up the courage one evening after I hear him return from a late errand. I wait for a few minutes after he's gone into his room before I pad across the living space. I hesitate, trying to drum up the courage to knock.

My bare toes dig into the plush carpet outside his door. I hover, feeling my heart thudding wildly in my chest. I take a deep breath and knock against the glossy grey surface with timid raps.

"Yeah?" Wil's voice sets my pulse racing even more.

I rehearse my question one last time in my head, then cough to clear my throat. "Uh, can I ask you something?"

A few seconds later, the door swings open, and all the words evaporate from my mind as Wil's face appears, surrounded by a halo of tousled hair.

"How you doing?" He looks at me, smile dimpling.

I struggle for coherent thought. "I . . . uh . . . I . . ."

Seeing my struggle, Wil's smile deepens. "Do you need help with the Watcher assignment?"

My eyes widen in surprise. "You knew about that?"

Wil's eye roll says it all. "Of course." He ducks back into his room and emerges seconds later with his VR visor and gloves.

"You been having a lot of trouble?" He returns to where I'm standing, wringing my hands together anxiously.

"I've been stuck for weeks."

"You took weeks to ask?" The disbelieving look on Wil's face makes me feel like a Lover has just sprung me disobeying the rules. I rush to explain.

"It's just that I didn't want to bother you, and you've been away so much, and . . . well . . ."

"Dorm Leader knows how to keep a Watcher Apprentice busy." Fitting the gloves onto his hands, Wil guides me toward the VR rigs. "If you ask me, I think she's afraid we might"—he lowers his voice and leans in so close I can smell the intoxicating scent of his skin—"fraternize."

I jolt backward, and Wil's grin widens. With a playful spring in his step, he leaps away to his VR station, twirling his visor in his fingers. I follow, slightly dazed. My hand wanders up to my ear. There is a lingering tingling sensation where his breath brushed my skin.

Oblivious, Wil climbs into his VR chair. "I told her she

should know by now that we're faithful Elites. We would never break Elite rules, would we?" He winks at me. "Come on, show me what you've got."

I stand there frozen for a few seconds. Wil thinks we could... fraternize? "But Elites don't... do that," I stay on the subject. "And Watchers..."

"Watchers see everything." Wil's visor is perched on his head. He gives me a look that is suddenly stern and serious. "So we shouldn't even be having this conversation."

Muddled by his words, I fumble with my gloves and fit the visor on my head. I'm not sure why I'm apologizing, since he brought the subject up, but I do it anyway. "Sorry."

When the visor drops over my eyes, the Watcher Dorm disappears, and the sea of people fades back into view. This time, Wil stands beside me, his Watcher uniform transformed into a virtual party suit. The thumping wall of music assaults our ears.

"So where are you having problems?" he asks, surveying the crowd at the Triumph stage. "The Haterman giving you the slip?"

"The music is the worst." I grit my teeth against the onslaught of hypnotic vibes. "I am having trouble trying to find him before I lose it."

"Easy fix." He waves his hands together, and the scene whirls, leaving me lightheaded. We land on the stage, looking out toward a million faces.

"Wait, what—?" I throw myself behind Wil's back to hide from the crowd. Wil laughs.

"This is VR, idiot. Nobody can actually see you."

"Oh." I feel foolish. "I knew that." I step out from behind him.

Wil points at the mass in front of us. "You are the Watcher, so you are in charge of what you see. So what do you see?"

I scan the crowd. In their Triumph costumes, everyone is a riot of color. Everyone's eyes are turned toward the DJ on the stage, who waves one hand in the air while the other clasps a set of headphones against his ear. The crowd moves in time, creating waves of undulating bodies. The beat pounds along with hypnotic force. I'm surrounded and enveloped in the pulsating rhythm, carried away by the sound like a leaf floating down a river. I begin to sway along, my body obeying the hypnotic tune.

"Snap out of it." Wil taps me on the arm. "Watchers don't fall for that."

I give myself a little shake. "Sorry. It's just so . . ."

"Yeah. That's what the Collective designs it to do. But in this assignment, you need to show you're not affected the same way normal people are."

"But I am normal." The pull to lose myself in the nothingness of beat and bass is almost impossible to resist. "I'm just like them."

"No, you're not."

I feel pressure on my suit where Wil grasps my arms. He turns me to face him gently. "You're the most outstanding person I've ever met, Apprentice Flick."

Mesmerized, it takes a few seconds for his words to sink in.

Accented by VR, Wil's green eyes shine vividly into mine, and for the first time I notice how realistic Watcher graphics are. "Stay with me," he pleads. His words force the music out of my mind, replacing the electronic beats with the heady thumps of my racing heartbeat.

"Okay," I say, determination loud and clear in my words. Wil's gentle pressure on my arms remains like an anchor, holding me fast to the real world while everyone in the crowd loses their minds. I go back to scanning the heads of the multitude.

"There!" I exclaim, pointing at a place near a side aisle and within a few rows of the stage. A hunched figure in a black cap stands alone, unmoved by the beats. Wil lets go of my arms.

"You know what to do," he says tersely. "And I know you can do it."

Using the VR controls, I reach out and zoom in on the figure to get a better look. Hidden from the people nearby by the visor of his plain black baseball cap, the figure's face turns toward the stage. He's wearing a black surgical mask, but around his eyes I catch a hint of the twisted scowl that marks the Haterman in all of our exercises.

With a quick flick of my fingers, I mark him and step back. In less than a minute the Love Squad have surrounded the hooded person. The VR sim sends me a congratulations message, and I whip my VR glasses off my head in triumph.

"We did it!" I do a little victory dance at my VR station. "Finally! Thank you!"

I turn to smile at Wil, but he's walking without a word to the kitchen. He pulls a bottle of water out of the fridge, opens it, and drinks, all with his back to me. All my happy feelings deflate.

"What's wrong?" I say, following him into the kitchen area.

He wipes his mouth with the back of his hand and shrugs, looking aloof. "Nothing. What's wrong with you?" His eyes go everywhere around the room, but avoid looking at me.

"Back there, you said—"

Wil's expression darkens. "What?"

"You said . . . you said that—"

"Oh that. I said what I needed to say to get you out of that trance," he says, face blank. "Don't get any ideas."

"Oh." My elation shatters into a million tiny pieces. "I thought . . ."

He waves his water bottle in the air dismissively. "You think too much. I needed to get the job done. It worked. Job done."

Embarrassed, I shrink back.

Wil saunters toward the lounge, throwing himself across the broad cushions. "Watchers can't let their emotions get in the way of their work, Flick. If you want to survive, you need to learn how to switch them off."

"So you were p-pretending?"

An infinitesimal shake of his head. "You're a smart girl." His gaze flicks up at the surveillance cameras, but he won't look me in the eye.

I stand, rooted to the spot by indecision and confusion. Is he playing me or not? He takes another sip of his water bottle, face shut down.

"But you said—"

A wave of his hand cuts off my protest. "You must have some infotab work to do," he remarks. "Messages or something."

"Whatever." Swiveling on my heels, I turn away and stomp toward the lift. The sudden urge to get out of this stifling room overwhelms me. I stab at the lift button like a madwoman.

"Don't stay out too late!" Wil calls as the lift doors open.

"Like you'd care," I shout at him in my mind, refusing to glance back.

THE MEMORY OF WIL'S MOOD CHANGE follows me all the way out into the cool evening air. A cold breeze frosts my cheeks, and I wrap my arms around my shoulders. My uniform is designed for the climate-controlled interior, not the cool of a turning season.

Lit into flame, my feelings rage against Wil. But not for long. The further I walk, the more my thoughts become self-accusatory. I didn't see it coming. But then, why would a guy like him even bother with someone like me? I should have expected it.

I squeeze my eyes shut as if that could somehow stop the memories. Guilt weighs me down, razor sharp and suffocating, and I can't run to a mental simulation of Wil to save me anymore. All I get from him is confusion.

Picking up pace, I walk briskly through the entrance to the obstacle course. The night sky is hidden from view by the tree canopy, leaving me in deep shadow. I don't know where I'm going, and I don't even know if I'm allowed to be out here at this time of night, but I don't care.

"I'm not naive," I complain loudly to no one in particular. Above me, the leaves rustle in the breeze, as if to quieten me down.

"*Shush,*" they seem to say. "*Shush shush shush.*"

I turn onto the little dirt path that runs alongside the obstacle course and feel the soft earth spring back beneath my feet. The air smells of mud and grass and wet foliage. I breathe it in deeply, feeling my shoulders relax just a little bit. A fragment of an old memory trickles into my mind, prodded into existence by the smell.

Memory date: Unknown
Memory time: Late

In the dark, I grab hold of Dadda's hand. We're walking faster than my legs can handle, but night sky cools my hot face. The leafy smell tickles my nose.

"I can't see. It's scary," I say, voice quivering.

"Shh, my darling," whispers Mumma.

"Not far now, dear heart." Dadda's voice is deep and calming. "Nighttime is like daytime to the Composer, so don't be afraid. He is with us. Always."

The cold wet slap of a branch on my face snaps me out of my reverie. Slightly dazed, I look around. I'm not on the obstacle course anymore. The thicket closes in, hemming me in on all sides. The pungent nighttime scent of woodland and earth brings the old memories into clearer definition.

"Where are we going, Dadda?"

"To safety, love. We need to move quietly so that only Lyric can hear us. Can you do that?"

I nod, feeling solemn. My weary little feet shuffle along beside Dadda. I want him to pick me up and carry me on his shoulders, but he is carrying a large pack on his back, so there is no room.

When I come to my senses, the door to the underground bunker lies open like a yawning mouth. My fitness tracker must have come within range of the automatic door system while my mind was miles away.

I give myself a little shake. *What am I doing?*

A cool, stale breath of air wafts up from the stairwell, smelling of rusted metal and dust. Before I know what I'm doing, my feet have stepped through the opening, guiding me onto the spiral staircase. I tread softly on the metal steps, heading down the yellow-lit tube.

When I reach the landing where Hodge took me all those weeks ago, I bypass the door that leads to Akela's underground office. The guilt is too much. Behind that door I learned I was a murderer, and Wil? Well, I have no idea what's going on with him right now either.

The off-key, discordant melody gets louder in my head.

Grasping the handrail for support, I descend deeper and deeper into the bunker. The air gets hotter and stuffier the lower I go. Eventually, feeling too dizzy to go on, I pause to let it subside. An unexpected sound makes the breath catch in my throat and fear clasp a cold grip on my heart.

Somewhere down below are voices. Lots of them.

For a second I think about fleeing back up the stairwell to safety, but the thought of running back into Wil stops me. Then another sound joins the first, and my heart starts racing with panic. Another set of footsteps has joined the stairwell and is descending toward me.

I curse silently and look up into the darkness as if I can magically see through solid steel. All that happens is the footsteps get nearer.

Taking a deep breath, I tiptoe down, heading for Love knows

what. When I run out of staircase, I curse silently again. Ahead, a long concrete hall stretches away, lit by dim red pools of emergency lights. A series of doorways lines the corridor, and they're all closed except one. Tentatively, I test the door handle closest to the stairs. It refuses to budge.

The footsteps grow louder. As quickly as I can, I test the door handles along the hall, hoping that somehow I can find a broom closet or abandoned storeroom to use as a hiding place. All I manage to do is pincer myself between two disasters. Ahead, the muffled sounds of conversation grow clearer, emanating from the single open doorway. Behind me, the footsteps clunk nearer and nearer. I shrink down the hall, reluctantly allowing myself to be squeezed between the two sources of noise.

A bark of laughter makes me jump. In my alarm, I back so far away from the stairwell that I am now staring directly into the open room. A circle of Elite Apprentices turn in my direction, faces aghast. At the same moment on the staircase, Hodge's face swings into view.

He gasps. "What are you doing here?"

"I was . . . uh . . . I was . . ."

"Harper? Who is this?" A willowy Apprentice emerges from the room. Her hair is a fine, silky black, and her brown eyes glisten in the dim light.

"Harper? Who . . . What?" I stammer, looking from Hodge to this strange girl and back again.

"Sorry, Viola," Hodge apologizes. "This is Cadence."

Understanding dawns in her eyes.

"The one—"

Hodge gives an abrupt nod.

"Cadence. You're welcome here," the girl called Viola smiles with such warm welcome that my fear subsides a little. "Do you want to come in?"

Struck dumb, and with Hodge blocking my only way out, I nod and allow myself to be drawn into the small underground room.

11

The insidious nature of Hate is that it masquerades as the very thing we are attempting to achieve by our own government's effort: Love. Therefore, we must utilize every ounce of our power to stamp it out. We have enlightened ourselves to the point of knowing the ultimate mode of being. We are only dragged back into the age of terror when we allow ourselves to be swayed by pleasant-sounding poison disguised as an opinion.
   (Elite Watcher Training Manual, 51st edition, page 103)

"SO WAIT—YOU'RE SIRENS?" I ASK FOR THE third time.

Viola nods, still smiling. "That's right."

"You all get together and talk about that Composer person."

"Uh-huh."

"And Lyric," I say, remembering another name Mumma and Dadda had used.

Viola's smile remains patient. "And the Muse. Yes."

"What do you say?" I venture to ask.

"Well, we sing," says a smaller Apprentice who seems to be made of skin, bones, and sinew. He flashes a toothy grin at me. "I'm Fife, by the way. I mean, that's not my Elite name, but you don't need to know that."

I look at them bewildered. "You're not worried I'd report you?"

Hodge snorts. "You'd have to explain your contraband fitness tracker first."

"I wouldn't report you," I blurt hurriedly, seeing the worry lines on Viola's face. "I've seen the Realignment chambers and—" My words fizzle away in a shudder.

"That's okay, Cadence. If Harper trusts you, then I do," Viola says finally. "Why don't you tell us your story?"

Ten pairs of eyes focus on me.

I shift in the hard plastic seat, feeling a tiny ember of panic. "Uh. What do you want to know?"

"How about you start with why you wouldn't check your messages," grunts Hodge.

"Let her be, Harper," Viola chides, laying a hand on Hodge's knee. "She's here now. That's a good thing."

Hodge gently dislodges her hand, but he doesn't speak.

"Did you get memories of the Before?" Viola prompts.

"Before Nursery Dorm?" I ask.

"That's the Before," Fife notes. "Did you have a weird Before? Was it scary? Did they beat you up?"

"Fife, don't." Viola throws a warning glance at the scrawny Apprentice before morphing into a smile back at me. "Yes, Cadence. Before you were in the Nursery Dorms." She puts a hand to her chest. "I was picked up by a Love Squad patrol from my parents' overcar out on Love Highway. Fife here was taken from his backyard. Harper—"

"She already knows mine," Hodge interrupts.

Viola gives him a look of surprise. "Really? Well, that's wonderful!" When her smile flashes back to me, she's showing extra teeth.

Before I know it, I am sharing my story, from the darkened hiding place to the grasping fists of the Love Squad ripping me away from Mumma. But I don't tell them how I later voted for her death in the Hater's Pavilion Show.

"We're so sorry that happened to you," Viola says. A trio of girls near her nod their heads sympathetically.

You wouldn't say that if you knew what I was really like.

"You had a terrible Before," one of the girls agrees.

I look around at them. "But what does it mean?" I ask. "I've got all this stuff in my head I can't understand. Like tonight, I remembered that I was with my . . . my dad, and he said that the Composer is always with us, but I have no idea what he's talking about."

The expressions on the faces around me range from amusement to pity.

I lower my head, feeling embarrassed. "Sorry, that's a dumb thing to say."

"This is a safe place, Cadence," Viola says reassuringly. "We want you to feel like you can say what's on your heart, and we aren't here to judge you."

A girl with short blonde hair leans forward. "She might understand better if we let her hear the Song."

"Great idea, Allegra. How about this one?"

Without warning, the most amazing sound comes from Viola's mouth. Her voice rings out in the room in clear, bell-like tones. A melody that is sweet and stirring, lilting with a sound that makes me want to weep and laugh all at once. The broken, out-of-tune melody in my head hiccups.

Prompted by her words, the rest of the group joins in, harmonies swelling around the space in tones that bring tears to my eyes. The words flow from their mouths with a strength that brings all of my senses to life. Men's deep voices complement the lighter female tones, weaving a rich tapestry of music.

> This is how we know what love is,
> Lyric laid down his life for us . . .

They sing the words several times over, and as the words

sink in, I feel enveloped in love and warmth and something I can't quite describe. It's like the first touch of sun on a spring morning, or the soft glow on waking just before the rest of the world tumbles in.

In the words, I feel connected to other voices, too. An invisible host of singers. A choir beyond a veil somewhere, all raising their voices to the Composer. When the song finishes, my cheeks are wet, and my heart is full.

Viola and the group sit in silence for a few minutes, eyes closed. I wait for something to happen, but when it doesn't, my discomfort returns. Unwanted memories barge in like unwelcome visitors: Mumma, bloodied and beaten. My hands, poised over the red Watcher button as I condemn another Lover to Embracement and death.

The just-finished song battles in my head with the broken melody that's been singing itself through my thoughts for weeks. A small voice of panic wells up from somewhere deep inside me, urging me to run from the room.

You don't belong here, the small voice screams into my growing disquiet.

Viola begins to speak, her eyes still closed. "We are notes in the Composer's Song."

Allegra and others nod and murmur their agreement.

Viola continues. "The Composer gave us the Song to sing. We were composed in harmony with the universe . . ."

More murmurs of agreement. Two of the boys begin to hum, their deep voices forming a stirring bass behind Viola's words. I fight back a laugh of derision. Harmony? My universe has no harmony. Stolen from my family, brainwashed and unloved by the so-called Love Collective. My closest friends turned on me. Now I'm condemned as a Watcher to select people for execution and imprisonment. If I had to describe my current existence, harmony would be the last word I would choose.

Viola's voice rises with increasing passion. "But we broke that harmony long ago." Her voice trembles with what sounds like a deep inner grief. "People believed they could be better if they composed alone."

The hummed tune from the small group becomes mournful, and I pause my self-accusations to listen. Viola's impassioned speech continues over the music. "And so the notes were scattered, the harmony vanished, the song broken and lost."

My inner melody grows louder, limping and off-key. It competes with the group's singing. Like an oily sludge coating the river's surface, my inner brokenness taints everything it touches. I glance around, wondering if anyone else hears the broken melody. It's so loud, it seems to be transmitting through my ears.

Viola's words flow toward me like the beam from a lighthouse. "In a time long ago, the Composer wrote himself into the tune—became Lyric—to mend the music he had first composed."

My head spins in a tornado of confusion. Lyric was . . . the Composer written into the Song? But how?

"What we could not do, Lyric did. Lyric sang the Composer's perfect tune. When we deserved to be silenced forever, Lyric bore the silence, became mute for us."

The humming cuts out, and the group is left in an eerie, darkened space. I feel the weight of Viola's words. What could she mean? What silence did Lyric endure instead of me?

The answer comes to me in the darkness. An unwanted vision of a woman, broken and bleeding in front of a baying crowd. My hand, poised above an infotab ready to vote for my own mother's execution. The word sings through my heart with the searing pain of a knife wound: *murderer.*

I killed my own mother. I deserve to die. I should be silenced.

Like a dying gasp, the cacophony of my own broken song splutters and stops. The weight of guilt bears down on me so heavily that I almost don't hear Viola begin again. But as if an invisible hand rests on my shoulder to guide me, I feel my eyes drawn toward her.

"What we could not do for ourselves, Lyric did to save us. He took the full burden of the Composer's anger, so we can experience the grace of the Composer's Song. Sirens are the children of Lyric. Without Lyric, we are broken instruments. But through Lyric, we become part of Lyric's mending, we become the notes were created to be, we . . ."

The pound of my heart is so loud in my ears that Viola's words become muffled. The Composer, the Song, the Lyric. Words from my forgotten childhood that seem like so much incomprehensible nonsense. Yet I can't explain the complete meltdown of my emotions. Am I getting sick? I desperately need some air.

The words from a dream return to me. *I came to make you clean.* Lyric. Lyric said that.

I am too broken, I think. But in reply, I feel the softest brush of love.

You only need to let me, the voice says again.

Harmonies erupt around the group, swelling even louder than before and drowning out my internal cacophony.

> This is how we know what love is,
> Lyric laid down his life for us.
> And we also ought to love as
> Lyric loved us first.
> Brothers, sisters, sharing joy
> Feeding hungry, quenching thirst.
> Love in truth and act
> Not just in word alone,
> As the Composer taught us:
> His love is truth, his presence peace
> Greater in us as we believe.
> One day Lyric's country
> Shall we with eyes perceive.

It's as different to the mindless hypnotism I felt in the VR as night is to day. The words seem to echo through history. In this music I don't lose myself. I find myself as I really am: failures, weaknesses, evil, and all.

The music carries something else, too. A Someone who has been waiting for me. Composer, Lyric, and Muse, the three/one who has my times held tightly in his hands. The Someone who has offered to heal my broken melody, replacing it with his own.

In the Sirens' music, it's as if the Composer himself is singing to me, his arms held out wide waiting for my embrace. Eyes knowing and compassionate. Voice clear as crystal, true and right and so sweet my ears hurt to hear.

As soon as the song finishes, the words burst out of me: "How do I get . . . that?"

Viola giggles, but it's not a mocking kind of laugh like I'm used to. It's a giggle of pure pleasure. Hodge beams too—an open, friendly smile that I've never seen before.

"Well," he says. "I've been hoping you'd ask that—"

A shadow darkens the doorway. "What did I miss?"

At the sound of his voice, I turn, ashen-faced. Wil stands at the entrance, arms held wide and face beaming. Seemingly oblivious to my inner turmoil, he looks around, his dimpled smile wide and confident. Hodge's face returns to its normal, stony scowl.

"You made it!" Fife holds his hand up, and Wil gives him a high five.

"Finally!" Allegra claps her hands delightedly. "X, you've been away so long we were starting to think you weren't coming."

Wil tosses his head, doing a brilliant impression of a famous streaming star. "Sorry. Had some business to sort up top. You seemed to be in the middle of something. Don't let me stop you."

With a confident strut, he crosses the room to sit in the last vacant seat, directly across the circle from me and beside Allegra. Her face goes pink, and she smiles happily at him.

Viola explains. "Cadence was just asking us about the Composer, and we were going to help her out."

Embarrassment kicks in, and I stand up, ready to run. "Don't worry about it. I think I probably need to get back now, anyway. Another time?" I start backing away toward the door.

"Let me walk you out," Hodge says, getting to his feet. At the same moment, Wil leaps up.

"This might be my fault," he says lightly. "Cadence, do you mind if we have a word?"

"If it's what I think it is—" Hodge speaks over Wil's continued prattle, but I interrupt both of them.

"No need, either of you." My voice is clipped and brusque. "I'll see myself out. Hod—I mean Harper, or whatever your name is, I promise I'll read my messages this time. Thank you everyone. Really. I am . . . I am so . . ." Anxiety has now robbed my lungs of air. "I have to . . ."

Leaving behind confused glances and worried murmurs, I dash out of the room. Footsteps echo down the hall behind me, so I speed my pace. Just as I reach the stairwell, a hand brushes my elbow.

"Cadence," Hodge says quietly. "Please. Wait."

I spin on my heels, crossing my arms protectively.

"Are you okay?" In his eyes, I see concern. Pity. And something else I can't quite understand.

"I'm fine."

"You don't look fine."

My memories splash around in my head in messy currents. Like a drowning child, I reach out for the memory.

His love is truth, his presence peace
Greater in us as we believe.

Suddenly I break. "Help me, Hodge," I say, almost desperate.

Confusion fills Hodge's face. "With what?"

"I want to know more of that music. I don't know why, but for some reason I just need it. Please."

As I talk, Hodge's slow smile creases the scar at the side of his face.

"That is something I can help with." He starts to guide me back to the meeting room, but my feet stay planted on the first step, welded in place by fear.

When his hands feel the resistance from my arm he turns back, surprised. "What—?"

"Not there."

Hodge's brow furrows. He looks to the open doorway then back to me again. "Is it Wil?" he demands. "What did he—?"

"No, it's nothing. Don't worry," I say quickly. In Hodge's face I can see a return of the murderous intentions, and I don't want to be responsible for Wil being injured.

Hodge looks somewhat relieved. "Well, how about we go to the office upstairs? I can explain there."

"That sounds wonderful."

12

One of the best ways to achieve peace is to first define the parameters of the conflict in such a way as to ensure victory. Therefore, Approved Lexicon was an inspired invention of our Supreme Executive. In the wars against Hate, we lost ground due to the ill-advised use of forbidden language. Haters were able to turn our words against us and use them to cast aspersions on the very heart of our great mission. It was an unfortunate necessity that our beloved leaders had to remove certain terms from collective memory.
  (Elite Watcher Training Manual, 51st edition, page 54)

"IT'S LIKE THIS," HODGE SAYS WHEN I'M seated comfortably in Akela's bunker office. "A Siren is a part of the Composer's symphony. No, even closer. A Siren is part of his family. Loved. Get it?"

"He wouldn't want me, though." My fingers twist around each other. "I've done . . . things."

"Look at me, Cadence," Hodge says gently. When I look up, his expression is soft. "The phrase 'I've done . . . things' is something all of us can say."

"Not as bad as me," I choke out. "I . . . I report people to be arrested. I get them killed. I mean, . . . my own mother, for Love's sake."

The cacophony in my head gets worse, like a thousand instruments rioting. But it's not a thousand instruments. It's a thousand layered memories. My own thoughts and actions accuse me at every turn, dragging me toward a pit of despair so deep I could drown. I cup my hands over my ears, even though it's a futile gesture.

Hodge grimaces. "I heard that too."

"You have no idea how much I—wait. What?" I say. I point at my left ear. "You can hear this mess in my head right now?"

"No." His smile is rueful. "But I know the kind of thing you're hearing. It means you're aware. You've woken up to your own music now that the Collective's memory block is gone."

An ache throbs in my chest. I knew it. "My own music? This hateful noise is . . . is me?"

"It's a good thing," Hodge assures me. "Most Collective citizens go on with their lives while that plays below their range of hearing. They might get a vague sense of something being wrong every now and then. But they just put the app in front of their faces to forget."

"How can I stop being aware?" I plead.

"You can't."

"But—"

Hodge leans back against Akela's desk. "You could try and run. Drown it out with the Collective soundscapes. Keep yourself busy with all the tasks they give you, and whatnot. But it won't fix your inner music."

As if to reinforce the point, it crashes loudly again into my ears. "Help me," I gasp.

"I can't help. But Lyric can."

"He won't help me." I'm trying not to cry. "I'm not in his family."

"You can be." Hodge's voice is full of emotion.

"What makes you so sure?" I say, shocked to see his eyes are wet.

Clearing his throat, he begins singing in a beautifully deep voice. The melody is simple, and Hodge's words bounce in hollow echoes across the concrete. But as the song flows from his lips, a strange thing begins to happen.

The walls of my inner defences begin to falter. Like a river, the crystal clear music cuts a path towards my soul. The avalanche of discordant memories slows to a trickle. As I begin to calm and my heartbeat slows, a face hovers in my mind, his eyes warm and full of love.

Lyric.

"Cadence, I came to make you clean," he says again, and my heart aches to hear it.

Hodge finishes his song and the image fades with the echoes.

I stare at him, unable to speak. Does he know what he just did to me?

"Lyric takes your broken melody and replaces it with his own. That's how you become a Siren," he says.

Me? A Siren? Ridiculous. All those people downstairs are *nice*. As soon as they find out what I have done, they'll throw me out, for sure. I could never be one of them.

Viola's song replays through my head then, competing with the off-key mess that is my own internal music. Lyric's face reappears in my thoughts, too, pushing back the onslaught of noise. As the image of his face grows clearer, a yearning grips me with a fierce hunger.

Dare I give in? Dare I let Lyric take over my music and fix it? Can I really find peace and get rid of this riot in my head?

"I-I'm not sure," I stammer, and as if I invited it, the off-key music blares loudly. I wince.

"Lyric doesn't force you to follow him," Hodge says softly. "You can stay as you are."

I let out a bitter laugh, pointing at my ears. "No one would want *this*."

"Then what do you want?" Hodge asks.

I don't have to think about that answer. "I want to be me again."

"Then ask Lyric to heal your music. Then you can be who the Composer made you to be."

I bite the inside of my cheek, searching for the answer. Why am I so reluctant? I feel exposed and broken. It seems impossible that I could ever get away from this horrible noise.

Downstairs, though. Down in that room with the Sirens, they welcomed me and they sang in a way that made my heart ache. It was so new and yet so familiar at the same time. I could have been in my parents' secret meeting, sitting on Mumma's lap while Dadda sang the songs.

"It's home," I say, suddenly realising exactly what I've needed all along. "I want Lyric to be my home."

"Then ask him," Hodge says.

So I do. The moment the words leave my mouth, everything changes. An inner burst of light burns away all the pain and guilt. The broken music that had been coating my thoughts the way an oil slick coats the river is washed away by a melody as clear as the purest spring water.

I search my memories, but it's as if the broken tones never existed. The music singing through them all now is alive. He has a name.

I am the Muse, the spring water sings to me in crystal tones.

I stare at Hodge with wide-eyed joy. "It's gone! H-how can it just happen?"

Hodge shakes his head. "It wasn't easy for Lyric. But his sacrifice means you can enjoy this as the Composer's gift."

In the silence of the secret bunker, I let the Muse sing to me. A small whisper at first, it grows on the wings of the pure crystal song, carrying the Composer's words into my heart:

You are loved.

You are mine.

Understanding is like a star exploding into existence. I'm not

Kerr Flick anymore, Memory Freak and mother-killer. I have become a Siren, a follower of Lyric. Beloved by the Composer. Companion of the Muse.

I am Cadence.

DEAR FRIENDS, LOVE COMES FROM THE *Composer*
So let us love like him...

I wake the next morning, music soaring through my mind in such sweet notes that I feel more fully alive than I ever thought possible.

Composer's children sing as one.
From death brought back to life.

The fragment trails off. Why can't I remember more? I must know more of this music. I must find as much of the Song as I can, or I will explode.

Lyric said, "Love your enemies,
And do good to those who curse you . . ."

Sitting up in my bunk, I lift my infotab from its charging station and immediately load up the Siren app. A torrent of conversations and messages scroll down the rudimentary screen, and I devour them hungrily.

A few names I recognize: Harper, Allegra, Viola. Akela, too. Under her Siren codename, Akela has been reaching out to me. But I had been too stubborn to pay attention.

Not anymore. I type the message as quickly as my fingers will allow:

Dear Zed,

I am so sorry I ignored you. I know now what I was missing. Forgive me?

—Cadence

If I could, I would wait for a reply, but my day has to start. So I reluctantly log off and get ready for a day of Watcher exercises.

At the end of the day, I log back on and find the reply:

All is forgiven. Talk soon. Zed.

IT'S ANOTHER FEW DAYS BEFORE AKELA CAN make time to meet with me. By the time our predawn meeting arrives, I'm so impatient that I don't even wait until the bunker door closes behind us.

"I have questions." I burst in.

Akela leans back in her chair, looking more relaxed than I've seen her for a long time. "Yes?"

"Lyric."

"That's a name, not a question."

"I need to know everything."

Akela listens to me for an hour, patiently answering with wise and careful words. At the end, she delights me by teaching me another fragment of the Song.

"Is there any more?" I ask.

Akela's smile fades a little. "Oh yes, yet much of it has been scattered. But I will teach you all that I know, if you are willing."

"Please," I reply, eyes shining.

She pulls out a small white object from her desk drawer. "Do you think you'd be able to listen to this now?"

It's the antique music player, the one I flung across the bunker floor. Sheepishly, I reach out for it. "I'm sorry about that," I say, afraid to meet her eyes.

"I apologize for trying to make you listen too soon," she replies. "Just don't throw it again, okay?"

I laugh and uncoil the cord.

"You'll have no problem remembering it all, so listen once,

then leave it back here." She taps the drawer of her desk, then glances at her fitness tracker. "We'll meet each week for lessons, if I can make it. Look for my invitations in the app. I'll have to keep the times irregular to avoid suspicion."

"Yes, Dorm—I mean, Zed."

Akela's mouth twitches. "It takes some getting used to, doesn't it?"

IT'S HARD GOING BACK TO THE WATCHER Dorm, trying to act as if nothing has happened. I want to laugh and sing and dance. But little prompts from the Muse help me along. Even so, it's impossible not to smile. Akela's lesson has filled me with a warmth I don't think I've ever felt.

"Lyric loves you . . ."

It's much later in the day when I get a chance to check my infotab. There's a message from Wil.

C. Can we talk?

I ignore that one and spend a little time on the Siren chat. My silence only seems to infuriate Wil, and a torrent of messages follows in the space of half an hour.

You need to let me talk to you.
I'm sorry.
Can we talk?
Need to talk to you C.
Stop ignoring me.
I know you're reading these messages.
Look, I don't know how many times I need to say it, but I'm sorry.
Can't we just talk about it and move on?
Cadence. I'm sorry.
I know I shouldn't have said what I said. I didn't mean it.

I get a guilty pleasure watching those messages trickle down the screen. Wil—confident, popular, center-of-the-universe Wil—is unsettled.

Cadence, are you listening?

I'm sorry Cadence. Please.

CADENCE TALK TO ME.

I PROMISE I WON'T DO IT AGAIN.

SOOOOOOOOORRRRRRRRRRRYYYYYYYYYYYYYY

"He's probably never been ignored before," I snort, going back to check the messages one more time.

Cadence, you are a truly extraordinary person, and—oh, forget it.

Sorry.

Really.

A final message drains away the smug feelings I had been enjoying, leaving me with a nervous thrill:

I'll be waiting for you at the tree.

"You'll be waiting a long time." Disgusted, I throw my infotab down on my bed and storm out of the room. Trust Wil to ruin my fun with actual plans. But when I stomp into the living area, I stop dead. He's not at the tree, he's standing two meters from my door.

"We need to talk," he says, pinning me on the spot with the force of his green eyes. And disgustingly, despicably, infuriatingly, I nod. Almost as if I'm out of my body watching from a distance.

"Fine," I say.

THE ATRIUM IS ALIVE WITH PEOPLE. A GROUP of Elites precariously balance on ladders around the room, erecting long banners and brightly colored bunting. I spot Pim in the distance, holding a large bundle of glittery streamers under a sign that reads, "Triumph of Love Forever" in giant, silvery letters. She spots me walking and goes to wave but nearly drops her streamers and has to madly try and rescue them from unravelling all over the floor.

Sunlight slants through the windows with the bright glow of midmorning. I glance at my fitness tracker. Lunch is an hour away.

"This is ridiculous," I say to myself. "I have work to finish."

I spin on my heels, ready to walk back to my room and disappear into VR. But Wil is suddenly beside me, propelling me forward with a guiding hand on my elbow. I try to dislodge it, but his grip is firm.

"Smile for the cameras, Flick," he says under his breath.

"You're not helping your cause," I spit back at him through my gritted teeth.

Instead of replying, he flashes me a bright, friendly smile. I turn my head away from him, unable to change my direction without making a public scene.

He marches me along leaf-strewn paths, heading below the tree canopy to where the obstacle course entrance looms. Birds chirp above our heads. I want to slow down and pay attention to their music, but Wil leads me in.

"I bet I can beat your obstacle course time!" His tone is so flamingly plastic I'm amazed he isn't melting. I manage to dislodge my elbow from his grip and take off, searching overhead for the birds and their chirping.

"Flick," Wil calls. "Wait."

Reluctantly I turn. "This better be good."

Wil attempts a dashing smile, then sees the look on my face and thinks better of it. "Can we go down and talk? I don't want to be standing here in case—"

"Here is just fine."

"I was hoping to explain."

"What is there to explain? I obviously got the wrong

impression, so—" I don't get any further because Wil is bending low, baring his neck at me.

"What are you doing?" I snap, looking down at the back of his head.

"Hit me."

Surprise drains the heat out of my anger. "What?"

"I deserve it. Hit me. It'll make you feel better."

"No." I back away from him confused. "I wouldn't—"

He straightens back into an upright position, looking miserable. "Of course you wouldn't. You're too good."

Wil comes so close that his face is nearly on mine. His hand gently brushes against my cheek, and my thoughts evaporate under the warm tingling of his skin. I know I should be upset, but against my will, my body reacts to him. For a moment all I know is explosive sensations going off all over me.

Then surprisingly, shockingly, he draws me into a hug. Nestled against Wil's chest I feel the warmth of his body pressed against mine, the strength of the arms that encircle my back. I hear the solid, regular thump of his heartbeat. Smell the clean scent of his uniform mixed with the smell of his skin. His chin rests on my head.

My mind is dazed, and my heart is pounding.

Wil draws away so that he can glance down at me. "Forget what I said back in our room that night. I couldn't be honest in front of the cameras. This—" With the gentlest of touches, he caresses my cheek with his thumb. "This is how I really feel about you."

My head is still swimming. "But you said . . . I mean, it was . . ."

"I know. I'm sorry," he mutters. "But you know how the Collective is. If they thought that two Watcher Apprentices were fraternizing outside Triumph season, well . . . we wouldn't be Watchers anymore, would we?"

"I-I guess not," I say reluctantly.

"Believe me. It was hard for me to treat you like that." His voice deepens. "I almost didn't go through with it."

My head is spinning. Part of me is rejoicing. After all, this is all I've wanted since those lonely days in the bunker. But another part of me is feeling hurt and confused. Unbidden, two opposing memories rise into view: Wil's face hovering close to mine, and then his scowl in the Watcher Dorm, aloof and dismissive.

I step backward. "How can I believe you? Maybe you're just pretending now."

"There are no cameras here, Kerr."

A strain of song wafts through my memory then, reminding me of the sweet sensation I had in the Sirens meeting. My whole being is filled with a sudden longing to go back and surround myself with the safe little Sirens group. Back there I felt known and loved. Back there felt . . . safe. None of this mind-boggling confusion Wil is making me feel right now.

"No." With determination, I pull myself away from him and look back in the direction of the Academy building. Somewhere out there, beyond the trees that hide us from view, Apprentices are no doubt still erecting the Triumph festival decorations.

"Wil, this is wrong. We could be Realigned. I-I need to go." Somewhere are the cameras that will protect me from any more of his advances. Hodge and Akela are out there somewhere, too, with more of the Song to teach me.

"Please." The pleading in his voice draws my gaze back to his face. His green eyes bore into mine. Once again, my heart starts beating wildly. Wil closes in again. "I never . . . I've never met anyone with your memory before. You keep surprising me with . . ."

The daze of tumultuous emotions builds inside my head, and my thoughts are reduced to fragments. Fraternizing. We can't fraternize. But he likes me. But back in the dorm he said . . . but then he . . . he hugged me . . . and now his eyes . . . and his lips . . .

"Stop," I put a hand up to halt my thoughts more than anything. "No more. I can't deal with this."

Wil moves back, still gazing at me. To my disgust, a pathetic part of me feels sad at the distance he puts between us. I clench my fists down by my hips to stop myself from reaching out for him.

"I'm sorry," he says. Stupidly, my body leans forward. Wil's face softens. "I know I've probably messed everything up right now, but I actually need your help."

I startle in surprise. "My help? How?"

"Zed's going to ask you to do something for her soon."

I balk at the mention of Akela's codename. "How did you know about that?"

He raises one eyebrow at me.

"Of course." I look at him. "What about it?"

"When she asks you, can you say yes?"

I look away. "It depends on what she—" Wil grabs my hand, and all of my nerves zing into ultra-high alert at the same time my conscious thought descends into a garbled mess. Again.

"She's going to ask you to leave the dorms. With . . . with me." He looks down at my hand, clasped in his warm fingers.

"What are you talking about?"

"Just think about it, okay?"

I search his face for a clue to help me understand what he's saying, but my body is a mess of electric nerves. Unable to put two words together, I nod.

"Thank you, Kerr." Wil's sunshine-filled smile dawns again, warming my heart. He drops my hand and turns for the dorm building. I nearly reach out to snatch his hand back again.

"We can't stay out here," he says over his shoulder, walking away from me. The distance between us yawns as wide as a chasm. "You'd better get back."

Before I can protest, he has sped away, leaving me in the obstacle course alone with nothing but confusion for company.

13

Watch not only what a citizen says, but what they do not say. For in the spaces between words, a person can betray their disloyalty. A skilled Watcher will be able to draw accurate conclusions from complete silence, and find a Hater even when nothing has been said.
  (Elite Watcher Training Manual, 51st edition, page 122)

HEADING FOR THE ATRIUM, I KEEP MY STEPS slow so I don't shadow Wil. Pim still teeters on the ladder, stretching glittery streamers out across the walls so that they form a silvery waterfall. Apprentices wander around in small groups, heads bent over infotabs or laughing in casual conversation.

My heart is almost exploding, but the world seems unchanged. It doesn't seem fair. In the distance, Wil stops beside the lift and briefly turns. His eyes lock on mine, and my heart goes into overdrive. At the last second I veer away to my right, unwilling to be Wil's obedient puppy.

"This is how we know what love is . . ."

I pull the Song fragment back into my head to calm my nerves. The words bring a sense of peace. They ground me. Wil's influence seems to weaken a little, and my resolve strengthens. I go to the dining room, away from temptation.

Downstairs, the kitchen is a hive of activity. Workers in blue uniforms supervise food robots, who pour more protein goop onto plates along a slowly revolving production line. Behind the dining area, the gym is full. Apprentices run on treadmills or lift weights, faces glistening with sweat.

Near the floor-to-ceiling glass walls, Hodge is in the middle of some particularly heavy deadlifts. As he rises from a squat, he looks up and sees me. Dropping the weighted bar to the floor, he lifts a hand in greeting. I head toward him, relieved to have some kind of destination at last.

When I open the gym door, the stench of sweat hits me like a wall. I wrinkle my nose. Heavy thuds and clanking weights pepper the room like a staccato, off-rhythm marching tune. Hodge steps out from the cloud of body odor, dabbing a small white towel at his face.

"Hey." He flashes a smile. "You looking for someone?"

"You," I reply, feeling sheepish.

Hodge's eyes dart at the ceiling and back to me. "Why?"

"I, uh . . . I . . ." I inwardly curse myself for being so stupid. Of course the first reason that pops into my head is the Song. But I can't say that in front of the ever-watching cameras. I also can't tell him that I actually stumbled down here just to avoid being stuck alone in a room with Wil.

"Missing your old dorm room crew, eh?" Hodge prompts in an overly bright voice.

"Yes!" I say with forced emphasis for the sake of the cameras. "I just wanted to find out how they're doing."

"Doing well," Hodge responds. "Everyone is giving their best, as all good Elites should."

"How are Loa and Yip?" I continue the banal conversation.

"Fine. Just fine. They'll make excellent commanding officers one day."

"They're good at their job." I pour on the praise.

"They are. Lover Fuschious has accelerated their training already. Which is why I hardly see them."

"That's amazing."

Hodge nods.

"So . . . how about . . ."

"Sif?"

I let out an awkward laugh. "Yes. Is she okay?"

"She's a very dedicated Apprentice." The tone of Hodge's voice is bright, but there's tension about his mouth. I don't ask any more.

With my fake line of questioning exhausted, I rock back and forth on my heels, scanning my brain for something to say that isn't forbidden or dangerous. But all I want to say is how excited I am about what Akela has been teaching me. And how Wil's face won't leave my thoughts. None of which I can talk about.

So I keep rocking back and forth, wracking my brain for some kind of topic to talk about. Our awkwardness grows as the silence lengthens. Hodge looks off to the side, a weird kind of uncertainty in his face.

I slap my hands against my hips. "Well, now that I've caught up with the news, I guess I'd better get going then. Okay, bye." I give an embarrassed little wave and turned away. I pace out of the dining room with as much speed as I can muster, cringing as I go.

"Smooth," I chide myself on the way out.

ALTHOUGH I CAN'T COMPLETELY AVOID THE Watcher Dorm, I spend every spare moment of the rest of the day haunting the atrium area like a ghost. Outside the tall glass windows, night falls. Orange beams of light stream down to the concrete paths, turning the hedges a strange yellow-brown.

The frenetic activity of decorating slows, replaced by crisp efficiency. Time for the nightly lecture approaches. I take my place against a wall while the cadres line up ready to listen. More time with crowds means less chance of Wil.

Framed by silver streamers, the projection wall lights up once more, and Supreme Lover Midgate's face looms over the gathering.

"Good evening, my Lovelies. May you follow your dreams and find yourselves in the universe. I love you all, I mean it.

"My Lovelies, our Triumph season preparations are proceeding with great success. This year looks to be the most love-filled festival we have ever seen. My thanks go to all of the hardworking Lovelies who give up their time and energy to provide us with the most life-affirming event of the entire year. So to express my thanks, and the grateful thanks of the entire Executive, we are pleased to announce an unprecedented gift-giving bonus this year. All eligible Lovelies will receive free entrance to the Love City parade, as well as a commemorative cup."

I start to tune out, lulled into a dreamy state by a combination of mental exhaustion and persistent memories. At times like this, it's hard to push aside the replays of every similar situation I've been through before. All the nightly lectures. All the promises of Triumph of Love presents. All the pomp and ceremony of the only time in the year when we get to have a party.

MEMORY DATE: EIGHT YEARS AGO

Memory location: Nursery Dorm 492

"My Lovelies, our Triumph season preparations are proceeding with great success . . ."

MEMORY DATE: FIVE YEARS AGO
Memory location: Nursery Dorm 492
"My thanks go to all of the hardworking Lovelies who give up their time and energy to provide us with the most life-affirming event of the entire year . . ."

—

MEMORY DATE: SEVEN YEARS AGO
Memory location: Nursery Dorm 492
"All eligible Lovelies will receive free entrance to the Love City parade, as well as a commemorative placemat . . ."

SHE NEEDS TO GET A NEW SCRIPT, I THINK TO myself. After Crucible's excruciating training exercise, I don't dare let my lips move.

"You are all my Lovelies. I mean it."

Supreme Lover Midgate smiles beatifically, and the giant screen pauses. With a burst of the Love Collective anthem, the vision fades, and the rigid groups of Apprentices melt back into life again. I lean against the cool concrete wall, waiting as they mingle and then dissipate down the stairs toward their dorms. A few turn curious glances toward me, but for the most part their eyes slide over my indigo collar, and they walk away without a backward glance.

Pim steps out from a small group of Engine Roomers and

strolls over to where I'm standing. "Hunting Haters?" she asks brightly.

"Just wanting to enjoy being around people," I reply.

"You sound worried."

"Oh no. Not at all. I just spend so much time alone that it's good to get out and feel like you're in a crowd every now and then."

"Oh."

"You were busy." I nod up at the silver streamers now adorning the space.

"What? The decorations? Yes, we're rehearsing with this space. Next week it's the Love City stages."

I look at her. "You really are going to Love City?"

Pim's eyes light up. "Oh, Kerr, it's going to be so wonderful. They've shown us maps of the whole Triumph plan, and we get to be out there in it, setting things up behind the stage. I may even get to meet . . . Carell Hummer!"

Pim's face glows with so much excitement that I can't help but smile back. "That sounds brilliant. How are you going to get across town?"

"We've got Love Squad escorts," Pim says, bouncing on her feet. "Sif and Yip are in the team. Their first Triumph mission, too."

A small stab of envy pricks at my conscience. The Watcher Dorm might be large, but it's still enclosed within the circular boundary of Elite Academy. I've never been to Love City except via screens. What would it be like to be there?

"I'm sure it will be good."

"Oh, I can't wait. We've been planning the layout and everything for ages. All of the equipment needs to be moved from the warehouses to the parks and—"

"Sounds great." My voice must betray me, because Pim stops, looking abashed.

"I'm sorry, Kerr. I didn't mean—"

"Oh, don't worry about me," I say breezily. "I'm just missing you guys, that's all." I don't tell her it's probably for the best that I'm isolated right now. Joining the Sirens was huge. Now the news of Wil's conversation wants to bubble up out of me all the time. But I can't tell anyone about anything. It makes me want to explode.

Pim gives me a kind smile. "We miss you, too. It just hasn't been the same since . . . Well, you know."

"Is Sif still being, uh, diligent?"

Pim lowers her head close to mine and her voice drops to a whisper. "You didn't hear this from me. But even Fuschious is getting a little impatient with her constant reports."

"I can't imagine that."

"Chu broke off all contact. He won't even look at her."

"What?" I'm surprised. "But he was going to try and . . . and fraternize."

"I know. But when he has to be in the same space as Sif, he acts as if she's not even there. Spends all his days and nights locked up in the Coding room. Love knows what he's working on. I think he just hangs around in there because it's the only place she'll never ambush him."

"I can't believe he would give up so easily," I say.

"You would believe it if you'd been here."

"Do you wish she would come back?"

"Wishes are for app monkeys," Pim says with a sudden flip in her demeanor. A false veneer of a smile plasters across her face. "We got more important business to attend to haven't we, Apprentice Watcher? Like Beauty Sleep, which is fast approaching."

"True. I'd better be heading back." I force myself to look like the formal and upright Watcher I'm supposed to be. I give a nod to where the lift doors wait for me like chrome sentinels.

"Love all, be all, Apprentice." Pim salutes. I nod and let her go. She chases after the last few Apprentices heading down to the dorms, and I am left basically alone with my thoughts.

In the late-evening gloom, the vast concrete atrium descends into a near-silent sanctuary. The distant hum of voices rises again from the stairwells below. A quiet whoosh of air circulates from the vents high in the ceiling above. In the dim light, silver streamers glint with a spooky kind of fervor.

Lost in my thoughts, I stare out the windows. A Love Squad night patrol marches purposefully along the path outside. They move like a multi-limbed insect, arms and legs in perfect unison as they snake away through the grounds. Under their black helmets it's impossible to tell who the Apprentices are. But their presence is enough to turn me back toward the lifts.

·

In the former days, we entrusted our fate to the unfeeling eyes of an artificial intelligence. We felt ourselves safe as it patrolled via algorithm and automation. It was that folly which allowed us to nearly be defeated. We will never make that mistake again. Humans will always remain essential to the Watcher mission.
(Elite Watcher Training Manual, 51st edition, page 36)

"WELL DONE, WATCHER."

The soothing electronic tones of the AI ring in my ears. I've done my job again. No matter how many times I tell myself I am just obeying orders, I still can't shake a horrible nauseated feeling that closes in on me every time.

Lights in the room dim. Before the screen goes completely dark, I hurry for the exit. Sometimes it feels as if the ghosts of the people I'm reporting chase me out. Every face of every person I've handed in is permanently imprinted in my memory.

What was Akela thinking, allowing the daughter of Haters to be placed in the Watchers cadre? Am I being punished for something? Surely she could have stepped in to prevent Crucible from torturing me like this.

MEMORY DATE: FIVE WEEKS AGO

Memory location: Secret bunker

"Crucible wants me to be a Watcher." I shudder, clasping my upper arms and rubbing them against the cold seeping in to my bones.

"Really?" Wil's voice sounds far too bright and chirpy for such news.

I glare at him. "You're liking this?"

He quirks a smile. "You could make the cameras look the other way."

EVEN MY MEMORIES ARE CONSPIRING against me.

The Watcher living space doesn't make me feel any better. Maybe it's supposed to be a safe cocoon, but it feels like a suffocating pillow placed over my face. I can't breathe.

Not alone. I am with you always.

Lyric's soft and gentle song leaves me with a unique feeling of warmth. It's only a small reassurance, but it's enough to blunt the knife-edge of my sadness. Absently I reach out for the Song fragments I remember. The melodies flow in, light-filled but brief.

This is how we know what love is . . .

In the beginning was the Lyric . . .

WHEN I COME TO MY SENSES, I AM LEANING on the window sill, staring at the green expanse below. Ant-like Apprentices scurry along paths and into drill fields. My heart feels light, and the heavy sense of loneliness I was feeling has evaporated.

A small ping from the elevator drags my gaze away from the window. Dorm Leader steps into the room.

"You're keeping busy, I see," she says with a wry twist to her lips.

I drop my head, shamed that I've been caught daydreaming. "I embrace myself in penitence, Dorm Leader."

"Join me at the conference desk," she says, striding over to the expansive table. "We need to talk."

I square my shoulders and take a seat, my back straight and hands clasped nervously in my lap. Akela sits down, steepling her fingers below her chin.

"First of all, my apologies for being absent so often these days. Executive Lover Crucible is inspecting the Elite education system personally, and I have a lot of . . . extra responsibilities."

A brief wave of exhaustion passes over her face. I wonder what Crucible has been doing to keep her so busy.

"That's all right, Dorm Leader. I have plenty to be getting on with."

"Good. Well, I have been assessing your lessons," she says, giving me an uncomfortable and appraising look, "and I think we have a problem."

My heart sinks. "Am I not good enough to be a Watcher?"

"Not yet." Akela's blunt statement is like a slap in the face. "But don't worry too much. I think there is a way to fix it."

"I will do whatever is required of me," I say, lowering my eyes in what I hope is a good imitation of submission.

"The main problem is that you haven't had enough experience of the real world. I've spoken to Executive Lover Crucible about this, and he has wisely suggested that we give you some more . . . realistic training."

A million possible scenarios race through my mind. What could Crucible have planned this time? Horrors sprout in my imagination, leaving me feeling faintly ill.

I lean forward. "I can work harder on my VR, Dorm Leader, if you could just give me a chance. I know I can—"

"The problem is that you're seeing the world as if it's a textbook," she says, ignoring me. "You need to experience people to be able to know them. And to know them, you have to get amongst them."

Akela holds out her infotab so I can see the screen. My face must look confused because she shakes her head and points emphatically at the image of buildings and overcars in Love City. "Out there."

I absorb the words slowly, turning them over in my head like a strange artifact I have just discovered under a rock. "Out where?"

"In Love City. Call it field training." Akela smiles. "You'll observe people in their daily work, learn how Love Citizens behave and act so that you can more easily pick up any aberrations when you're back in the observation room."

A weird, dizzy sensation gurgles up from somewhere in my stomach. My hands grip the table so hard my knuckles go white. I open my mouth, the words of denial ready on my lips. Then the memory of Wil on the obstacle course stops me in my tracks:

"Zed's going to ask you to do something for her soon . . . When she asks you, can you say yes?"

Akela lays her hands on the desk. "I wouldn't be sending you alone. Your Watcher senior will be going with you."

"Wil?"

"Yes."

"Oh."

Heat rises to my cheeks. A thought war begins to rage in my head between safety and the chance to see Wil alone again. Self-doubt battles desire. Fear battles anticipation.

"I live to serve the Collective," I say, anxiety making my words too loud for this empty room.

Akela's shoulders relax. "Good," she smiles again. "When Wil has finished his tasks in the Administration wing, I will bring him here and brief you both. In the meantime, you have some reading material on your infotab."

"Yes, Dorm Leader," I nod, seeing in her expression the significant emphasis. From her tone, it's clear that there's more to this mission than meets the eye.

"YOU WANT HER TO DO WHAT?" VIOLA squeaks. "But that's so dangerous!"

At Viola's outburst, the Siren gathering descends into a rumble of voices.

"There's another side though." Hodge gives me a reassuring wink when Viola isn't looking. "You know we're missing parts of the Song. Big chunks of it. Cadence's memory—"

"She could hold the entire Song in her head and still have room for more," Wil agrees. I can't look at him, but I can feel his eyes on me.

"Can't we just get media players to record everything?" Piccolo asks. The pale Apprentice looks like he hasn't seen sun in years. Thin wisps of black hair only accentuate his pallid complexion.

Wil shakes his head, a look of disdain on his face. "And let the devices be hacked? Or fall into the wrong hands? Are you mental?"

"Believe me," Akela says. "That has been attempted."

The room has been electrified by Akela's announcement, which dropped on the Sirens like a bomb. Around the circle, all I can see are shocked faces and worried looks. All except for Loa and Yip. Yip gives me a look of grudging admiration, and Loa's face is impossible to decipher.

Akela is watching us all from her chair, her face determined but understanding. "Data sticks can be useful," she tells us. "But our history with them is mostly negative. Almost every one was detected, and the people behind the voices disappeared. The only reason we still have the orientation data stick is because I keep it down in the bunker at all times. Cadence's extraordinary memory provides us with an unprecedented opportunity to gather the information together for the first time, in a format that can't be traced by the Love Collective AI."

Hodge looks around the room. "If Akela wants this to happen, then we can trust that she knows what she's doing," he says.

"It's a wonderful opportunity." Allegra seems to force a smile. "Think about how great it would be to know more of the Song!"

A few of the Sirens murmur agreement.

"Yeah," Fife says. "I'm sick of the bits we keep singing. I need something new."

"Fife!" Allegra gasps, horrified. Fife makes a face at her.

Beside him, Piccolo seems troubled. "You're asking her to find Sirens in Love City. Love City! She's never even left Elite Academy, let alone found her way to the secret underground."

"She'll have me to guide her," Wil retorts, sending off another riot of flutterings in my stomach.

"But she's barely joined us," Viola protests.

Piccolo shakes his head. "It's way dangerous."

Wil turns on him, angry. "So you'd prefer the Sirens to be hunted to extinction, then?"

Akela raises a hand. "We cannot delay any longer," she says. "Executive Lover Crucible made her a Watcher. So let's make the best of the mess that's been handed to us. It may yet work to our advantage, and we can recover the entire Song for the first time since the wars."

"How can we know she'll be able to do it?" Piccolo splutters.

"She will do it." Akela's voice is quiet but firm. "I have the utmost confidence in her abilities."

I have listened to all this in embarrassed silence. I've never enjoyed being the center of attention, and now is no exception.

"With Cadence on the team and the Composer at our backs, the Mission is secure," declares Hodge, surprising me with the warmth in his tone.

The Mission. All I have to do is travel across Love City with Wil under the cover of being Watcher Apprentices on field training. Along the way, Akela has organized for us to meet up with other Sirens and gather Song fragments together. It would be simple if it weren't for the threat of imminent death and torture.

"Are you absolutely sure there is no other way?" Viola pleads. I almost speak up then, ready to join in with Viola's anxious doubts. But I can't back out now.

"I said I'd do it," I say aloud. Silence falls on the room.

"Thank you, Cadence," Akela says gravely.

"We have faith in you." Hodge smiles in a way that I think is supposed to be reassuring, but it looks slightly out of place on his gruff and scarred face.

"I hope I won't let you down," I say. My eyes flick toward

Wil, and his eyes gleam in triumph. In spite of my nerves, I can't help feeling a twinge of excitement.

You and me. He mouths the words so silently that I wonder if I imagined it. But the wink that follows leaves no room for doubt. Guilty pleasure fuses into every corner of my being as I absorb the meaning behind his message. I respond with the tiniest smile.

You and me, I think.

I'VE BEEN TO THE ENTRANCE LOUNGE MANY times since arriving in Elite Academy. I've sat on the orange couches, staring at the tree-lined drive beyond the glass. I've listened to the tinkling sounds of the intricate sculptures that hang from the cavernous ceiling. But for the first time in my life, I'm standing at the doors, about to step into the wide, unknown world beyond.

Wil waits for me while I take deep, calming breaths.

"Ready?" he asks.

"Yes!" I sound way more brave than I feel.

Wil waves his wrist ID over a console beside the doors, and they swing open. A cool breeze brushes my face, bringing the nose-tickling scent of dust and concrete along with a distant whine of traffic. Morning sun glints off the silvery light poles, making the whole avenue twinkle.

Wil gives me a quick thumbs-up, and we step out together onto the pristine white concrete path.

"Where are the people?" I ask, staring at the deserted landscape.

Wil grimaces. "Safe in their living pods, no doubt."

"But I thought Love City was always busy."

"It will be. But we're not in the center of Love City yet. Out here, everyone pretty much keeps to themselves."

"Oh. So how–?"

"The overcar will be here in a minute," Wil states, staring into the distance. There's an edge to his voice that I don't understand.

Feeling awkward, I take the opportunity to stare back at the Elite Academy building. A towering slab of white concrete wall rises high above our heads, curving slowly away. It forms a solid white arch against a cloudless blue sky.

"No windows," I observe.

"Huh?" Wil glances up.

"Nothing."

"You nervous?" His eyes narrow at me.

"No reason to be."

"That's what they all say."

I raise a cynical eyebrow at him. "So how many Apprentices have you taken to Triumph, then?"

Wil's smirk returns. "Wouldn't you like to know?"

"I wouldn't ask if I didn't want to know."

He leans toward me, so close I can smell the clean scent of his uniform. "Only one."

I take a small step back. This seems to offend Wil, who puts on a wounded expression. He looks so crestfallen that I feel like I need to apologize.

"I'm sorry. I didn't mean to offend you."

"Yeah, well, you did." His shoulders stiffen, and he speaks gruffly over his shoulder. He strides away. We proceed like this for most of the driveway–him marching in stiff, angry steps and me trotting along like a chastened puppy behind him. Then he stops so suddenly that I collide with his back.

"The overcar's here," Wil says as a sleek silver blob of metal glides around the corner with a soft electric hum. When it stops, a door slides open with a smooth whine, revealing a comfortable seating area at the rear of a low wall. In front of the wall sits a driver, curious eyes turned back toward us. Her dark hair is hidden under a white cap.

"Party of two to the city?" she asks.

"That's us," Wil replies, stepping in to the plush interior without a sideways glance. I put on my best and brightest smile.

"Thank you," I say, slotting myself into the back seat in a way that puts as much distance between Wil and me as possible.

"Love all, be all." Wil waves his ID over a small panel in the wall. The panel lights flash green, and a small message scrolls across the ceiling of the overcar:

JOURNEY PAID. LOVE ALL, BE ALL.

"Don't forget your restraints," the driver says, turning toward the road.

I look around, confused.

Leaing over me, Wil pulls a long black strap from beside my shoulder. My heart beats faster. With expert, nimble fingers he clasps the strap into a buckle beside my hip and then shifts away.

The overcar gives a subtle jolt, and then whispers into motion, turning onto a wide, near-deserted highway. Tall concrete barriers painted in vivid scenes along the side of the highway block our view of the city beyond. But no amount of exciting new scenery is enough to calm the storm raging through my mind.

I don't quite understand why Wil isn't talking to me, or why I feel as if I've deeply offended him. But he is the only thing familiar, and with a jarring revelation, I realize that I would do whatever it takes to get him to talk to me normally again.

15

You may wonder why our citizens spend so much of their time on their infotabs, or why they must wear AR units when in public streets. Why are they affectionately (yet not officially) called "app monkeys" by those who know better? This is for their own good. We wish to keep their minds on happy things, so that they do not feel mistreated when food scarcity strikes the city. Distraction is our most potent medicine.

Watchers should take special note of those who are not distracted. Is a citizen without their tablet companion? Are they spending more time watching the crowds than accruing Love Points? These are the citizens to watch with special care. A citizen who will not obey the call to be entertained by us is a citizen who may well be in the grip of Hate's nefarious influence.

(Elite Watcher Training Manual, 51st edition, page 140)

THE BUSTLING STREET IS FULL OF SILVERY-white overcars and solid black vans, all gliding with an electric hum down the jet black road. Sidewalks overflow with Love City citizens, a melting pot of white outfits, navy blue service uniforms and the occasional rainbow-colored menial worker. Everyone stares into the distance, seeming to take no notice of the people in front of them.

"What's their deal?" I venture to ask Wil.

Many of the Lovers wear a small glass visor over their eyes. Some of them carry miniature glass rectangles across their noses. A few white-robed Lovers walk with bare faces but eyes that glow as if their irises are made of blue LEDs.

"What do you think?" he says impatiently. "They're earning Love Points."

"By staring?"

Wil rolls his eyes. "The AR in their headsets."

"Oh," I breathe, suddenly feeling stupid. Of course.

MEMORY DATE: CE 2272.311 (NINE YEARS AGO)
Memory location: Nursery Dorm 492

Lover Zink holds up a small glass loop. "When you graduate to do the work of the Love Collective, children, you are given a gift."

"Ooh," *says the class. Lover Zink fits the loop over his head. Beneath the glass, his eyes are magnified, and Apprentice Bez roars with laughter.*

"Three laps before dinner, Apprentice," *Lover Zink chides, looking at Bez over the top of his glass headset.*

"I embrace myself in penitence, Lover Zink," *Apprentice Bez says miserably.*

Lover Zink clears his throat. "All sorts of games and information and news will appear in front of you as you walk," *he says, flicking a display onto the big screen in front of the room. Another round of gasps circles the room. Our classroom is now covered in bright rainbow-colored graphics, advertisements, and entertainment options. Each Apprentice is replaced with an advertising sign that glows and twirls in the air. A big red rectangle in the top left corner shines with* "LP=10,435."

"See?" *Lover Zink smiles.* "Doing the work of the Love Collective is rewarding, isn't it?"

"WHY ARE WE WALKING SO FAR?" I SIDESTEP a rather grumpy-looking man. If I hadn't moved, I'm sure I'd be flat on my back on the pavement, trampled underfoot.

"Dorm Leader's mission is to watch the crowds, remember?" Wil replies, giving me a cryptic look. "Besides, the overcar doesn't need to know where we're going."

Of course, I've never been to Love City before, and so my eyes keep being drawn upward, awed by what I see. Towering apartment blocks and offices surround us—glass and concrete prisms rising so high into the sky, they cast long shadows across the road.

"That must be where the app monkeys live," I say, then give myself a little shake. Almost everyone uses the term, but it still isn't Approved Lexicon. A momentary stab of fear clutches at my chest, and I glance nervously from side to side. But the crowd just flows along, mesmerized by whatever visions their headsets are projecting.

Walking from block to block, the river of people moves around us with such speed that it drags Wil and me apart. At an expansive intersection where traffic lights beam down on the crisscrossing public, Wil stops. "Take my hand," he says, holding out his palm. "It's too dangerous to lose each other here."

I reach out and grasp his hand, and his warm fingers enfold my own. This time, when he sets off again, we stay close. I try to ignore the electric feelings going off from the contact and distract myself by watching the city. Love City at Triumph time is a riot of color. Banners unfurl from lampposts along the streets. They match the ribbonlike LED screens wrapped around buildings. A parade of light flickers around the screens, announcing Love Collective slogans:

Love all, be all.
A party like no other.
Triumph Festival: Love always defeats Hate.
Expel the Haters from our midst. Triumph in Love.
Supreme Lover Midgate wishes you a triumphant season.

Wil guides me through the crush. Our grey uniforms stand out amongst the sea of white and navy, but it looks as if everyone is too app-obsessed to notice. I tighten my grip on Wil's hand. He shoots a surprised look at me, then slows his pace so that we can walk side by side.

Eventually the crowds thin, and the streets narrow. The buildings look less glossy and more rugged. Fewer white uniforms pass us, replaced with more navy and rainbow suits.

Wil finally halts in front of an old-fashioned building made of large yellow blocks of stone. An archway over the entrance bears a sign, Love Hotel: Rooms by the Hour. When Wil begins to lead me through the archway, alarms go off in my head.

"Wait! What do you think—?" I pull away from the door and try to disengage his hand.

But he whirls me around so that I am caught close against his body. My back is pressed against the archway wall. Wil's face hovers only an inch away from mine, and he leans his free hand against the stone just behind my head. Passersby would assume we were in the middle of a lovers' embrace.

He leans down to murmur into my ear. "Play along. You'll understand soon."

Tearing my gaze away from his lips, I stare into his eyes for a few seconds, trying to work out what is happening. He's so close that I can't focus. Too close.

"We can't fraternize," I hiss, straining against his arm.

His smile is slow and inviting, but he steps back and pulls me through the slowly revolving door.

We enter a darkened lobby. Light from a high window to the street illuminates a stream of dust motes that dance in the sunbeam. Ancient leather couches form squares around low glass tables, and a few fake plants dot the space, covered in dust. The floor is cracked and worn but bears the marks of ancient luxury, with gold trim and marble patterns leading to a mahogany reception desk.

I get the feeling that people once spent a lot of money here. It doesn't take a genius to see those days are long gone now. The whole place reeks of age.

Releasing my grip, Wil places his hand in the small of my back, guiding me to where a lone worker sits behind the reception counter. The worker's greasy pink hair is a strong contrast to his navy blue service uniform. He looks up from an infotab stream as we approach, boredom transforming into annoyance.

"Yes?"

"We have a booking," Wil says smoothly, drawing me closer to his side. "The name's Burr."

The reception worker looks both of us up and down, his scowl deepening as he spots our Apprentice uniforms. He lets out a long, bored sigh and starts ferreting around in a drawer behind the counter. "Freaking Triumph season. Typical."

Feeling a sudden rush of anger, I open my mouth to protest, *I'm not that kind of Apprentice!* But a warning tap of Wil's hand on my back closes my mouth again. The reception worker pulls a small cardboard envelope from the drawer and slaps it down on the wooden counter.

"ID." He lifts up a scanner and points it at Wil's wrist. Wil smiles.

"You'll find it's been prepaid," he says smoothly, keeping his ID bars carefully hidden. The reception worker frowns and turns to the cracked old console beside him.

"So it is," he says, grumpily. "Room 637. You got two hours."

"Thank you. Love all, be all," Wil replies, sweeping the cardboard envelope into his hand and simultaneously guiding me away from the reception counter toward a bank of stainless steel elevator doors.

"What do you think you're doing?" I hiss at Wil through clenched teeth.

"Taking you for two hours of Triumph passion," he replies. Startled, I pull away. He clasps me closer. "Kidding! Just kidding. Sheesh," he mutters darkly, irritation clearly visible beneath his fake smile. "You're no fun at all."

In the elevator, Wil pulls a small rectangular card from the envelope and scans it across a black console. A green light flashes, and he presses the number six on the lift. Wringing my hands together, I feel a rising sense of panic. Wil keeps a safe distance between us during the elevator ride.

Room 637 turns out to be a dingy cube of a room that contains a large bed, a wall-like vision screen, microscopic bathroom, and a strange, shadowy figure sitting in an armchair in the corner. The figure moves to stand as we enter, and I have to stifle a scream. Frightened, I back into Wil, who lets out a soft chuckle.

"Melody." Wil smiles, inching past me and holding his arms out wide. The person steps from the shadows, becoming a rounded middle-aged woman in a blue service uniform, her grey hair pulled back into a tight bun. When she smiles back at Wil, small wrinkles crease the corners of her eyes. He makes a twisting motion with his fingers, and with a start I realize it's the same Lyric's tree movement Akela used months ago. My surprise increases when Melody returns the signal.

"You made it," she says, wrapping her arms around Wil in a warm, motherly hug. "I was beginning to wonder if I'd got the day wrong."

"Triumph season," Wil replies. "It's crazy out there today."

"Figures. Every lone Lover must be trying to get their costumes sorted before the big party starts."

"Yup."

"So this is your friend?" Melody says, turning to me for the first time. Her smile is warm and friendly, and I feel myself beginning to relax for the first time all day.

"Cadence," I say, holding out a hand in greeting. Instead of taking it, Melody wraps me in her soft hug. The gentle floral scent of her clothes reminds me of Mumma after laundry day. Against my will, my eyes sting with unwanted tears.

"We've been praying for this day," she says over my shoulder, then holds me at arm's length. "You're pretty, too. You should snap this one up before she's taken, boy."

Wil laughs. "Already on it, Melody."

I scowl at him. "And I don't get any say in this?"

"Nope," he says, the familiar cheeky expression creasing his handsome face.

"Girl even blushes pretty." Melody giggles.

"That's what I think," Wil agrees.

"So did you bring me here just to embarrass me?" I say, hating the way they both are looking at me right now.

Wil grins. "Only quiet place we could find without cameras."

"Even the Executive needs a place to get away from the Watchers every now and then," Melody finishes, walking back to the shadowy corner and pulling something out from behind a cushion on the armchair. When she returns to the lit area of the room, I can see that she is carrying a tiny black stick in her hand, wrapped in a thin black cord.

"This," she says, grasping my hand and placing the black stick into it. "It's our chapter's edition. I'd sing for you, except my voice couldn't carry a tune even if my life depended on it. So Danse risked his life to record these. He would be here himself 'cept he got a shift at the last minute. So we had to take a risk. It's an antique."

I look down at the stick and begin to unravel the earbuds.

"Should take you 'bout an hour." Melody bustles toward the door. "After that, I take that little stick and melt it into oblivion."

"You aren't staying?" I ask, feeling a little nervous about being left alone in the room with Wil.

"Can't, sweetie. I got rooms to clean." A brief look of disgust crosses Melody's face. "You just go ahead make yourselves comfortable, and leave that stick under the armchair cushion when you go. I'll be back soon as I can."

Wil glances at her. "Is that safe?"

"Safer than taking it with you," Melody responds. "I'm working this floor all day alone, so nobody but me's here to find it."

"Thank you for doing this," I tell her.

Melody suddenly clasps my hands in her own. "No. Thank you. You have no idea how . . ."—her eyes brim with tears—"how good it will be to have the Song whole again after all this time."

She clears her throat and drops my hands. "Well, gotta go earn my dinner. You be good, you hear?" she says with forced cheerfulness. "Don't go doing what these animals do when they think nobody's looking."

"Melody!" Wil gasps in shock. "Would we ever do anything like that?"

"Oh, I'm not worried about her," Melody says with a dismissive wave. She pokes Wil in the chest. "It's you with your hot-head smile and dangerous face. You keep to yourself, mister. You hear?"

Wil gives a great impression of being suitably chastised. "Yes, ma'am. I'll behave."

A wicked gleam in his eye says otherwise.

Melody doesn't seem to notice. "Good. Cadence, you make sure you learn that Song good and well. Don't let this charmer distract you, all right?"

"Yes, ma'am." Out of habit, I begin to give her a salute, then catch myself just in time.

Melody's mouth twitches, and then she is gone.

The room falls into an awkward silence. Standing in front

of the armchair, I twirl the earbuds in my fingers. I can't look Wil in the eye.

"Have fun," Wil says, taking a step toward the door.

Shocked, I look at him. "What?"

"I've got to go and meet someone." His hand rests on the door handle.

"Who?" The word sounds sharper than I mean to.

Wil gives me a shrug. "Best if you don't know. And don't tell Melody."

"But what if she comes back and sees you're not here?"

"Tell her I'm in the bathroom," he says, closing the tiny bathroom door. "Upset stomach or something. That'll keep her away."

"When will you be back?"

"In plenty of time to escort you home. Don't worry."

"Okay." It's impossible to keep the note of disappointment out of my voice.

Crossing over to me, he stares intently into my eyes. "I will come back." Slowly his face lowers toward me, but I duck around the back of the chair, putting some space between us.

"Excellent. Good. I'll see you then," I say, embarrassed and immediately hating myself for being such a coward.

"Don't open the door for anyone," he says. The door latches again with a heavy click.

"I'm not a child," I mutter, sitting down on the armchair. I fit the earbuds into my ears.

AN HOUR LATER, I'VE MADE IT THROUGH MOST of the recording. Danse turns out to have a deep baritone voice that leaves my senses tingling. Although he sings unaccompanied, I feel as if I've been to a concert.

> "Let the children come," Lyric said.
> And opened his arms out wide.
> "They are the Composer's Beloved," he said.
> And for them Lyric died.

The music ends, and silence falls like a heavy blanket over the room. Beside the armchair, the charcoal-colored curtains block out any light from outside. But the Muse's words shine brighter than the sun, and I let myself bathe in their warmth. I play it over again, just because I can.

"Let the children come," Lyric said.

In every note of the melody, I now see Lyric, the Composer spun into song. *I wish I could meet him,* I think. The words come softly back, like an answering melody sung into my ear:

> In Lyric's country, we may sing
> Free of fear or threat or woe.
> In Lyric's country we are known
> And in his name we go.
> Sing for joy, children sing,
> Lyric's country is our home.
> You are known, chosen, loved,
> With the Composer as your King.

The Muse's voice is unmistakable. Loving, soft, and strong.

Minutes tick by. I begin to feel uneasy. The time limit for our booking is drawing near, and Wil hasn't returned.

"Where did he go?" I wonder for the umpteenth time. I place my ear against the door. In the distance a vacuum cleaner drones quietly, and a vidscreen soundtrack blares across the hall. But no footsteps approach.

I glance back at the clock. Ten minutes remain.

With a frustrated growl, I throw myself onto the bed, flicking on the vidscreen with the remote. A menu glows onto the wall—a price list for entertainment options that seem tailored to the seedy tastes of hotel clientele. Wrinkling my nose, I flick the vidscreen off again.

I swing my arms around to try and get some blood flowing back through my body. The movement ruffles the heavy curtain beside me, and a sliver of light beams in.

Curious, I walk to the edge of the curtain and tickle the folds of fabric slightly away from the wall. Sunlight nearly blinds me. I blink, letting my eyes slowly adjust to the view outside.

The window overlooks a courtyard of sorts—a square of pavement surrounded by tall buildings. Beams of sun reflect off the windows, throwing the courtyard into shadow.

I draw back toward the protective gloom of my hiding place, when a movement catches my eye. Pulling the curtain closer so that only a tiny fraction of an opening remains, I search for the source.

The building opposite is even older than the ones I saw on my walk through the city. The concrete exterior is painted with fading apricot colors that have peeled away in large sections to reveal grey- and rust-colored patches. Boxy square windows are mostly empty. Except one.

In an apartment a few floors below me, two people stand in a bare room, empty save for a threadbare couch and a low brown table. The smaller figure cowers before a larger man, who has one arm high above his head. He brings his hand down viciously upon the side of the other's face.

I cry out.

Panicked, I shrink back behind the curtain, even though I know they can't hear me through the double-glazed windows. After a few seconds, I risk another peek. The smaller figure has fallen, and I can see now it's a woman. She has one elbow resting on the table for support. The other arm hangs limply at her side. A trickle of blood runs down her face, which is upturned toward the man, full of terror.

The man raises his hand again. I cannot hear what he is saying, but his face is contorted in rage and spite. He shouts at her, bellowing words that don't make it to my ears. Then he brings his hand down again. The woman is knocked to the floor, and I scream.

Horrified, I can't watch any longer. I shrink back from the curtains and begin to pace the floor.

"I've got to do something." I turn and return across the tiny space of carpet beside the bed. Flicking on the vidscreen only brings up a basic menu system that gives me a choice between Adult Entertainment, Room Service Menu, and Weather Report.

"Useless," I mutter, flicking the remote off again. My pacing resumes. Somewhere out there beyond the curtains, a woman is possibly dying, and I am doing precisely nothing about it.

"Where's Wil?" I fume. All of a sudden, the door lock beeps and clicks open. I leap into the chair, seeking the shadows. Adrenaline courses through my system. Melody hurries into the room.

"My dear, we need to get out of here," she says breathlessly.

16

Language is a weapon in the hands of Haters. What we consider to be right and true and good, they twist for their own evil purposes. It does not follow that just because a citizen uses the right words, they are therefore speaking with the right intent. Haters know Approved Lexicon just as well as faithful citizens.
(Elite Watcher Training Manual, 51st edition, page 92)

WHEN I TRY TO EXPLAIN WIL'S ABSENCE, Melody throws her hands in the air.

"If I get my hands on that boy—oh, never mind. The manager is on his way to check you out." She looks around. "Have you got the . . . ?"

Fishing the memory stick out from under my seat, I nod. Melody hurriedly pulls back the covers of the bed, messing the sheets in a way that leaves me blushing.

"The manager is already suspicious about two Apprentices using the . . . facilities," Melody says with an embarrassed smile. "Don't want to make him call in the Squad."

I pass her the small media player, which she zips into a pocket under her apron. We exit the room.

At the end of the hall, Melody stops beside a housekeepers' cart, a metal contraption equipped with cleaning supplies, towels, and a bright yellow trash bag.

She waves me toward an open door. "This is the room I'm cleaning right now, so you can hide in here until he's gone."

Mute with worry, I step into the vacant space. The heavy curtains are open, and a white beam of sunlight filters through the privacy screen onto the neatly made-up bed. This faces the opposite view from my room. From here I can see the street below, crowds of citizens milling in all directions.

Melody guides me around a corner into an armchair and picks up the nozzle of her vacuum cleaner. With a flick of a switch, we're surrounded by a humming whine. She looks at me and puts a finger to her lips.

I'll be right back, she mouths silently. Then she bustles out.

Down the hall, she speaks with a man, their voices reduced to nonsense by the vacuum cleaner's drone. But I can tell the man is angry as Melody's apology disappears under his aggressive intonations. A few minutes later, she waddles back into the room.

"Dealt with him. Now we just have to get you somewhere safe."

"Are we going without Wil?" I ask, feeling a vague flutter of panic.

"Just follow me, and we'll be okay." Melody's face is set, and my vague flutter of panic solidifies into a solid, rising wave.

We hurry back down the corridor to the fire stairs. Propping the door open, Melody places another warning finger over her lips and then ushers me through to the stairwell. We descend. By the time we reach the bottom, Melody's breath is labored, and her face is sweaty and red. She leans against the wall.

"This . . . is . . . where . . . you go," she puffs, waving me ahead. Doubtful, I glance at her before pushing through the exit door. It makes an echoing clank and opens onto a wide loading dock lined with laundry bags and folded cardboard boxes.

"This . . . way . . ." huffs Melody, pointing me toward a darkened recess where rows of shelving line the walls. I hang back.

"I don't . . ."

"No need for that," says a voice from the street.

I spin around. Wil skips up the steps of the loading dock, a wide smile on his face. "I was on my way to meet you. How did you get here?" His uniform looks ruffled, and there's a mark on the side of his face.

"Where were you?" My anger wells up from the depths of my fear.

"No time," Melody says, ushering me toward him. "You should both be gone."

Wil smiles with a relaxed confidence I don't feel, and reaches for my hand.

I brush past him, indignant. "We should be getting back."

"Of course, my lady," Wil replies, a quirk at the corner of his mouth. Before I know it, he has swept my arm under his own and leads me away from the hotel, whistling an unfamiliar tune as we walk into the sunshine.

WE'RE IN A CITY PARK WHEN MY IMPATIENCE gets the better of me.

"Where were you?" I demand, looking nervously around us for any sign of eavesdroppers. Wil eases off the pressure on my arm, and I take a step back to be able to breathe again.

He runs a hand through his hair and gives me an apologetic look. "I'm sorry. My business took longer than expected."

"What business?" I press. "We were on an errand together. You were supposed to—"

Wil places a single finger on his lips, and I stop mid-sentence. "I was going to wait, but now seems like the right time," he says. His eyes don't leave my face. "I know you're angry and you probably won't want this, but . . ."

He lifts his hand, and a small silver locket on a fine chain drops from his fingers, dangling in the air in front of me. The small necklace gleams in the afternoon sunlight, a perfect orb of metal. I stare at it, dumbfounded.

Wil's face looks crestfallen. "I was right. You don't want it." He pulls the locket back, scrunching it into his fist.

Ashamed, I make a sudden grab for his hand. "No!" I stammer. "I don't . . . I mean . . . I mean, you just caught me by surprise. What is it?"

Wil's crooked smile sends off a wild fluttering in my insides. "It's for you. I know it's not much. I don't have much. But I just wanted to give you something that showed how I feel about you." He opens his palm where the locket sits like a pool of silvery liquid.

Openmouthed, I gape at him then at the locket. "I don't know what to say."

"Say you like it," Wil quips. He toys with the chain's clasp and then holds it up, open in front of me like an invitation. "It will fit under your uniform, and nobody but me will know it's there. It can be our secret."

At my wordless nod, Wil links the clasp behind my neck.

"There," he says with a satisfied smile. "My secret girl."

My hand trembles as I hold the locket up. It is an oval shape, no bigger than my thumb. I fit my fingernail into the ridge that runs around the edge, ready to flick it open.

Wil's hand closes around mine. "There's nothing inside. But I hope that you'll think of me when you see it," he says.

He rests his hands on my shoulders, forcing my eyes to meet his. Green eyes, unblinking. Pools of color so deep I could drown in them. Somewhere in the distant reaches of my mind, a small voice of warning cries out, but I ignore it, transfixed by the Apprentice before me.

Wil's face is solemn. "You are important to me, Kerr. Do you know that?"

"I'm nobody special," I say awkwardly, staring at my feet.

Wil cups my chin in his hand, lifting my face again. "That's rubbish, and you know it. If we weren't in public, I'd . . ." He is suddenly transfixed by something over my shoulder.

"We have to go," he says abruptly. Instinctively, my head begins to turn to see what grabbed his attention, but he immediately pulls me away.

"Come on," he says, all businesslike again. I only have a few seconds to shove the locket inside my uniform before we're nearly jogging along the path toward another street in the distance. "The overcar will be waiting for us."

"What's wrong?" I ask, confused.

He just shakes his head. "Not here."

I hurry to keep up. We pass through the stone gate of the park and emerge back onto the street. Wil looks behind us and speeds our pace.

"The overcar is on the next corner," he says. "We need to move."

As we turn onto the path, I take the opportunity to look behind me. At first glance, the park looks normal. Small groups of linen-clad citizens mill around, enjoying the afternoon sunshine. Nothing looks out of place, as far as I can tell.

Using my Watcher instincts, I search again. In the distance, I see them: two men at the far end of the park. Dressed in the normal white linen uniform of the business class, they stroll along the path as if they are out for an afternoon walk. But their steps are a little too fast for a relaxed walker, and the way they cast glances at us leaves a cold, prickling fear at the back of my neck.

"Who are they?"

He silences me. "Don't look suspicious." He throws his arm around my neck, propelling me forward along the pavement.

I catch sight of a passerby watching us, one eyebrow raised. "This is worse," I yank away. "Two Apprentices fraternizing? What were you thinking?"

"Never mind." Wil is tense. "We're almost there."

In the distance ahead, a silver blob idles beside the path. A small red light gleams on the roof, indicating that it's booked. Our ride is waiting. I glance back again. The two men have thrown off all illusions of being out for a stroll. They're running.

"Wil." I grab his wrist. "They're gaining."

Wil lets out a string of curses that shock me. He pulls me into a run. We reach the overcar as the two men burst from the park onto the pavement. Panting heavily, Wil rips the door open and leaps in behind me.

With a swift swipe of his ID on the panel, he turns to the driver, pasting on a polite smile that doesn't quite work. "We're running late to get back to our Academy. Any chance you could make it a quick ride? Please?"

The driver nods and speeds off, throwing me backward into the seat. The two men have stopped near the corner, frustration written large on their faces. They watch us drive away, eyes never leaving us until we turn a corner, out of their sight.

I start to ask again but am silenced by a warning scowl from Wil. His face is pale, and beads of sweat have broken out across his forehead.

"They'll know we're from the Academy," I whisper.

"Shut up! Can you just let me think!" Wil's voice so harsh that I shrink back. Seeing the expression on my face, he calms. "I'm sorry." It doesn't sound sincere.

My hand floats up toward the locket hidden beneath my uniform. I almost want to rip it off and throw it back at him. But the image of those two men staring after us leaves me frozen in fear, so I just clasp the locket against my skin.

The ride continues in a tense silence. Wil has become a stranger, ashen-faced and shaking.

In the silent opulence of the overcar's plush interior, I have questions that find no answers.

"IN LYRIC'S COUNTRY, WE MAY SING
free of fear or threat or woe.
In Lyric's country we are known
And so in his name we go.

"Sing for joy, children sing,
Lyric's country is our home.
You are known, chosen, loved,
With the Composer as your King."

Akela leans back in her chair. The last echoes of the song fade from the concrete bunker walls. Her face glows.

"You have done well, Cadence," she tells me with a wide smile. "That was exactly what I had hoped you'd bring to us. It was so good to hear it again."

"Thank you, Dorm Leader."

"Tomorrow I will have you sing it to our Sirens. Then we will prepare for your next field trip."

My heart stills. "When?"

"In three days. Crucible has picked another location for you to visit, and I found a nearby Siren cell. They have much of the same material as us, but there are some additional pieces we haven't been able to hear for some time. Your cover will be that you're investigating life in the industrial zones."

"How do you know where these people are?" I ask curiously.

Akela shakes her head. "The less you know, the safer it is."

"Is . . . is Wil coming too?"

"Is there a reason he shouldn't?"

I swallow nervously. "No, I just wanted to check. That's all."

"She needs me to hold her hand." Wil remains jovial. The

back of his hand brushes mine in a way that sends all of my nerves zinging. I fight back the impulse to clutch at the silver locket again.

Akela's glare darts at him. "None of that, Wil."

"What?" Holding his palms up, Wil's face is a mask of wounded innocence.

The concern on Akela's face deepens. "I know it's Triumph of Love season and the rules are relaxed. But priority number one right now is to find the Song. Don't get distracted."

"Well, you did put the two of us in a room together."

"And I can remove you both just as easily. So behave."

"You know me." Wil grins. "I always behave."

"Until recently." Akela looks from Wil to me and back again. "But now I'm thinking you need a chaperone."

"But—" I blurt out, feeling my face flushing with embarrassment.

"Akela, that's not necessary," Wil says.

"Those responses don't make me feel any more confident." She gives us a distinctly suspicious look.

We share an anxious glance. "Look," Wil says. "It's true that we . . . we do enjoy each other's company." Akela's eyes narrow but Wil rushes on. "I know what you're going to say, but we can be trusted. When we're on mission, we're on mission. We wouldn't risk everyone's lives just to fraternize. Elites focus on the goal, not the game, remember?"

The sincerity in his voice rings around the room, and even I begin to feel convinced. His words seem to have an effect on Akela, too.

After a few more tense seconds, she reluctantly nods. "All right. But this is your final warning. The mission comes first. If I get even a whiff of misbehavior or distraction from either of you, I will find someone else to escort Cadence." She eyes us sharply. "Do you understand?"

I nod vigorously. "Yes, Dorm Leader."

"Of course," Wil assures her.

"That means here on campus, up in your rooms, out there in

Love City—everywhere," Akela says pointedly. "Don't do anything that will make me regret trusting you. Okay?"

"Okay," we both say together.

"The Composer be with you both." She rises, dismissing us.

LATER THAT NIGHT, I HIDE IN MY BUNK, SCOOTING back against the wall as far as I can to avoid the surveillance camera. Then I pull the chain up around my neck to take a closer look. The silver is smooth against my fingers. Tiny white spots from the ceiling lights are reflected on the curved silver face like stars. I tilt the locket back and forward, watching the light dance across the surface.

"Why would he give me something like this?" I wonder. The answer brings a flush of heat to my face.

"You are important to me, Kerr. Do you know that?"

I fit a fingernail in the thin groove around the edge of the locket, looking for a way to open it. But it remains shut as if soldered together. Resigned, I give up. He told me it was empty, so I guess that's proof.

Apart from my parents and the regular Triumph propaganda merch, nobody has ever given me a present. It must mean that I am special to Wil. The thought warms me from the inside out, and I let myself replay the day in my head. It feels good to remember the soft, warm glow of hearing the Song. I push aside the little voice of concern and deliberately ignore the memory of the two men who pursued us. I must have imagined it. It wasn't real. Only the locket and Wil's words mean anything right now.

"My secret girl."

Clasping the locket in my fingers, I fall asleep. That night, I dream irrational and wildly romantic dreams of a future where Wil and I get to grow old together. But every time we settle, two mysterious shadows hunt us, turning the dream into a nightmare.

17

A Watcher's first loyalty is to the Supreme Executive. A command from the Executive is as much the dear wish of a Watcher as the Watcher's own thoughts. In fact, a Watcher must seek to rid themselves of independent thought, and desire only to be a vessel of the Supreme Executive. For it is in this deep symbiosis that the Love Collective will truly function to its full potential.
(Elite Watcher Training Manual, 51st edition, page 176)

THE NEXT MORNING, EXECUTIVE LOVER Crucible appears in the Watcher Dorm, a greasy look of satisfaction on his withered face.

"I will be supervising your lessons from now on," he says after I have nearly prostrated myself in greeting. As if to prove his point, he waves a thin white infotab in his desiccated hand.

I school my face into blank acceptance, but my mind goes into overdrive. Crucible is here? Why not Akela? "Of course, Executive Lover," I say, hoping he can't see any distaste in my expression. Crucible always looks me up and down as if I'm a tasty morsel he wants to devour.

"May I ask why?" I ask primly.

"You may not."

I wish Dorm Leader was here. Or Wil.

"Find me ten Haters before lunch," Crucible commands,

pointing to the Watcher room door. "I have set you coordinates and locations. All you need to do is inform on the attendees."

"Yes, Executive Lover." I bow, fighting off mutinous thoughts. My least favorite person is sending me to my least favorite place. Why is he so confident I'll find Haters, anyway? What do I do if they're all innocent?

Crucible dismisses me with a curt nod, and I force my steps into the darkened, soundproof hellhole that is my workspace for the day. I lock the door behind me for good measure.

"Welcome, Apprentice Flick," the announcer's voice sounds as if she's trying to soothe me to sleep. But the lights below and around me become the pulsating lasers of a nightclub.

Bodies jump up and down to the throbbing beat and bass, faces lost in the mesmerizing power of the music. One entire wall of the club is taken up by a mirror-lined bar, where Lovers in black outfits serve drinks to a drunken crowd. I swoop between cameras, seeking quiet corners where small pockets of patrons interact, heads close together. In the tiny corridor leading to a bathroom, I catch a dealer palming a small package of contraband to another customer. Red flag numbers one and two.

"Small fry, Apprentice," Crucible squawks in my ear. "Get me something decent, not this piffle."

Alarmed, I don't bother waiting for the Squad to appear but move upstairs to a room behind thick-carpeted walls. A series of gold letters announce VIPs Only. The beats are muffled to the level of dull thuds. More vivid are the sounds of clinking glass and laughter. A semicircle of lounges sit around a central table, littered with bottles and half-eaten plates of expensive food.

In one gilded corner, a large man reclines on a leather lounge, his white linen suit a glaring contrast to the black decor around him. His face is bloated and flushed, and he rubs at his bald head with chubby fingers. Two navy-clad women lean toward him, hungry smiles on their faces. They feed the VIP grapes—delicacies worth more than most Lovers would earn in a year. His laughter bounces around the room as if he doesn't care that he just swallowed an apartment's worth of credits.

To the left of the bald man, a crowlike figure perches uncomfortably on a spacious leather couch. He looks very out of place in this debauched gathering. His figure is trim, but his face looks worn beneath the regulation-style black hair that spikes up around the top of his head. Two small gold bands around his collar tell me he has an important position in the Hall of Love.

"Oh relax, Zee," croons the grapes man. "At least have one drink, for Love's sake! You haven't even said hello to our beauties." He makes a loud smooching sound, his moistened lips puckering toward one of the women.

"Why did you invite me here, sir?" Lover Zee asks, looking as if he had swallowed something spiky and unpleasant.

The large man lets out a bellowing laugh. "Why wouldn't I invite the newly appointed Under Secretary to the Security Sub Commissariat? Really, Zee, you have no idea how far you've come in these last few months."

"Speaking of that, Chief Lover, I—"

"Here. Have a grape." The Chief pushes one of the women so hard she flies at Lover Zee with a distressed squeak. Zee catches her clumsily on his lap, then drops her as if she were a burning ember. The woman lands awkwardly and skulks away into a lounge on the other side of the room.

Wiping his hands nervously on his pants, Zee stands. "Thank you so much for the invitation, Chief Lover, but I really must be going. I can't . . . There's somewhere I have to be. You are my tribe, all of you. I mean it." Zee's eyes dart from side to side.

The Chief Lover snorts as Lover Zee nearly runs from the room. "Looks like we've got another over-starched recruit on our hands. Too conscientious by half."

A wave of laughter cackles around the guests.

"Where should we transfer him to, I wonder?" the Chief Lover taps his chin. "Warehouse patrols? Rural supervision?" Each of his suggestions is met by another round of jeers.

Crucible's voice crackles through the speakers. "Flag the whole room," he croaks. "Fareyn can just find himself a new Security Sub Commissariat, for all I care."

"Sir?" I squeak.

"There's more than enough there to fill your quota," Crucible's disembodied voice snaps. "Flag 'em."

Fingers shaking, I follow his orders, leaving only the two navy-uniformed women unchecked. It's not their fault they had to work this room. In the status display on my screen, I see the Love Squad signal approaching. No doubt the whole place will be shut down in a few minutes.

"I said *all* of them," Crucible bellows through the speakers. I jump in fright. "Sir?"

"Are you deaf?" His harsh voice takes on an incredulous tone.

I bow to the air in front of me. "No, sir. I mean, yes, sir. I live to serve the Love Collective, sir."

Hands shaking, I hover over the two women's faces. My heart is screaming at me to stop. They don't deserve this. But Crucible has ordered it. I cannot disobey his order, especially not if I want to keep my own head. Feeling slightly sick, I press the red button twice, and the whole room is finally highlighted in accusatory colors.

"Target acquired," croons a soft female voice. "Love Squad proceeding to location."

Nausea builds. I know Crucible wants me to witness the arrest, Watcher that I am, to ensure that all flagged citizens are properly apprehended and removed from the room. But I really want to take it all back. Or run away until there is no breath left in my lungs.

Dreading the inevitable, I swing around the room, listening

for any treasonous conversations. Apart from the Chief Lover's jibe at Lover Zee, all of the talk seems innocuous. Trivial competitions and betting on the next Lovers' Pavilion show. The occasional lascivious comment directed at the two women, who pretend that they're enjoying themselves while sharing secret looks of disgust.

Doors burst open, shattering the heartiness of the room. A dozen black figures explode into the space. With practiced precision, the soldiers drag frightened partygoers away. The fat man struggles to rise from his cushioned bed, angry protests on his lips.

"Now see here," he begins.

He gets no further because a Love Squad officer immobilizes him with a swift jab. It takes four officers to lift him out. Before long, only toppled glass bottles and a distant thumping beat remain.

"I'll allow you a pass," Crucible's desiccated voice crackles. "But only just. Get back to VR and practice drills."

CRUCIBLE'S TRAINING REGIMEN SOON becomes a habit. Every day I spend hours upon hours finding people using the Watcher sphere. I work until my hand cramps and my ankles ache. Crucible won't allow any rest.

Snapping out of another intellectual party where I've flagged four philosophers Crucible detested, he sends me to watch a street scene. Although I'm sure he wants me to follow the well-dressed group emerging from a designer store, a man in dirty linen clothes draws my attention.

Unseen by the Lovers around him, the man runs through the streets as if being pursued. Glancing over his shoulder, he bumps into a Lover's shoulder. The Lover overbalances. Their glass goggles fly from their heads and the Lover crashes to the ground in a white linen heap. But the man in dirty clothes runs off, his arms in a rough gesture of apology.

The injured Lover shouts. But the crowd of Lovers, still so caught up in their own AR goggle world, barely register anything. A few Lovers hear the sound and stare around them. But the AR is too powerful, so nobody sees anything. The injured Lover lurches into traffic to retrieve his glass visor. Meanwhile, the figure in grubby clothing disappears down an alley.

I turn away, pushing the vision back to the designer store.

"Follow him," Crucible commands, voice dripping with displeasure.

"Yes, Executive Lover."

I shift the controls and seek out the grubby figure again. The software connects the separate cameras seamlessly, so it feels as if I'm in a drone, flying behind the man as he flees toward a dead end. Concrete walls hem him in between trash piles and broken furniture. Just when I'm about to lock on to his figure with the red circle, he crouches and slides down into a large stormwater drain, disappearing from sight.

"Executive Lover?" I call, knowing he is watching me from outside the room.

"Yes, Apprentice?" Crucible's voice is rife with irritation.

"This suspect has disappeared into the drain system."

"Send in the biological measures," he commands. Confused, I look around the sphere in front of me for some kind of clue as to what he's talking about. He must be watching me because he makes a frustrated clucking noise.

"Code 50-34," he informs me impatiently. "Call it in with the coordinates, and the Hall will send in a tracker drone."

"Oh," I say, feeling stupid. I follow Crucible's instructions and wait to hear from the Hall's communication channel. I have to ask. "Sir, why have I never heard of it before?"

"They're only for subterranean work. Strictly speaking, they were decommissioned a few years ago. But I've sent a message explaining that your request is at my authority. You won't have any problems."

Sure enough, after a delay which stretches out for minutes, a terse reply comes back through the audio channel. "Executive request granted. Biological measure dispatched."

I spend a few more minutes watching the entrance to the drain but see nothing.

Crucible, again, is closely observing me. "You won't see anything from there," he mocks. "When the drone is finished with him, there won't be much left to embrace. Get on with the next case."

I give an obedient nod as my body goes numb. What did I just do?

WHEN AKELA FINALLY CALLS ME IN FOR A briefing in the secret bunker, I blurt out my problems as soon as I'm through the door.

"I can't do it anymore."

Akela frowns. "What's wrong?"

"I can't stop seeing them, Akela. Every face is still up here." I tap at my temple. "Can you even begin to know what that's like? I remember every single one of the people I have reported. How can I live with that on my conscience?"

Akela doesn't answer.

I pour my frustration into the silence. "Before I got my memories, you said I was completely the wrong person to be a Watcher. And you're right. Today Crucible made me send in biological measures for a fugitive." Akela's face pales. "It's . . . it's killing me." My eyes sting with tears. Akela reaches out to comfort me, but I avoid her. "How long do I have to keep doing this? I can't spend the rest of my life in darkened rooms informing on people. Their blood is on my hands." I thrust out my palms, half expecting to see them stained red.

"You can protect people, too."

"How? Crucible's always breathing down my neck, thanks to this audit. If I don't report every suspicious person I find, *I'll* be arrested."

"I know it's hard, Cadence, but—"

"No. You don't know," I nearly shout. Her pained look brings a stab of guilt. Of all people in this universe, it's Akela who knows how hard it is to be a Siren in plain sight. She knows that more than anyone.

"I'm sorry." I rub at a dull ache that is starting to throb in my temple.

"Don't get me wrong, Cadence. I'm sorry you have to go through this struggle. But the situation is dire. With the Executive more suspicious than ever, I'm afraid we have no alternative."

"I need to get out of here. Put me into the Coders cadre. I can write hidden code for you, hack into systems. I can make sure the Sirens are safe from the surveillance algorithms without having to report anyone. You saw my Filtering results. Coding was my best score."

She runs a hand wearily across her face. "You can't go on field trips if you're a Coder."

Reality finally hits, and I slump down into a chair. "Oh."

Akela watches me, her expression thoughtful.

A heaviness settles on me. If I can't leave the Academy, then I can't get the Song. If I can't go looking for the Song, then I can't hang out with Wil either. Or sing for other Sirens.

"You see the dilemma now? Getting you field trips was the payoff."

"So I either have to report people or give up collecting Song fragments?" I ask.

Lyric help me.

"There's a line in Lyric's saga that seems appropriate right now," Akela remarks.

"What is it?"

She starts to sing softly. It still echoes around the concrete walls. "'Throw your cares on him because he cares for you.'"

"How?"

She sighs. "I always get into trouble when I try and do the Composer's work for him. It's best to let him be him."

"Can he do anything?"

"'Greater is the Muse in you than the one who is in the world,'" Akela sings again. "I hold on to that one a lot when I'm worried."

A sudden thought shines in my head like a beacon. A brief glimpse of a woman's fearful face illuminated in a window, cowering as a man raises his fist toward her. My last excursion to Love City, and the scene I couldn't forget.

"What if—I mean, what if there is a way I can redirect the squads?" I ask.

"What do you mean?"

"I mean, can I send them to arrest people who are actually hurting others, instead of people like Sirens? Crucible keeps on making me watch intellectuals at parties. Could I focus on catching people who are hurting other people for real? You know, like people who beat other people up or take their stuff."

"Mm," Akela demurs. "Didn't he say he didn't want small fry?"

"Yeah, but—"

"That's going to be tough," she says. But she is obviously thinking.

I watch her hopefully.

Akela puts her fingers together. "You'll have to send him a lot of targets."

"It's not perfect," I admit. "But, in having to look at them, it's the only way I can stay sane."

18

They have been told it was a war that threatened their serene and secure way of life. But it was not war that caused us to lose almost all of our technology. The disaster that befell us, when we were nearly obliterated into Stone Age primitivism, was brought upon us by our own lack of vigilance. It was the hubris of our own self-congratulation that nearly ruined us. Had we been more watchful, we may not have allowed the threat to gain a foothold in the first place.
(Elite Watcher Training Manual, 51st edition, page 222)

MY NEWFOUND PLAN BEGINS EARLY THE next morning. I get up an hour early and go to the Watcher room as quickly as I can. The process makes my skin crawl, but I need to get my quota before Crucible arrives.

It's all too easy to find violence in Love City. My first visit is to the apartment I saw from the hotel room. I flag the man who I saw attacking his flatmate, but in an apartment two floors up I spot another. Soon, I am flying around alleyways and tenements, flagging drug dealers and thieves. Violence simmers barely below the peaceful surface of Love City. I feel as if I've lifted a rock and discovered a bugs' nest crawling in the shadows.

"So much for the Love Collective Precepts." I flick the red

button on a man who is standing over a fallen figure, blood dripping from the knife in his hand. Crucible would call him "small fry," but I figure that if I can find enough of them, he won't be able to complain.

When Crucible finally arrives, I emerge from the Watcher room with my face carefully expressing the appropriate level of solemn obedience. He narrows his eyes, evaluating me as I report my findings: double my usual daily quota. Withered fingers flicking across his infotab, he begins to interrogate me about the criminals I have reported.

"This one?" he rasps, pointing to a man I found in the marketplace.

"Suspicious Anti-Love activities," I reply, giving the official transgression category.

"Huh." Distaste is written on Crucible's face, but he flicks across his screen again. "What about this one?"

"Treason. He killed someone."

A grey eyebrow on Crucible's face rises. "Really? Who did he kill?"

"I believe it was another shop vendor. From what I could tell, they had an argument about stealing one another's customers."

"That's not treason." Crucible snorts derisively.

"The victim was wearing a Love Collective flag, Executive Lover."

The sharp, evaluating stare is directed at me again. "Hm."

"Has this fulfilled my quota, Executive Lover?" I stare at a point over his head.

"You have clearly been diligent." Crucible is still flicking at his screen. Finally, with a tired sigh, he casts his infotab onto the cushion of the lounge beside him. "That will be enough for this morning," he says. "VR drills for the rest of the day."

I nod, feeling triumphant. "Of course, Executive Lover."

BY THE END OF EACH DAY, MY BODY IS ZINGING with tension, but my brain is completely exhausted. I fall into a fitful sleep, peppered by nightmare dreams that involve my parents being interrogated and arrested. The worst nightmare is when I find myself standing in the witness dock while they are standing in the accused chamber. I wake up in a cold sweat more often than not and have to drag my exhausted body out of bed in the morning.

Today, when I shuffle into the common room, Wil is in the kitchen area, scoffing down a bowl of protein cereal.

"You look terrible," he says between mouthfuls.

"Thanks a lot." I stagger for the fridge to grab a bottle of water.

"Okay, see you." He sets the bowl down.

"Where are you going?" I ask. "It's only just 0600."

"Dorm Leader assignment."

I shake my head. "She's got you busy."

His eyes shift sideways. "Yeah. Yeah, she does." Before I can say anything more, he bolts from the room.

I'm too tired to do an early Watcher run, so the time spent waiting for Executive Lover Crucible is excruciating. I wish Dorm Leader wasn't too busy with the demands of his inspection to be here. Her presence is calming, even if she can't openly back me up.

But today, Crucible doesn't arrive by the usual start time. At 0800, the room's announcement system chimes with a soft *ding* to remind me to begin work.

After a quick deliberation, I step up to the VR booth, letting my headset fall down over my eyes. I know Crucible well enough by now to know that he would not be happy to find me standing around doing nothing when he turns up.

Safely cocooned in VR, I swoop back into the Triumph festival training exercise. It's easy now to find several Haters in the hypnotized, dancing crowd. I just wish that every exercise didn't keep reminding me of uncomfortable memories. The way Wil rescued, then confused me. The fact that I have to report real people for Embracement. The way I seem to be purchasing my own safety at the price of other people's lives.

I run through the training exercise five times before risking a break. When I emerge from VR, the Watcher Dorm is still silent and empty.

"Where is Executive Lover Crucible?" I ask the vacant air. The AI gives me no reply, so I wander into my room to collect my infotab. Hiding back in the safety of my bunk, I flick over to the Siren message system to see if Akela has left me any clue.

Mission with X coming. Wait for signal, is all the information I get from her. But a chat conversation seems to be raging between the other Sirens.

Viola: *Ugh. Triumph fever. My eyes!!!*

Allegra: *I know. It's like the entire Academy forgot how to control themselves.*

Hodge: *Only a few weeks left. Hang in there.*

Viola: *YOU AREN'T IN MY BUNK ROOM.*

Allegra: *Dining room is worse.*

Viola: *It's gross.*

Hodge: *It's only bad because Elites know this is their one chance to fraternize each year.*

Allegra: *Well, they're certainly making up for lost time. Blergh.*

Fife: *I can kinda understand it.*

Viola: *ARE YOU JOKING???*

Hodge: *Cool down. Go run on the obstacle course or something.*

Fife: *The obstacle course is full of them, so watch your step.*

Viola: *Can't we just hang out together at meals? I need a break.*

Hodge: *You know the drill, V.*

Allegra: *BUT WHY??????*

I flick the infotab off and safely stow it back in the charging dock. I wonder what's going on.

Straightening my uniform, I decide to go for a walk. It's time to see for myself what has horrified my Siren comrades so much.

The lift delivers me to the atrium with silent efficiency, and the doors open to something that jolts me. All around the open space, small groups of Elite Apprentices mingle. Faces pressed together, arms locked around each other. It's all so shocking that I almost turn around and retreat back to the safety of my dorm.

I avert my eyes and focus on the direction of the dining room, taking care to step around couples sitting on the stairs as I descend. The usual lunchtime hum emanates through the doorways, but the sight that greets me is just as bad as the atrium.

Triumph fever has hit.

Sidling up to one another in line, couples snuggle in small pockets, heads together and arms entwined. The atmosphere of the room is uncomfortably charged with pheromones and desire. I start to retreat, but a bright, familiar smile catches my eye.

"Flick! Hi!" Cam calls from a nearby table. Farr sits on Rook's lap, twining her fingers in his short sandy hair. Pim is beside an unfamiliar black-haired Apprentice who leans into her with a hungry smile. Chu has his arm around Sif, who looks so different I nearly don't recognize her. The old cheeky smile is back, and her eyes are wide as she gazes lovingly up into Chu's face. I stop dead, stunned by the image.

"I know. It's sickening." Cam looks distinctly uncomfortable as he follows my gaze.

"I thought he was avoiding her."

Cam merely shrugs. "He played her well. All that mean treatment made her crazy, so when he finally spoke to her, she nearly jumped on him right then and there."

I stare at them. "Interesting strategy."

"Yeah, well I think I'm the only person who can't wait for Triumph season to be done," he grumbles.

You're not the only one.

"Haven't you found someone?" I ask innocently.

"Not yet. Are you free?" Cam smiles.

I inch away from him. "Uh, no."

"Figures," he sighs, looking crestfallen. "I don't know what I'm doing wrong. Everyone else seems to have found a Triumph buddy."

Sif looks up from her canoodling, and a shadow crosses her face when she recognizes me. "Oh. It's you."

"How are you, Sif?" I ask, keeping my voice carefully even.

She turns back to gaze at Chu. "Busy," she replies curtly. Chu doesn't even turn, but smiles back at her with an adoring expression.

I feel the ache of the distance that has grown between us. Our easy friendship seems like an age ago now.

"I'd better get back," I say quietly.

Cam grabs my wrist. "Can't you keep me company for a while?"

I press my lips together. "I can't."

"I'm going to die alone." Cam looks miserable. "And nobody cares."

"I do care, Cam. Really. But if I don't get my training quota done, I'm in trouble."

"Fine. Go."

With a last apologetic look, I turn to leave. "Sorry," I say again.

"Whatever." Cam slumps in his seat.

THE WATCHER DORM'S SILENCE IS A WELCOME relief after the visual onslaught that is the dining hall in Triumph season. My shoulders relax the moment I step into the cool interior. It's quiet. The lights are dim. The VR chambers are empty, waiting like silent sentinels against one wall.

Wil sits alone at one end of the table, as still as stone. He looks up at me, and my heart does its flip-flops again.

"Love all, be all, Apprentice," I say carefully.

He stands slowly, face streaked with shadow. "It's time," he says, and it doesn't take a genius to know what he's talking about.

"When?" I reply.

"Now."

"Okay."

The air is humid and cloudy as we step out of the Academy for the second time in my life. Like the last mission, a sleek silver overcar turns up to meet us. With us comfortably seated inside, it glides down the drive, turning in the opposite direction from our first mission. I'm startled, but I know better than to say anything in front of the driver. Instead, I watch the highway walls pass by, drinking in the occasional suburban views and hoping there might be a chance that Wil would talk to me again. The locket rests snugly against my collarbone, hidden from view.

To pass the time, I let some Song fragments ramble through my head. The Muse's whispers calm me and lift my thoughts away from the Triumph tumult and into a quieter plane. The more the Muse sings, the less chaos I find. Worries that were pressing against my thoughts now don't seem as important anymore.

"Is it much further?" I ask, watching the grey sky above the highway barriers. Bulbous shapes ebb and flow in the soft vapor. There might be a storm later.

"Twenty minutes, or so. Not too far," Wil says. "The warehouse district is downriver."

"I know." My voice is calm and happy. I glance at Wil to find he is giving me a confused look.

"Are you okay?" he asks.

"Yeah." I smile. In my head, I'm replaying the Song fragments I learned last time. They float around like a flock of birds, swooping melodies and mind-bending poetry mingling in a symphony of wonder.

Wil's hand brushes mine, and the flock scatters.

After twenty minutes, the overcar turns off the highway. We glide past huge rectangular blocks that form concrete warehouses. Workers in brown shuffle in and out of warehouse doors. Large vehicles thunder down the road nearby, belching black smoke into the air.

The overcar heads down a road that slopes toward a brown ribbon of water. In front of us, the river meanders through the warehouse district like a chasm, cutting between white concrete buildings and separating teams of workers from each other. A few low barges putter along the river, decks crammed with containers.

"Pull over here," Wil says, leaning forward.

The driver nods, and pulls to the side of the road. We get out into the afternoon haze, and the warm air brings the scent of diesel fuel, rusted metal, and sulfur.

"That's not pleasant," I say, trying in vain to stop the smell from getting into my nose.

"Kind of glad Watchers stay in the Hall of Love," Wil agrees, face wrinkling in disgust.

We head toward the river. Wide concrete docks line the waterfront, and barges gently rock against their thick rope tethers. Machinery chugs out of the warehouses, carrying containers and boxes from the giant open doors out to the waiting boats. In our grey-and-indigo uniforms, we stand out easily. A few faces turn to us in curiosity, and I feel a nervous twinge of fear.

"Is it safe?" I whisper to Wil.

"Nothing ever is," he informs me. "As long as you remember that, you've got half a chance to survive."

19

A Watcher's task may be simple, but it is deceptively so. Watchers never make mistakes. Their judgement is final, and their decision is irrevocable. This is not because they themselves are perfect. But it is because they have trained and practiced until an error is impossible.
(Elite Watcher Training Manual, 51st edition, page 101)

THE SECRET MEETING PLACE TURNS OUT TO be somewhere in a food processing warehouse. We're greeted at the door by the warehouse manager, an older man with a wisp of greying hair across the top of his head.

"Ah, the Watchers in Training are here." He smiles, though he wrings his hands nervously. "Come in, come in. I'm Lover Benz. I'll be conducting your tour this morning. It is a great honor to have you with us."

He ushers us into a packing room, where tubes of protein food are boxed by robotic arms along a conveyor belt. A few workers hustle around, supervising the machinery and moving boxes into larger containers for transport.

"You'll be wanting to learn about our food production processes, wouldn't you?" he asks in a voice that's just a touch too loud.

"Yes," Wil says.

The old man's obvious acting makes me cringe. Anyone feeling suspicious would see through him in a heartbeat. But the rest of the workers go on as if nothing has been said. If anything, they appear too nervous to make eye contact with us.

After a long and tedious tour of every production line, office and storage facility in the building, the manager leads us down to a dim basement area. When I think we can't go any further. Benz stops beside a large stainless steel wall. The area is deserted and smells of damp timber and metal. Opposite the steel wall, a row of thick, warm jackets hangs from a series of hooks.

Lover Benz's smile disappears. He lifts a jacket from one of the hooks and holds it out to Wil. His eyes flicker to the thick, insulated door set into the steel wall.

"This is one of our food storage rooms," he says quietly, glancing up and down the corridor. "I think you'll learn some interesting facts in here. You'll need these, though."

Wil takes the jacket from Benz's hands. A doubtful look crosses his face, but he pulls the thick coat on anyway. Benz picks out a slightly smaller one for me. The jacket is so thick that I begin sweating almost immediately. A bulge in one of the pockets turns out to be a snug pair of warm gloves. I fit them over my hands.

When Benz has donned his jacket, he pulls on a solid steel lever built into the door. With a crackling noise and a rush of cool air, the thick door breaks from its seal. We step over the threshold into a vast chilled room and make our way between rows of steel shelving that are illuminated by dim blue lights.

The air is so cold my breath comes out in misty clouds. All around me, thick insulated boxes bulge with vegetables and fruits, some of which I have never seen before.

"Wow." I lift a bulbous green vegetable from one box.

"I wouldn't do that if I were you," Benz lets me know.

"We often have to arrest workers who try and steal the food from here."

I instantly drop the vegetable. "Sorry."

"No harm done. But if anyone asks, we came in here to discuss the problem of worker theft, not what we're really about to do," he says. I feel a brief flash of alarm. Then his fingers curl into Lyric's tree signal, and my shoulders relax.

"Down here," he says, nodding over his shoulder to a section of the cool room hidden behind a wall of boxes. Long plastic strips hanging from the ceiling form a kind of doorway, and we push through into a small square of concrete that contains two wooden chairs.

"Zed tells me you can remember things," Lover Benz says to me.

Wil nods. "I've never seen anything like it."

"I don't know about that." I blush.

"Could you share something with me?" Lover Benz's question is almost shy. "It's been so long since I—"

"If we have time," Wil interrupts. "I think we'd better hear your fragments first."

"I would love to." I intentionally ignore Wil's impatience.

"No, he's right," Lover Benz says reluctantly. "We haven't much time. Take a seat. If we're here too long, you'll end up with frostbite. Or they'll send someone down to check on us."

Wil and I sit, and Benz leans against one of the rows of cardboard boxes. In a soft tenor voice, he begins to sing. Notes echo off the cool room walls. My memory records the words and the melody, and the Muse begins to stir my heart in response. It's a story of Lyric. As odd as our surroundings may be, hearing this music feels like the most natural thing in the world to be doing right now.

> Lyric, though in nature the Composer himself
> Did not snatch at his rank, nor use it for gain.

> But reduced himself to nothing for us
> Walked as we walked, Composer sung into flesh.
> Though he sang stars into existence,
> He let men hang him on the tree.
> Loving those who hated him
> Though the blind could not see.
> Fully Composer, Fully Song in harmony
> Opening our eyes to love,
> From death to set us free.

When Lover Benz finishes, my toes are numb with cold. But my eagerness to hear more is stronger.

"I-is t-there a-any m-more?" My hopeful voice comes through chattering teeth.

"Not now," Benz says with a quick smile. "We have to get you out of here before the cold gets to you. Also, if we stay here too long, the security team might get suspicious and wonder why the cool room cameras are switched off."

"B-better get m-moving then," Wil says briskly. We maneuver back through the rows of vegetables, and Lover Benz pushes the heavy door open again, letting us out into the warm air of the basement corridor. We take off our jackets and leave them back on the hooks. Then we go back up into the main warehouse upstairs. I pause and turn to our guide.

"Thank you for teaching us that," I say, then stop in shock. A quick glance tells me I've blurted out in front of at least two different cameras. Lover Benz's face pales.

"Ah, yes . . . yes," Wil says loudly. "We will be sure to watch out for vegetable thieves more carefully in the future."

"I would never have known about the concealment techniques until you told us," I add with a nervously forced laugh.

Lover Benz frowns. "It's no laughing matter. The Love Collective cannot afford to lose such precious commodities to the black market," he says stiffly. "Love all, be all."

With stilted steps, he turns and marches away from us. I salute at his back, feeling miserable.

"Come on." Wil pulls at me. I let him guide me out of the warehouse and into the open air. The sunshine is almost mocking in its brightness. I want to apologize to Wil, but black camera eyes stare down at us from almost every building. There's nothing for it but to pretend I didn't just nearly expose our whole operation. Time to make-believe that I'm a loyal and hardworking Watcher Apprentice, not a failure who is desperately wishing the ground would open up and swallow her whole.

I'M SO CAUGHT UP IN MY OWN SELF-accusations that I become a passenger to Wil's direction, letting him walk us through the streets without question. Only when a shadow falls across my path do I surface from my reverie.

"Where are we?" I stare at a wall of unfamiliar warehouses. Somehow we have ended up in a narrow four-way intersection, surrounded by identical concrete blocks and beaten-up garbage disposal units. There's an acrid smell of urine and refuse. The only signs nearby are the green glowing Exit labels above the occasional door. The whole place looks eerie and deserted.

"This is our next stop." Wil heads toward an empty loading dock.

"What—?"

Wil waves me silent with his hand. "Shh."

He stops and turns to me. "I almost forgot." And with a slow and enticing smile, he leans into me. I'm so startled that I freeze. His hand rests on the back of my neck, and his green eyes fix me in place like I'm cemented to the pavement. Then he pulls me to his chest. Once again I feel the solid warmth of his ribs, hear his heartbeat thumping slowly and calmly. When he pushes me away, I'm left gaping like a dying fish.

"What was —?" I stammer. My heartbeat pounds thunderously in my ears. He's already turned away.

The loading dock spreads before us. The interior is dark and shadowy. A Love Squad detail could be hiding in there, and we wouldn't know until they pounced on us.

Already feeling tense, I nearly scream when someone steps toward us from a dark corner. Clad in a brown uniform, his face is pockmarked and red. A sheen of sweat covers his forehead, and his hair is receding. He squints over Wil's shoulder, shooting suspicious glares in my direction. I shrink back.

"You were supposed to be alone," he snarls at Wil and spits on the ground as if to reinforce his point.

Wil just shrugs, looking calm and confident. "What have you got for me?" he asks.

The man stares me up and down. I hold my breath. Then he cocks his head toward the shadows behind him. Wil steps forward. I make a move to follow. The man nearly hisses.

"Not her."

Wil turns to me with a wide smile that I'm sure is meant to be comforting.

I look from him to the scowling man and back again. "Wil? What is going on?" I thought I was supposed to be learning Song fragments, so why am I not allowed to be a part of this?

Wil's voice is soft and soothing. "It's okay, Apprentice. I won't be long. Wait for me."

I nod speechlessly. They disappear into the darkness, and I hear a soft rumble as they discuss something that's obviously too important for me to know. After it's clear that I won't be able to hear anything, I wander back out into the light, leaning against the factory wall. The scent of garbage is pungent.

Wil's behavior has sent me on another tailspin. The more I try and think my way through his actions, the less sense they make. But the memory of his hug still lingers down my body. My neck still feels the touch of his fingers. My cheeks still remember the soft press of his uniform against my face. I keep that memory in the forefront of my mind, and it comforts me. We might be out here in a strange part of Love City, but he will protect me.

After a few more minutes of hushed murmurs and urgent whispers, Wil strolls out. He flashes a tense smile when he spots me, running his finger around the inside of his indigo collar. I let him walk all the way over to me. The Elite uniform shows off just a hint of his muscular frame.

"Shall we go?" he says brightly. Feeling embarrassed about my private thoughts, I don't say anything, fearful he might accidentally be able to read my mind. His smile doesn't waver. "It's okay. There's no reason to worry. We should probably get back to our ride, though."

"What's going on? Who was that guy?"

Wil closes his eyes, looking pained. "Why do you not trust me?"

I rush to reassure him. "No, I do, really I do. It's just that—"

"Thanks. At least I know where I stand." Wil turns away from me.

"Wait," I call as he widens the distance between us. "I didn't mean to—"

Wil ignores me and continues to walk away down the road toward a distant intersection. His pace is so fast that I have to trot along to keep up with him.

"I'm sorry," I say.

"Forget it, Flick."

The way his face has shut down fills me with dread.

I try and explain again, but he gives me the silent treatment. He doesn't speak all the way back to the waiting silver bullet of an overcar. He sits silent and tense, staring away from me for the entire trip home. And when we arrive back at the Academy, he goes off to his sleeping quarters without even so much as a backward glance.

Completely miserable and confused, I throw myself onto my own bunk, letting the hopelessness blossom into a dark cloud. I reach inside my uniform, searching for the familiar silver chain, but then jerk upright.

Wil's locket has gone missing, which just seems to top off an already stinking end to the day.

"Figures," I moan.

20

The greatest threat to our Collective began in obscurity. Therefore, we must never ignore the obscure places in our quest for peace. Rebellion does not foment in the open. It requires shadows to be neglected in order to gather strength. So we must never allow the shadows to linger. Watchers must sweep every corner of the Collective to expose Hate where it crouches. Night will not hide it from us. We never sleep.
(Elite Watcher Training Manual, 51st edition, page 223)

WHEN WE REPORT BACK TO DORM LEADER, Wil does all the talking. "She said, 'Thank you for teaching us that' in front of the whole warehouse. I mean, we covered for her, but it was too close."

Akela greets this news with pursed lips. She stares at some blank spot on her bunker desk. My nerves descend into an agony of foreboding.

"It should be okay," she says, finally. My flash of relief dies with her next words. "The warehouse manager should be safe, but I want you to practice your loyalty phrases before the next mission. Small things can be fatal."

"Yes, Dorm Leader," I say, temporarily abashed. "But Wil—"

Wil interrupts loudly. "I've given her plenty of chances, but she's slipping. Maybe she's just inexperienced, but these missions are too important. We can't afford to bring the squads down on the Sirens."

Akela gives him a long, penetrating stare. I hold my breath. He's right. I've ruined everything, even the mission. Absently, my fingers stray to the place where the locket had rested against my skin.

"I'm sorry," I say limply.

"Everyone has near misses, Cadence," Akela says. "Even X here knows that. Which is why—" she pauses. "Never mind."

"Oh, don't get me wrong," Wil inserts. "I'm happy for her to accompany me if that is your wish. But with the sensitivity of everything right now, maybe you *should* let me go alone."

"No."

Wil's eyes flash with anger. "But—"

The look on Akela's face is enough to silence Wil. She stares at him with a look so full of steel and flint that he shrinks a little.

Feeling awkward, I rush to make excuses. "If it's better for the mission, I don't have to go. I don't want to make Wil uncomfortable."

"You *are* the mission, Cadence." All hints of Akela's hardness evaporate from her gaze as she looks at me. "Without your memory, we would be lost."

"Then I will work harder. I promise."

"I trust you," she says to me. "In fact, on the next mission, I'm sending you and Hodge. Wil remains here."

"What?" Wil explodes so suddenly that it makes me jump. "You can't do that!"

"You and I need to have a little chat, Wil," Akela says with an edge in her tone. "And the next mission is the least of your worries."

Pinned by her stare, Wil's face reddens. A mutinous anger flashes across his expression, then is gone. "Yes, Dorm Leader."

I flinch at the hard way he uses Akela's formal title.

"Enough of that. Let's move on. I can't wait to hear the fragment you found this mission."

"I have some work to do," Wil says. Without waiting for permission, he turns and stalks from the room.

Akela seems undisturbed by his sudden exit. "Would you sing it for me?"

My attention has drifted out the door with my departing companion, so it takes a superhuman effort to fake a smile. "Of course."

She settles herself in, leaning back in her desk chair to listen. I begin. I'd much rather be running after Wil, but I realize this is important too.

> Lyric, though in nature the Composer himself
> Did not snatch at his rank, nor use it for gain.
> But reduced himself to nothing for us
> Walked as we walked, Composer sung into flesh . . .

"I don't get it," I say when the song is done.

Akela closes her eyes for a moment, humming the tune I've just sung. "Your father would have explained beautifully," she says. "He had a wonderful gift for words."

She leans forward on her desk, hands clasped in front of her. "Lyric is human. But Lyric is also the Composer. He's the solution to all this." Her arm makes a graceful arc, as if to sum up the whole universe.

"But things are still messed up." I say. *Like the way I messed up things with Wil, even though I don't know how I did it.*

"Yeah," Akela agrees. "Things are still messed up. But that's the Collective for you. They had the solution right in front of their faces, and they didn't want it."

"What do you mean?"

"Who do you think the Haterman is?"

I'm startled by the change in Akela's line of thought, but years of Nursery Dorm lessons immediately flow back into my mind.

"The Haterman wanted to destroy our world and filled it with hate and destruction—"

"Don't just recite the party line. In your own words. Who do you think the Haterman is?"

"He's the enemy of the Love Collective?"

"Think."

"I . . . I guess he's the one who caused all the trouble back in the Wars of Hate. He's the one we're taught to hunt for. The bad guy."

"But he's dead, so why keep on hunting for him?"

"I don't know. I thought he was real at first, but after a while I just figured he was a cartoon character they use in training."

"No," Akela says. "He's real." She sits gazing at me intently, and I know there's something I'm not getting right now that I really should understand. Then the pieces fall into place with a thunk.

"Lyric?" I say in disbelief. "*Lyric* is the Haterman?"

"Exactly."

Revulsion curdles in my stomach. Years of indoctrination battle with this new revelation. Memories swirl and swoop through my head, mixing sweet strains of song with the long-ingrained images of the ugly Haterman scowl.

Instinct urges me toward the door. The Haterman? I've been hunting for his ugly face in every VR exercise I've had this year. He's the enemy of everything we know and love about our Collective. Now Akela is telling me this guy is Lyric? What on earth can she be thinking?

"I can't believe you'd try and fool me into this," I say, feeling the sick sense of revulsion grow.

Moving faster than I've ever seen her, Akela is in front of me before my hand can close on the door handle. "Wait." She holds her hand out to me.

I try and brush her hand away. "Why follow someone like *that*? He's so . . . so creepy and so—"

"That's the Collective lying to you, and you know it." Her face is dead serious, but she isn't angry with me. It's enough to make me pause.

"But he's so angry," I argue. "You've seen him. They put Haterman masks on all the Haters at the . . ." A rush of unwelcome memory almost stops me mid-sentence. *Don't think about your mother. Just don't.* I squeeze my eyes shut for a second to try and blink it away. "At the Haters' Pavilion Show."

"Think, Cadence." Akela's doesn't let up. "Think of everything you know about him. You've even seen him."

"The Haterman's the . . . the worst. An animal." But even though faint nausea is churning around in my stomach, I know what she's talking about.

—

HE IS STANDING BEFORE ME ONCE MORE. HIS *coat is a color that shines brighter than my eyes can stand. His face is the same as I remember, loving and kind.*

"Who . . . who are you?" I ask, even though somewhere deep down I already know.

"I am Lyric," he replies.

—

A SMALL EMBER OF PEACE QUENCHES THE storm of revulsion that had been raging through me. "I remember," I breathe, grasping at my vision with every ounce of willpower I have. "He looked nothing like the Haterman."

"That's my point." Akela's voice is triumphant but sad.

"Sometimes the truth gets hidden when the powerful want to tell a different story."

"I don't get it." I move away from the door, back toward the desk.

Akela joins me.

"Lyric turned power on its head. Said that if we want to show love, we should love our enemies, not just the ones who are nice to us. If your whole world has been built on forcing everyone to like you and be like you, you don't want to hear things like that, do you?"

"So the Executive killed him?"

Akela gives a slow nod. "That's the story behind the Triumph festivals. Each year the Collective celebrates the day they had Lyric strung up on a tree. Of course, they don't want people asking inconvenient questions, so they rewrote the history books."

Something plays across her face, which seems completely at odds with what she's just told me.

"What's so funny?" I ask, feeling confused. "They burn the Haterman every year on the last day. What could be funny about that?"

"Was he dead in your vision?" Akela's eyes sparkle.

"No," I say slowly. "He was alive. Oh!"

"Not even death can stop the Composer."

My head whirls. "So where is he now? I mean, why isn't he here?"

Akela leans against the wall, arms crossed. "He's waiting."

"But why? If he's more powerful than the Love Collective, why doesn't he just bulldoze the whole place down?"

"You're thinking about power the Midgate way, not the Lyric way," Akela says. "You sang it before: 'But reduced himself to nothing for us.' Lyric had bigger plans than running a government."

"But he could—"

Her words ring out. "Power is in dying to yourself, not living to dominate."

"But that's weak," I protest.

"That just shows how much you still need to learn," Akela points out. "For your next mission, I'm going to introduce you to a Chief Siren. You'll be able to learn more from him, and you'll have a Siren group to belong to when I'm not around."

"They are going to get rid of you?" I ask, panicked.

Akela shakes her head. "Crucible's getting suspicious, but the Composer has my life song in his hands."

"But what if they do get to you? What if they arrest you?"

Akela smiles. "The Composer's plans aren't foiled by people's schemes."

"But what if they kill you?" The thought of Akela not being around has never really occurred to me before. With a lurch of anxiety, I suddenly realize how much she means to me.

"Nothing the Collective can throw at us will separate us from the Composer, Cadence," she says softly. "Not even death."

She runs her fingers across the edge of her desk, brushing against a Lyric's tree symbol ornament beside the lamp. "Death just brings us into his presence once and for all."

I SPEND THE NEXT FEW DAYS TRYING TO digest Akela's words. But I don't get much of a chance. When I'm not being put through a series of punishing tests and VR exercises by Crucible, I'm working on my drill practice or the acres of assignments he dumps on me between lessons. I try and rehearse the Song in my head at night, but by then my brain is so full of work that I'm too exhausted to think.

Wil treats me as if I don't deserve to exist. My every word seems to reinforce his disapproval.

"Wil, can we talk?" is met with stony silence.

"Wil, I'm sorry," never gets a reply. It's like I'm on permanent mute or something.

Eventually, I give up and descend into an emotional pit of self-loathing.

He took me on a mission. We were going fine. Then he took me to that weird warehouse. I thought he cared. But then . . . what? All I wanted was to know what was going on. So why do I feel like the worst person in the world?

One afternoon, unable to face Wil's unpredictable temper, I flee the VR room, searching for some peace. But the sun shines outside, drawing me into the warm, open spaces. On the drill yards, a group of Love Squad Apprentices wheel and march on the open field. Over on the far side of the open space, Sif and Zin step with laser-like precision, their steps and turns crisp and perfect.

Emotion catches in my throat at the sight of my former friend. On a day like today, I wish I could speak to her again. But what would she say? If I poured out my worries and fears, she'd most likely find some reason to blame me.

I am so lost in thought that I don't notice Hodge approaching until he's right next to me.

"You look distracted," he says, a warm smile in his tone. "Love all, be all."

"Hm? What? Oh, nothing," I mutter, dragging my eyes away from Sif. I give him a lazy salute. "May you follow your dreams and find yourself in the universe."

"How is training?" he asks. We stare out at the drill practice side by side.

"Excellent," I say distractedly. "It is such a privilege to be in the Watcher cadre, and I'm grateful to be there."

"Mm," Hodge says. I cast a sideways glance at him, and he's frowning out at the field. "Everything okay with your coworker?"

he asks in even tones. I catch the quick flick in his eyes and see something more than vague curiosity there.

"Wil?" *If only you knew,* I think. "I barely see him. He's . . . busy."

"Really?" Hodge's voice goes up in surprise. "I would have thought . . ."

You were thinking he would actually talk to me?

"Hodge, can I ask you a question?"

"Sure. Go ahead."

"Am I . . . Is there . . . Is there something wrong with me?" I ask, feeling a welling of emotion in my throat.

"What? No!" Hodge blinks at me. "Why would you think that?"

"No reason." I glance down at my shoes, scuffing the toes on the path.

"Apprentice Flick," Hodge says. "Look at me."

I rotate my head and meet his deep brown eyes. They search my face with such open concern that I almost lay out the whole story. But I don't.

He places a heavy hand on my shoulder. "You are a Watcher, aren't you?"

I nod.

"That means you're the best of the best," he says.

"But—"

"No buts, Flick," he interrupts. "Crucible is training you because you are exceptionally gifted. You don't get a visit from the Supreme Executive without being someone important."

I drop my eyes to the ground again, fighting back an unwanted wave of sadness. "Thanks." But his words fail to penetrate my internal wall of self-loathing.

In the distance, Sif and her squad reach the end of the field and smoothly wheel around in lockstep formations. Their chants are lost on the wind and arrive in our ears as a rhythmic, wordless cry.

"Is he . . . is he being good to you?" Hodge asks tentatively. "Wil, I mean."

A shrug is all I can manage.

I hear Hodge take a deep, slow breath. "If he hurts you, I'll—"

I throw my hands up. "No, he's fine. It's my fault. He hasn't done anything to me. At least—I mean, he wouldn't—" I catch myself blabbering nonsense and close my mouth.

Hodge narrows his eyes at me, suspicious. In a rush of panic, my words continue to flood out. "Wil's fine. Really he is. He's good. Doing well. Working hard for our Dorm Leader. He just doesn't have time to—I mean we're both busy with our own training right now, so there's no time for useless chatter, or anything like that. But he's fine. Really fine. Super fine."

"So he's fine, then?" Sarcasm drips from Hodge's voice.

"Yeah, he is. He hasn't spoken to me in a while. But that's my fault," I say, then wish I could take the words back.

Hodge's gaze holds more than a little suspicion. "I doubt that."

"It's true. I mean, we're fine." I wince. I sound like an idiot. The more I say it, the less impressed Hodge seems to be.

"Well, I'd better be getting back to training."

I nod.

I wait for him to leave, but he turns back to me. "Flick."

"Yes?" I look up at him.

"If anything . . . If there's ever anything you need to talk about. I . . . I'm happy to listen," he says.

"I'm fine, really," I lie. I reach out to pat his hand. "But thank you. That means a lot."

Hodge glances down at my hand. Then he looks back at me "Just one thing . . ."

"What?"

"Real men don't play games." He doesn't blink.

"What?"

He salutes. "Love all, be all, Watcher."

"Love all, be all," I repeat. My mind fills with unanswered questions, but Hodge is gone.

21

Hate never sleeps, we are told. Yet Haters sleep as Lovers do. They eat as Lovers eat. They frequent the same places of commerce Lovers frequent. They may even do the Collective's work with the same precision as Lovers. In almost every way they are indistinguishable from the loyalty we would expect from a Love Collective citizen. The only thing that distinguishes a Hater from a Lover is that the Watcher has identified them.
(Elite Watcher Training Manual, 51st edition, page 199)

I'M NOT SURE WHETHER HODGE'S WORDS have an effect, or whether I just run out of patience. Whatever the reason, I begin to avoid the Watcher Dorm as much as possible, even with the mountain of work Crucible has piled on. I just can't handle the thought of running into Wil anymore. I hate the way I fell for him. And I really, really hate the fact that I still want him to talk to me again.

The Triumph parade is less than a week away when the signal arrives and I am summoned to Akela's office. The plush carpet deadens the sound of my footsteps on the corridor. Getting to know Akela has dimmed my trepidation somewhat, but I am still nervous walking across the topmost level of Elite Academy.

Wil sits at his usual desk in the office. But this time, Hodge is also there, standing in the middle of the waiting room like a door guard. He has the practiced stillness of a Love Squad officer, but his presence forms a comforting buffer against the icy sweep of Wil's gaze, which briefly washes over me and then goes back to pretending I don't exist.

"Love all, be all." I salute into the quiet room.

Hodge salutes back. "Apprentice."

I smile. Hodge has a special way of speaking warmth into a single word. I think of the contrast between the two men. One dazzling but infuriating. The other . . . what? What is it about this Squad Apprentice that I find comforting? Perhaps it's the way the Muse seems to shine in him during our Siren meetings. I don't know for sure.

Akela's inner office door swings open, and all three of us straighten.

"You may enter," Wil speaks to his desk. His tone makes me feel like poking my tongue out at him, but I don't. Instead, I make a show of stepping up beside Hodge.

"Time for the big excursion," I say with an exaggerated grin.

Hodge's brows furrow a little. I get the hint, so as Wil continues to ignore us, we march in silence into Akela's room.

It's been ages, but the room is exactly as I remembered it, with two crucial changes. One: Akela is not here. Two: Crucible is.

The Executive Lover stands beside the tall windows, his hands clasped behind his back while he stares at the sun-soaked grounds below. When we step into the room, his face remains turned toward the view, but the wrinkles around his eyes crease in a look of eager anticipation.

"Executive Lover," I say. My hands shake a little as I salute, but that's the only hint of surprise in my demeanor. I resist the instinct to turn around and scan the rest of the room, just to make sure Akela isn't hiding behind a curtain or something.

Crucible continues to focus on something outside the windows. "You are ready?" A slow smile spreads on his face.

"Yes, Executive Lover."

Without a word of explanation, Crucible walks to the bookshelf behind Akela's desk. A section of the shelves swings open, revealing a richly decorated hallway. Akela's personality is everywhere from the plush carpet to the fine art on the walls, which only makes me more worried that she's not here in person.

At the end of the hall we reach a lift well, and Crucible leads us in. I worry all the way down, occasionally sending a few querying thoughts toward the Muse. Things like, "Help!" and "Please don't let us die today!"

Beside me, Hodge is a block of unreadable stone. Until I catch him giving me a side glance, that is. The quick eyebrow raise he gives me says everything.

This wasn't part of the plan.

From the lift, we enter a dim corridor that ends in a darkened arch. Our footsteps make sharp echoes on the concrete floor, which bounce shrilly off the glossy white tiles covering the walls and ceiling. Ahead, there's a faint smell of something that I have only once smelled in my life. Sure enough, we emerge from the archway onto the nearly silent train platform of Elite Academy. A single carriage waits there, sleek and shiny as an overcar and emblazoned with gold trimming. Crucible strides ahead and steps inside without so much as a backward glance.

"Come on." Hodge speeds his steps. We jump onto the train just as the doors begin to glide shut.

The interior is luxurious. Gold trim glitters on every surface. The middle of the carriage is taken up with a mahogany conference table and chairs. The end where we enter is furnished with a bar and lounge, complete with fat leather armchairs. Crucible has already installed himself in one.

"Hurry up and sit," he says irritably, waving me to a couch opposite. I perch on the edge, not quite sure if I can put my whole weight on something so expensive. Hodge sits beside me.

With a silent lurch, the train glides away into the darkness. Crucible shuts his eyes. For half an hour, Hodge and I sit in excruciating silence, sharing worried glances at each other. At the end of the journey, Crucible rouses himself enough to give us an imperious wave, ushering us ahead of him to the doors.

Unlike the Academy, this platform shows signs of more frequent use. A series of wet footprints stream across the concrete toward a wide moving staircase. Crucible takes us to a small lift beside it.

"Executive Lover, sir," Hodge says as the lift doors close us in. "I am honored to be in your presence today."

Crucible's grunt is begrudging. I figure he's heard Approved Lexicon so many times it's become meaningless.

Hodge continues. "If it does not trouble you, Executive Lover, I was wondering if you could tell us where we are?"

Crucible's eyebrows shoot up in surprise. "Did Dorm Leader not tell you?" he asks insincerely. The predatory smile on his face chills me to the bone. "Ah, yes. That's right. She had some *ridiculous* plan as to how you needed to witness Triumph preparations, blah blah blah." He waves his hand dismissively. "I had a much better idea."

At that moment, the lift doors open onto an expansive glass and concrete half dome. Four times the size of our assembly atrium, the far walls curve overhead in a lattice of laser-carved beams. Sunlight streams down on the polished concrete floor like glittering jewels. Opposite the outer dome wall and to our left, a vision screen as high as an apartment block projects the Supreme Executives' faces intermingled with scenes of Love Collective Triumph and slogans.

Love always Triumphs.
Haters will never succeed.
Love all. Be all.

Outside the dome and across a vast stone courtyard, a blindingly white building towers high above us.

Stunned into silence, my mouth goes dry. Hodge's face has become blank, like a guard who is not permitted to have thoughts of his own. And as if to confirm my thoughts, our Executive guide turns back toward us, his arms held wide above his head.

"Welcome to the Hall of Love," Crucible says, his wizened face wrinkling in a wide, benevolent smile.

MEMORY DATE: CE 2269.355

Memory location: Nursery Dorm 492, Assembly Hall

"Well, as promised in our Triumph celebrations, I'm happy to announce that all your dreams have come true. Thanks to your loyalty and diligence, you get to visit . . . the Hall of Love!"

The elated screams erupt so loudly a bunch of Apprentices sitting on the floor around me clamp their hands over their ears. Projected onto the vidscreen above us, a small group of Lovers jump up and down in a huddle. Joy shines in their faces. At the other side of the stage, Carell Hummer beams at them, enjoying the mayhem after his announcement. When the initial chaos dies down, Hummer places a hand on one of the men's shoulders.

"You seem pretty excited," Hummer says. "How has this win affected you?"

The man looks into the distance, his eyes lost in some kind of excited wonder. "Oh, this is . . . I mean it's . . . it's more than I ever could have dreamed of. I tried so hard for so many years, you know? This . . ." The man shakes his head a little. "The Hall of Love? Can you believe it? It's all I ever wanted. Thank you. Thank you!"

"IT'S AN HONOR. IT'S AN . . ."

"Smile, Flick," Hodge hisses through his gritted teeth.

"Trying," I whisper, forcing the grin onto my face so widely that my cheeks begin to ache.

This is the last place on earth I want to be. The steel fist of the Love Squad is commanded from here. Supreme Lover Midgate lives here. Everything about this place makes my skin crawl.

I never knew it was possible to keep functioning as a human being while you felt constant mid-level fear. Now I know. My heart is thumping so much that I can hear the flow of blood to my ears. I stopped rubbing my clammy palms against my uniform ages ago, because it was starting to leave telltale damp patches along my hips.

After Crucible has dragged us around so many corridors that my feet are starting to ache, he stops in front of another bank of lifts.

"You're going to enjoy this," he drawls without a hint of sarcasm.

I fight back the urge to claw my way through the nearest exit and nod. After a short travel upward, the lift opens in the center of a vast circular room, decorated in a similar fashion to the Watcher Dorm, but three times the size.

A series of high-definition scenes project on the dome-like ceiling above us: A towering scaffold under construction by an army of Engine Roomers, complete with enormous lighting rigs and vidscreens. A tent, where a group of performers wheel and spin in acrobatic dives and sweeps. Beside that, a projection shows the balsa wood figure of the Haterman being erected in the middle of a vast open space, readying the area for the closing ceremony of the Triumph celebrations. Nearby, squadrons of

Love Squad officers work with disciplined precision setting up a camp behind the Triumph grounds.

While I'm distracted by the vision above, a Lover steps onto the circular observation deck from a ring of desks below.

"Love all, be all, Executive Lover," she says, snapping her salute crisply. "Watcher Rank, reporting for duty. How may I assist you?" She takes in Hodge and me, her eyes pausing on my indigo collar. But she asks no questions.

Only Haters question the Love Collective.

"We are here for a tour," Crucible declares.

The woman nods. "As you desire, Executive Lover. What do you wish to see?"

He motions to me. "Apprentice Flick here is a Watcher in Training. Show her."

I stiffen, assaulted by fear again. *Watcher* Rank. Screens everywhere. This is Watcher headquarters?

Tearing my eyes away from the images on the ceiling, I take a better look at our surroundings. We stand on an inner circle that forms an observation deck of the whole facility, ringed by padded railings. A few steps down from the deck, another ring is formed by three rows of console desks. Lovers in indigo-lined white uniforms work silently at the consoles or move to the next ring where conference tables intermix with semicircular lounge areas and temporary sleeping pods. Outside the conference area is another walkway, where steps lead down to the outermost ring: hundreds of vidscreen Watcher cubicles that line the circular wall. The ring of cubicles is broken by four darkened hallways that lead out of the room like points on a compass. Every blank section of wall is taken up by a Love Collective flag.

"Welcome, Apprentice." Watcher Rank bows briefly to me. "May you follow your dreams and find yourself in the universe."

"Thanks be to the great minds of you all," I reply, trying hard to avoid looking at the lifts and my only chance to exit.

Watcher Rank leads us down from the observation deck.

"This is where signals are audited," she says in a low voice, pointing to the desks where a small group of Watchers meet. "Requests come in from the surveillance algorithms, and we double-check them before sending them on to the Love Squad."

"How do you do that?" I ask, curious.

Rank leads us to a console table, where a Watcher has just sat down. I watch as he logs in to the screen, fascinated as he navigates to an algorithm protocol. Hovering above the table, a series of faces appears in a grid formation. The Watcher begins flicking the images away, only to have them replaced with more.

"Most of the time we send them to a booth." She indicates the outer ring of screens. "The Coders have made the algorithms super-sensitive, but they occasionally need a more human appraisal." She takes us along to another group of desks. "Over here, Watchers are evaluated on a daily basis for quota parity."

I nod, pretending that I know what she's talking about. *It's an honor. It's an honor. It's . . .*

"The business end of the work is down here," she continues, waving at the outer ring of Watcher cubicles. "There are group surveillance rooms further down that hall." She points to one of the compass-point hallways nearby. "But most of the work happens out here."

"Where do the other halls lead?" I ask. "If that's not presumptuous of me to ask."

"Not at all. That one leads to our living quarters, and the other two to the Supreme Executive and the Security Sub Commissariat. They're the only ones who get to see us." She casts a quick look at Hodge and frowns.

My thoughts drift. Life seems so small here. Opulent and comfortable, for sure, but a life lived through the eyes of others.

"How long have you worked here?" I ask her.

"Fifteen years," the woman replies.

"What do you like most about it?" I ask courteously.

Watcher Rank pauses for a moment, as if I've asked her

something she wasn't expecting. "I like a job well done," she replies.

"What is 'a job well done,' Lover?" Crucible has appeared.

The woman stands a little taller and looks straight ahead at the Watcher screens. "To know that I have eliminated a few more Haterman acolytes, Executive Lover."

"Good." Crucible nods, satisfied. An icy finger of fear slides across my heart. *The Haterman isn't who you think he is,* I think, glancing at the woman. She just looks pleased at the praise.

In the nearest booth, a Watcher stands silhouetted against a vivid image of a Nursery Dorm drill yard. Nursery Apprentices wheel around on the artificial grass, mouths moving in unison. I can't hear what they're saying, but I can tell which chant it is:

Haters can't love!
Lovers don't hate!
Love Collective children
Will all embrace their fate!

Apart from the serial number printed high on the concrete wall (ND605), it could easily be my old dorm. The Watcher in the booth zooms in on a small boy in the middle of the pack, his scowl a contrast to the determined expressions of his peers. His lips don't move. A red circle appears over the boy's face, which means the Watcher has flagged him.

The blood drains from my face as I watch the guards lift the boy out of the middle of drill practice and carry him away. I don't get to see what happens next. The Watcher's view flicks to another Nursery Dorm somewhere else (ND144), where another group of students wheel and turn in identical drill marches on their own fake grass compound. I remember vividly the terror we felt any time those white uniforms stepped in to remove an Apprentice. This guy is inflicting that on those children as if it's a game.

I turn away from the Nursery Dorm and search for something

that won't make me want to vomit. A familiar skyline snatches my attention, drawing me toward a different booth.

Leaving the others behind me, I wander around the circle to get a better view. Onscreen, the sluggish brown ribbon of river meanders through the warehouse district. Controlling the flow of images, a stout Watcher pans along the road leading from the docks. She zooms in on a collection of loading bays, and I have to stifle a cry of recognition.

No way. I have walked that street. Or rather, Wil led me along that street, heading for the very warehouse where the surveillance has stopped.

A truck rumbles down the road, stopping in front of the loading bay where Wil met his secret contact. I hold my breath. The Watcher zooms into the darkened space, and despite the shadowy entrance, a crystal clear vision of the interior swings into view. A familiar man in a brown uniform steps out from an inner office. His hostile expression is one I will never forget.

Goosebumps prickle along my arms, and a cold tendril of fear freezes me on the spot.

Walk away, my brain urges my feet. But my body has gone into lockdown. My eyes are glued in place, and my feet are fixed to the floor.

A red circle hovers over the man's face. I want to push it away, but I can't do anything. He is doomed with the flick of a small red button. I am frozen to the spot, unable to turn or move from the horror I have to witness.

Watcher Rank comes up beside me.

"You are finding a lot of Haters here," I observe, but my throat is dry.

She follows my gaze, sounding proud. "We have to, Apprentice. The world would fall into chaos if we didn't do our jobs. Haters are everywhere."

"I can see that," I say, secretly wishing I could burn the whole place down.

22

Because Watchers have a vital mission, they have the second-highest level of privilege in the Love Collective. In recognition of the level of pressure and the extreme gravity of their position, Watchers receive a greater measure of the Love Collective's bounty. This is to remind them of the heights to which they have ascended. Only the Supreme Executive may access more in the Hall of Love. Only the Supreme Executive have a greater level of authority.

Watchers, therefore, should always remember this: what has been gained can all too easily be lost.

(Elite Watcher Training Manual, 51st edition, page 216)

"I'M GOING TO REPORT TO DORM LEADER," I say as soon as the train deposits us back at the Academy. Crucible sent us home without so much as a goodbye.

"I'll go with you," Hodge replies.

"Don't worry about it." I look at my fitness tracker. "It's nearly dinner time."

"I am a little hungry," Hodge admits. "Are you sure you don't want company?" he asks. His deep brown eyes search my face. There's not an ounce of the stonelike guard in his expression now. He's all warmth and friendliness.

I smile and shake my head. "I'll be fine. Thanks for the security detail today."

"That's my job," he says, but the smile transforms into concern. "I'm here if you need to talk later."

I just wave him away and press the button that will take me upstairs.

As usual, Akela's office door is shut, so I pass my wrist at the console. Nothing happens. I wave my wrist again.

A few seconds later, Wil's harsh voice rings through the speakers. "What?"

"Can I come in?"

"Why?"

"I need to talk to Dorm Leader."

"She's not in."

"When will she be back?"

"Love knows."

"So can I wait there?"

"She won't be back until tomorrow."

"Why didn't you say that before?"

"Whatever."

"Thanks," I say with as much sarcasm as I can muster.

Exasperated, I give up. Who am I kidding? His hostility hurts.

Back in the Watcher Dorm, I head for my bunk to check the infotab. There are no official messages, which only increases my agitation. I turn the device off and on again, making the secret swirl gesture with my forefinger. In the Siren app, I tap out a quick warning to everyone: *Just returned from the Hall of Love with Crucible. Be extra careful. You might be under surveillance.*

This sets off a flurry of worried responses from Allegra and Piccolo, which I can't handle right now. So I switch my infotab off and step out into the Academy again, not even bothering to come up with an excuse to cover my tracks.

I head for the dining hall. Everything looks normal. Relaxed.

"Maybe it's all in your head," I mutter to myself.

At that moment Sif steps into my line of sight. "Crazy girl talking to herself again?" A hint of a smile twitches at the corner of her mouth. It's a small thing, but that twitch reminds me of the Sif I used to know.

"It's been a big day." I stifle a yawn.

"Must have been. You look wasted."

I feel a twinge. It would be nice to have old Sif back again. She was the only someone I could talk to.

"Do you want to talk about it?" she says. I nearly fall over in surprise. This is *definitely* not new Sif.

I shake my head. I can't suddenly trust her just because she makes one little twitch at the end of a long day.

"I feel alone," I say, then clamp my hands over my mouth. Where did that come from? "I mean, I'm fine. Really fine. I had a special assignment today, and it was an amazing privilege. I am just tired now, that's all."

"Yeah. Right." Sif eyes me.

"No, it's true," I lie. "Crucible took me to visit somewhere today, and it was something I never thought I'd get to see. But I am tired, and I think I just need to get some Beauty Sleep."

I don't tell her my visit was to the Hall of Love.

"I'm not going to report you." Sif leans back on a dining bench, resting her hip against it. She looks more like the old Sif than ever. "If that's what you're worried about."

"There's nothing to report," I reply, my unblinking stare defying her to disagree.

Sif's shoulders slump, and she frowns. "Sorry. I know I've been . . . different lately."

"You've been . . ." I stop. I can't say what I was about to say. *You've been a monster.*

"Look, Flick," Sif says, and her use of my second name jars against me. This might be a trap. Perhaps she's getting me to trust her so I'll give her something to report on. Wild thoughts for sure. But right now anything is possible.

I paste a quick smile on my face. "Don't worry about me, Sif. I'm working hard for the Collective. I'll catch you later, okay?"

With as much composure as I can manage, I walk away. She doesn't follow. After I reach the exit, I glance back and see her staring at me, shoulders drooping. She looks so small standing alone in the middle of the dining hall. I almost want to go back and tell her everything.

But I don't. "Don't be an idiot, Flick," I tell myself.

THE DAY ARRIVES FOR THE OPENING ceremony of the Triumph of Love festival. It will be strange to see the festivities without a crowd of companions cheering around me.

—

MEMORY DATE: CE 2278.356 (FOUR YEARS ago)

Memory location: Nursery Dorm 492, Assembly Hall

The lights dim, and the low hum of conversation sputters into silence. Above our heads, the display begins to glow like a sunrise breaking over the Dorm wall. Music thumps into life—a throbbing, mind-numbing beat that fills our hearing until there is no space for conscious thought. As the music swells, the screen begins to flash with a mesmerizing series of shapes and colors. In minutes we are bobbing up and down, hearing nothing and knowing nothing except the screen and the show and the light and the festival. There is only Love. The Collective is all we live for.

I don't know how long we are caught up in that state, but eventually the beat stops and the light changes. As we slowly emerge from our musical sleep, shaking our heads and returning to our senses, Supreme Lover Midgate is there waiting for us. Her smile is familiar, and her blue eyes are piercing. As usual, she sits in her white armchair, hands folded neatly in her lap.

"Welcome to the Triumph of Love festival, my children. May you follow your dreams and find yourselves in the universe . . ."

With a whooping cheer, the crowd erupts as Supreme Lover Midgate waves us into the festival concert. We are soon entranced, watching a parade of live acts and animations. Death-defying stunts follow intricate dances and amazing feats of strength. Each new act is met with loud cheers and applause.

"This is the best night of my life!" Bez cheers from his white beanbag chair.

"You say that every year," Fedge scoffs.

"But this year I mean it!" Bez cries without a hint of irony.

—

EVERYTHING IS SILENT AROUND ME THIS year as the dawning light of the Triumph festival breaks over the vidscreen. For a moment I wonder if I should venture downstairs. But a slow, miserable laziness has descended on me. The beats of the music begin to thrum. Lights and colors flash across the screen, draining my resolve. It's easier to stay where I am. The lounge is just too comfortable . . .

Thump thump thump.

The music is really relaxing.

Thump thump thump.

I was . . . what was I doing again?

Thump thump thump.

Doesn't matter.

Thump thump thump.

"Wake up," a rough voice snarls in my ear. Hands are on my shoulders, shaking me. I slowly emerge from a fog and my eyes alight on a man's face hovering inches from my own. I feel like I know him from somewhere. His frown is deep, but there is worry in his vivid green eyes. "I thought you'd learned to handle this stuff," he says.

"What?" I mumble, feeling like my head is packed with stuffing. "What happened?"

Conscious thought slowly coalesces, like a camera struggling to find focus. It's Wil who's shaking me. He leans across the lounge, a knee on the cushion beside me. Behind his shoulder, the Triumph vidscreen explodes with a series of flashing lights and pounding beats that threaten to send me back into a hypnotic state. While the light show goes on, a soft voice croons, "The Love Collective is your parent. The Love Collective is your only hope . . ."

I shake my head once more, trying to eliminate the last strands of mental rope tying down my thoughts. The room has shifted since I was last alert. Night has fallen, and the picture window is a streak of black glass at the far end of the dorm.

"How long was I out?" I still feel in a fog.

"You should be on assignment." Wil collapses onto the cushion beside me. "Didn't Crucible give you work to do tonight?"

I rub at my forehead, trying to get my memory working again. "Um . . . no, I don't think so."

"Well, you're a Watcher. You're supposed to be working, not vague-ing out. Come on. We should go for a run to clear your head. Then we'll head to the observation room."

I narrow my eyes at Wil. "I thought you weren't speaking to me."

"Now's not the time for that." His stare bores into me with the force of a laser beam.

"So you *are* speaking to me?" I say, feeling a wave of relief that almost brings tears to my eyes.

He jumps back up from the lounge. "Come on," he says, tugging at my wrist. "Jog first. Then Watcher assignment."

Reluctantly, I allow myself to be lifted from my cushiony resting place. The last tendrils of mental fog still curl around my thoughts, making it hard to move.

"Wha—?"

He pulls me into the elevator and while it descends, I press my hands against the sides of my head, waiting for the last remnants of the daze to evaporate. It's almost completely gone when the elevator doors open on a hallway instead of the atrium. A glimmer of alarm forces me wide awake.

"Wait, where—?" I begin, but Wil places a silencing finger on his lips, which shuts my mouth. He guides me into a dormitory corridor. We're below the ground level, although I have no idea how far underground we are. I just follow Wil's lead and let him walk me through the subterranean halls until we emerge in a paved courtyard, lit by glowing orange LEDs.

Wil is giving a good impression of relaxed but purposeful ease, but I can tell there is something worrying him. A slight sheen of sweat glistens on his brow, which sets off little flickers of anxiety. But I keep my worries to myself.

When the Obstacle course trees safely hide us, Wil abruptly turns to me, eyes flashing.

"What on earth were you thinking?" he whispers harshly. "No, don't answer that. You *weren't* thinking, were you? Of all the—"

"Wait just a second," I splutter. "What is your problem? Last I checked you weren't speaking to me, so I didn't think you would care what I did. Besides, it's just the Triumph opening ceremony. What's the big deal?"

"What's the big deal? Did you not *see* the mental

programming going on there? If I hadn't arrived when I did, you'd be a vegetable by now. You should be thanking me."

"Mental programming?" I remember the soothing tones of the announcer's voice over the Triumph ceremony. "What—?"

Wil scoffs. "You still don't get it, do you? I knew it. You are completely useless without me around to keep on rescuing you. I stick my neck out for you every day, did you know that?" He steps nearer to me, his green eyes dark orbs in the dim shadows thrown by the trees around us. "I put my life at risk every day to keep you safe."

The look he gives me is intense, and in spite of myself I wish I could get back into his good graces. I just wish I didn't keep on making him mad all the time. A Watcher shouldn't need rescuing, but I can't seem to stop getting in trouble. Wil's right. If he hadn't been there, what would have happened to me?

"I'm sorry," I say, my lip quivering. "I messed up again. I should have—"

My words evaporate under the intensity of Wil's gaze. His chiseled features are intoxicating. Why would someone so incredible even bother with a Memory Freak like me? The thought makes my head spin. Like a thunderclap, I'm hit by the sudden realization that I don't want him to reject me again. But this thought brings on an irrational wave of anger. Why should I be so desperate? He didn't talk to me. He could at least have explained what I did wrong.

Wil's face softens. "I just want you to trust me."

Almost as quickly as it appears, my anger is swamped by a wave of regret, and I'm back to nearly bursting into tears again. I wonder if it is the effect of Wil ripping me out of the hypnotic state too early. Maybe the mental programming up there has left my feelings raw and vulnerable. Whatever the reason, as I speak, the words wobble under the weight of emotion in my voice. "I do. I do trust you, Wil."

A wry smile blooms on his face.

"You forgot this," he says, dangling a silver chain from his fingertips.

"My locket!" I exclaim, reaching hungrily for it. "Where did you find it?"

Wil shrugs. "You're very careless, you know."

"I was so upset when I lost it. I'm sorry."

"Never mind. It's back now. So you can relax." He waggles his finger at me. "But don't lose it again, okay?"

"I won't."

He leans forward to clasp the chain around my neck again. The nerves along my spine tingle as if electrified under his touch. I sniffle, and my pendulum-swing emotions threaten to drown me in a flood of tears. What is wrong with me?

"Don't cry," he chuckles. He reaches out for me, pulling me to his chest again. He holds me close, wrapping his arms around my back.

I try and stop, but tears leak from my eyes. "I thought you would never speak to me again," I say, sniffling. "It was so hard. Please don't be mad."

A knot of guilt and shame builds up within me. Wil's right to be angry. I missed the hypnotic elements of the Triumph festival and nearly paid dearly for it. If he hadn't been there—

I push away from his chest. "You're in danger," I say urgently. "I saw something, and you need to know."

"Let's go and talk," he says, and I know he means the bunker. With a small smile, he clasps my hand in his and guides me into the undergrowth. I let him lead me, my heart pounding.

23

There is one period during the year when our efforts must be redoubled. For the enemy knows that when we are at our most exultant, then we are at our most vulnerable. Haters would love nothing better than to drag us down to abject humiliation in the midst of our greatest celebration. What a "triumph" it would be if terror and fear could be sown amongst us at this moment!

Watchers must be extra vigilant during Triumph season. Haters will mewl about poverty or lack of resources or unemployment or some such. They will attempt to use our live entertainment for their own destructive propaganda. We must make every effort to ensure they have no voice.

(Elite Watcher Training Manual, 51st edition, page 118)

"WHAT DID YOU SEE?" WIL SAYS AS SOON AS the door to Akela's bunker office closes behind us. My hand still feels warm from where he held it. But he's moved further away into the room, waiting for my news. No thoughts of hugs or closeness now.

"Crucible took me to Watcher headquarters," I explain. "I saw someone being arrested. Well, I saw lots of people being arrested, but this one you need to know about."

"Who?"

"The guy in the warehouse. The one who didn't want me to meet him."

Wil lets off a string of curses.

"Are you sure?" he presses.

I raise an eyebrow and tap the side of my temple.

"You're sure." He starts to pace around the room, muttering to himself. He pauses. "What happened?"

"He was meeting a guy with a truck when the Watcher flagged him. That's all I saw. I don't know anything else."

Wil resumes his pacing, face stormy with rage.

"That means they're onto the plan." He curses again.

"They know we're collecting Song fragments?" I ask, feeling my throat constrict in fear.

"Not that one."

"There's a different plan?"

"Of course there's a different plan," he scorns.

He's almost scaring me. "Does Akela know about it?"

The snort Wil gives in reply tells me everything. "She doesn't need to know."

"Why not? They'd still blame her for it."

"Ah, Flick, you don't understand." Wil's pacing across the room grows agitated. "Nothing is going to change unless we change it." A fervor animates his face in a way I've never seen before. "All of this sneaking around in the dark is never going to get us anywhere. We have to fight. Don't you see?"

My mouth goes dry. "You were planning to . . . to fight the Collective?"

He throws his hands in the air. "They're killing us. We have to fight back."

"That sounds like Midgate's way, not Lyric's way."

"Rubbish. We have to do Lyric's work for him. He won't come back unless he can see that we're fighting the fight."

"But Akela said—"

"Akela is wasting time we don't have, Cadence," Wil says

tersely. "She just wants to quietly sing while the world burns. But we can't afford to just sit around and do nothing."

"I'm not doing nothing. I'm collecting the Song."

Wil pauses in his frenetic pacing for a moment. "For how long? You saw the Watcher operations on your *special* tour. Their eyes are everywhere. How long will it take to pick us off one by one?" He glances around the ceiling as if a thousand eyes might be watching us.

The thought makes the hairs rise along my arm. "Lyric will protect us," I say, voice faltering.

"Maybe. But think about what they did to us. To you." His hands are on my shoulders. "How many children will they steal and reprogram before we finally get it? We have a chance, Cadence. A once in a lifetime chance to overthrow the status quo. We can take back our rightful place in this nation. We can be free to meet together the way we want to be."

This is not my way, croons the Muse in my head.

In his current agitation, Wil looks dangerous. I decide to take the path of least resistance. If I can placate him for a few minutes, I might be able to defuse the situation and get out of here.

"But how?" I try to make my voice sound calm and interested.

"We are going to make a statement. One that finally gets the world to pay attention," he says cryptically. "One that could bring down this oppression and give us the freedom we've wanted for so long."

"What are you going to do?"

Wil searches my face. "The closing ceremony of the Triumph festival. Where do the Supreme Executive watch?"

"They're always in that VIP observation box," I reply.

Wil nods. That feverish glow in his face intensifies into a look of eager anticipation. "It's not just the Haterman effigy that's going to burn this year."

"That's treason," I breathe, horrified.

Wil gives me a look that drips with condescension. "The Supreme Executive are evil, so it's not treason," he says. "It's loyalty to justice."

"You're insane."

His bitter laugh is mirthless. "I've finally come to my senses, Flick." He steps away from me, resuming his manic walk around the room. "The Collective stole my family from me. Forced me into years of this mindless loyalty training. They're a cancer, eating away at us until we're empty shells that hold nothing but Love Collective slogans. I've had enough." Going over to Akela's desk, Wil pulls out the photo album he showed me months ago. "This is what they do," he says, thrusting the open pages toward me so I can see the bulldozer images. "This is the only language they know. Unless we speak their language, they'll never get it."

"But we're supposed to be like Lyric, not like them. We can't become murderers just because we're treated unfairly."

"We're not murderers," Wil scoffs. An eager smile creases his face. "We're the Composer's avenging angels, bringing his judgement on those who've failed."

"So your friends are Sirens, then?"

Wil's eyes flick from side to side. "It . . . it isn't just Sirens who have been mistreated by the Collective, you know."

My sense of dread grows. "So you're partnering with people who aren't Sirens?"

Wil shakes his head. "This is the right thing to do, and you know it." He points a finger at me. "You've been helping us do it, too."

"Me? I would never . . ." My words die as I see where his finger is pointing. My locket. With trembling fingers I lift the silver oval from its hiding place. Smooth and round, it rests coolly in my hand. "What does that have to do with—"

"I knew you were the right one to choose." Wil utters a

short laugh. "You're so naive you'd never question anything. So willing to please. You've kept our data safe all this time so I could take it to the people who need to use it."

"This is a data bank?" I drop the locket from my grasp as if it burns. The weight of the chain seems to bore into my neck. As the words pass my lips, I feel my heart breaking into a million tiny pieces. "What . . . what am I to you?"

"I had hoped you would join us," Wil said, his casual shrug crueler than a knife wound. "But even if you don't, you've done your job. You can't report us, because you'd be arrested as a co-conspirator. You can't get me arrested, because I'll have to tell them about the secret Siren chapters we've been visiting all over the city."

I grasp the locket tightly in my fist again, thoughts racing. What a moron I am. All of his flattery, his dizzying physical closeness, all of it was just a game. It was there all the time, and I refused to see.

"I can tell Akela."

Wil shrugs, unconcerned. "Go ahead."

The maelstrom of my internal conflict coalesces into a burst of white-hot rage. With a superhuman effort, I wrench the chain from my neck and throw it across the floor. It slides across the concrete, and bounces off Wil's feet.

"I won't be a part of this." The back of my neck burns, but I don't care. "I will *never* be a part of this."

I don't wait for him to respond. Gathering the remaining tatters of my self-respect, I turn and run out the door.

STAMPING THROUGH THE UNDERGROWTH, I formulate a plan. Wil's insane terrorist plot will bring us all down if we're not careful. Every single one of the Sirens could be arrested.

I have to find Akela. She is the only one who has the power to stop him. She needs to know her years of meticulous planning are in danger thanks to Wil's brainless desire to conquer the world.

I'm so angry and distracted that I nearly walk headlong into disaster. A branch snaps somewhere out beyond the veil of trees. The noise comes from a spot out on the obstacle course. I freeze. From the same location comes a faint crunch that can only be the sound of a boot on grass. Then it stops.

Crouching down, I train my eyes on the location of the noise. My heartbeat starts thudding in my ears so loudly I wonder if it could be heard in the darkness. The low bushes form an impenetrable screen. I can't see but I know there is at least one person out there. I thought all the other Apprentices were supposed to be in the atrium, hypnotized by the beats and the general vibe of the celebration. So who could be out in the darkness at this time of the night?

Moonlight filters through the leafy canopy overhead, casting ghostly shadows. With as much stealth as I can muster, I creep away from my last noisy position. There's a small indent behind dense foliage a few more meters away from the bunker entrance. In this near darkness, someone could walk within an arm's length of me and not know I was there.

For a few tense seconds, the only sounds that filter through the undergrowth are the soft sigh of leaves in the breeze and the muted thumps of Triumph music vibrating through the walls of the Academy building. Then a soft squelching tells me that a foot somewhere in the darkness has taken a slow step into the thicket. Another footfall follows soon after.

Help! I think to the Muse. Wil is still in the bunker, but he will probably return soon, and the last thing we need is to have our secret haven exposed to some random stranger.

There's a pause, and then I hear a quiet step. Another pause. Then a rattling of branches as if someone is pulling them back to clear the way. A few more steps crackle into the border of dense bush. Branches snap and whip back, growing louder with the effort. It sounds like the person—whoever it is—is heading for the direction of the bunker entrance, where my angry noises first erupted. I'm glad now that I shifted out of the way, or they'd find me in no time at all.

Help! I think again. *Now would be a good time!*

A sudden gust of wind ruffles the tree canopy, making the slivers of moonlight seem even more spooky. Trees sway and bend in the wind. The boughs creak.

My pursuer has heavy footsteps. It sounds like combat boots, the way the leaves and sticks crunch beneath their feet. Was there a Love Squad patrol out tonight that I didn't know about? I tense, ready to bolt away if I can, but it feels as if I won't get a chance. The footsteps are closing in.

The breeze intensifies, and I flatten myself further. Then, with a snap and a crash, a branch tumbles down from the treetops, loosened by the wind. It rustles down through the leaves, and lands on the ground with a thud, somewhere between me and the bunker entrance. I force myself to stay still, not wanting to let the slightest sound give away my position.

A deep, familiar voice curses—Fuschious. There's a pause. I hold my breath for a few seconds, waiting to hear what will come next. Above our heads, the wind gusts through the treetops again. Leaves rustle. Boughs creak. Another small twig snaps down through the branches, making rhythmic footstep-like rustles as it bounces off other tree limbs.

Meters away, Fuschious's footsteps begin to crunch through the undergrowth again. But this time, they're retreating. I listen as the sound squelches out into the obstacle course. I let out a long, shaky breath, my heart pounding wildly. Fuschious marches out of earshot, back toward the Academy. Only after

I've heard a small burst of music from the doors opening to the Academy do I let myself stand.

Trying to imitate the graceful steps of a Pleasure Tribe dancer, I make my slow way through the bush away from Fuschious, where the wide-open drill yards lie in silvery-grey rectangles. A weird, giddy feeling sends my mind into a spin.

I'm not brave enough to run into Fuschious, so I jog around the drill yards until my breath is ragged and the sweat pours down my face. Only then do I turn back for the Academy building.

Why was Fuschious out on the obstacle course? It was Triumph opening ceremony, so all the Love Squad Apprentices had to be in the crowd. That meant nobody was on security patrol. So maybe Fuschious stepped in to do his duty. But as a Love Collective citizen, shouldn't he have been watching the ceremony, too?

The longer I think about it, the scarier my thoughts become. Maybe Fuschious knew Wil and I were out there. Have Wil and I jeopardized our whole operation with this one, clandestine meeting?

There's no point trying to find Akela now. I race up to the Watcher Dorm, cocooning myself into the Watcher room as fast as I can. Now more than ever I need to put on a show for the cameras. I'm still mad at Wil but grateful he at least gave me the cover story when he woke me out of hypnosis. Now, if Fuschious asks why I was outside, I can sound plausible. What was I doing? Getting some air and clearing my head for an assignment. Why was I outside when everyone else was supposed to be at the Triumph opening ceremony?

"That's Watcher business. Which means it's none of yours." I practice saying.

The Watcher room whirls into life, and as if Crucible himself has commanded me, I look for thieves and gangsters to flag. There's enough shadowy behavior going on behind tents and marquees to keep me busy for hours: groups of scary-looking Lovers coercing smaller Lovers into darkened corners, drunken brawlers throwing careless punches, a man wandering the crowds with a large weapon that looks like a homemade knife of some sort.

I stay in the Watcher room until the early hours of the morning, when the vision shows me a sky tinged with soft yellowy-white light on the eastern horizon. Only then do I drag myself away, eyes dry and limbs stiff from standing so long in one place. I fall into bed, exhausted but also relieved.

By some miracle, I've managed to dodge a bullet, thanks to the falling of a chunk of wood. It can't have been sheer chance that turned Fuschious away at the last moment.

"Thank you," I breathe to the Muse. It's the only explanation I can fathom.

24

As a Watcher, you may feel at times that you have sacrificed your own freedom for the sake of your calling. This is true. But do not think of it as missing out. A protective fence may not move from its position, but that does not mean it has no value. Rather, it is in fulfilling its mandate that it achieves its highest purpose.
(Elite Watcher Training Manual, 51st edition, page 119)

YEARS OF SLEEP PROGRAMMING DON'T HELP me to rest. I'm haunted by threatening nightmares which wake me gasping and dripping with sweat. Fuschious chases me in most of them. Sometimes Wil leaps from a hole in the ground and grabs me by the ankle, then drags me into a bottomless pit where we fall and fall until I wake screaming.

By the time my alarm rings for breakfast, I am glad for the excuse to rise. In the bathroom, I splash my face with cool water, but it doesn't stop me looking haggard. In the mirror, my skin is sallow. Dark circles ring my eyes. I look more like a ghoul than a Watcher.

Downstairs, evidence of last night's party is everywhere. Silver streamers are strewn around the atrium floor, and only bedraggled slivers remain on the wall where Pim and her team carefully installed them weeks ago. The faint scent of sweat and body odor lingers in the air. Some Apprentices are curled in slumbering bundles on the floor, obviously partying so long into the night that they forgot to go to bed.

I pick my way carefully through the mess. Soft dance music still pumps through the speakers. A lone Elite sways near the vidscreen wall, lost in a trance with a faraway look on their upturned face.

My sleep-deprived bleary eyes and sallow complexion fit perfectly.

I spot Pim leaning against the wall near the dining room entrance, staring dreamily into the distance. She holds a large blue blob of something soft and squashy clasped against her body. I have to tap her on the shoulder to get her to snap out of her reverie.

"Oh! Hi, Flick," she says, her gaze fixed somewhere past my right shoulder. "How was your Triumph?"

If I'm honest, it's been a bust so far. But I'm not about to tell her that. "You look like you had fun," I say, deflecting attention.

Her face lights up. "Oh, Kerr, last night was the most amazing time. I got to go backstage at the big concert, and we were organizing the food trucks and catering for the performers, and I was so close I could almost touch them, and we stayed out all night, and I got to see Carell Hummer, and I think I'm so happy I could die right now."

She hugs her strange puffy cushion, a look of complete ecstasy on her face.

"Carell Hummer, hey?" I say. "Are his teeth as white as they are on the vidscreen?"

Pim's eyes mist over. "Whiter. He is—I mean, we get to see him larger than life up there." She nods in the direction of the atrium stairs. "But this . . . this was . . . He's just so perfect, Kerr. So polished and . . . Look! He gave me this. Well, his bodyguard did. But it's from him." She holds the cushion out to me. It's a cloud, with a large printed photo of Carell Hummer's smiling face in the middle. Stretched across the fabric, the enormous plastic smile looks hideous.

"Wow." I try to pretend like I'm impressed. "That's . . . that's something special."

Pim's so awestruck that my lackluster response can't burst her bubble. She takes the cushion back again, staring at the photo with open adoration. "I know, right? This is a limited edition. He said to us that only a privileged few get to take Carell Hummer home."

"Carell Hummer said that?" I'm a little shocked.

"No. His bodyguard did."

"Oh."

"But he was really there," she continues, eyes shining. "He turned up in his overcar, and he was right there, and he walked like . . . two meters away from me to get to the party room . . . Ah, it was amazing."

"Good for you." The mental image I'm getting is far less impressive than her ecstasy would suggest. "Want some food?"

"Oh, I couldn't possibly eat right now. I'm too excited!" She squeezes the cushion tightly to her chest.

"Right. You'll have to tell me more later, okay? I'm starving."

She looks crestfallen. "Okay." As quickly as it went, the smile is back on her face again. "I'll tell you about how the dancers came to our food truck. They were so sparkly and . . . and sweaty."

"I, uh, look forward to it." Giving her a small wave, I walk away to the dining hall. The last thing I want right now is a detailed account of Pim's exciting night at the food trucks.

The hall is sparsely populated, even though it's the breakfast hour. A smattering of Apprentices hunch over their tables, wearily scooping protein cereal into their mouths. Almost nobody is talking.

Viola is the only familiar face I can see. She sits alone on a table nearby, standing out from the surrounding tables with her freshly washed face and straight-backed posture.

I slide my tray onto the steel surface at the opposite end of her table. "Hi. I'm Apprentice Flick," I say engagingly, hoping she gets the hint. "Is anyone sitting here?"

Viola looks up in surprise. "What?" she says, slightly panicked. She recovers quickly. "Oh, Apprentice Flick, you say? It's nice to meet you. Love all, be all." She nods, giving me permission to sit down.

"Love all, be all. Sorry to bother you this morning," I continue, doing my best impression of a friendly stranger. "I just didn't want to sit alone."

"Of course. It's fine." She turns back to her breakfast.

"Where is everyone?"

"Sleeping it off, obviously," she remarks.

"I thought Elites were supposed to show no weakness."

She looks at me sharply. Did I go too far? "You must be a first year."

"How can you tell?"

"The others know the drill by now. When Triumph comes around, you can forget about classes or anything else. It's a party for two weeks solid. The second the closing ceremony is over, we all go back to life as if it never happened."

"This is the first Triumph festival I've been to since coming to Elite Academy," I can honestly say. "It's been . . . different."

"I imagine it has."

"Don't get me wrong. It's a privilege to be here at the Academy," I hurry to assure any invisible ears that might be listening. "It's just . . ."

"It just takes some getting used to," she finishes, giving me a smile.

"Yes, it really does." With that, I focus on my own plate. I desperately want to let her know about my conversation with Wil, but I know I can't out in the open with what feels like a thousand eyes watching us. But last night sets off internal panic alarms every time I think of it.

As I lift my spoon to my mouth Lover Fuschious marches in. All corded muscle and testosterone bulging beneath his uniform, he's impossible to ignore. His eyes narrow as they scan the room.

I try to act natural, but my hand is trembling. There's only one reason he'd be down here in the Apprentices' dining hall.

He's here to find me.

"Are you okay?" Viola asks.

"What?" I drag my eyes away from Fuschious.

Viola's eyes are concerned. "You don't look well."

"I'm not feeling all that good," I say truthfully.

A mental scan of my options doesn't give me much hope. If I stand up, I draw attention to myself. If I pretend I'm leaving, I draw attention to myself. If I do anything to get out of the dining hall and away from Fuschious's threatening presence, I draw his attention straight at me.

I stare down helplessly at my protein goop. Guess I sit.

"How was last night for you?" I ask with forced brightness. "After the opening ceremony."

Viola studies me a brief moment, then plays along. "Me? Oh, I celebrated like everyone else, but then I had some Coding to catch up on, so I went back to the lab and put my head down for a few hours."

"You're a Coder?" I really am surprised. I had Viola pegged for an Engine Room health specialist. Out of the corner of my eye, I see Fuschious wandering away from us, which gives me a chance to breathe.

Viola nods. "I graduate at the end of this year. They have assigned me to a Love City corporation, so I'll be moving there soon."

"Oh really?" I feel a sudden sadness. I've hardly begun to know Viola at all. "Wow."

"It's exciting to finally be able to get out into the Collective." Viola smile is a perfect imitation of loyalty. "Don't worry. One day you'll be out there, too."

I catch sight of Fuschious turning at the end of the room to head back our way. Averting my gaze, I duck my head and scoop a spoonful of protein into my mouth. In my distress, the effect is catastrophic. My throat, constricted in fear, rejects the cereal. I cough and splutter, trying to force it down. The noise draws Fuschious's beady eyes straight at me. I look quickly down at my food, but the damage is done. With a homing drone's sense of purpose, he marches deliberately at our table.

"Watcher Apprentice Flick?" Fuschious's voice sounds as if his words had to be forced through gritted teeth. "Come with me."

I stand with exaggerated slowness, covering my abject terror with an expression that I hope conveys mild surprise. "Love abounds and abides, Lover Fuschious. Where are we going?"

"Just follow," he commands and then starts to leave. I flash a quick look of alarm at Viola before I follow. But she doesn't help. She can only watch helplessly. I throw all caution to the wind and give a panicked Siren signal to her behind my back. I know it's a long shot, but it's all I've got. Somehow the Sirens need to know that things are not right. They need to know something momentous is going on.

I just hope I'm still around to be able to tell them in person.

MEMORY DATE: TWO HUNDRED AND TEN *days ago*
Memory location: Elite Academy, Hall 53

"You got too much nerve, Apprentice." Fuschious jabs his thick finger into my collarbone. "Listen well, since you're obviously a bit slow. The Love Collective don't abide people who step outta line. Got that?"

"Oh, I get it."

Fuschious's hand comes out of nowhere and cuffs me across the side of my face. The slap knocks me sideways. I reel against the wall, struggling to keep my balance. It takes every ounce of my self-control not to cry out.

I AM NOT THAT PERSON ANYMORE. I AM A Watcher in Training, not some wet-behind-the-ears Apprentice who's barely arrived in Elite Academy.

Fuschious wouldn't dare slap me this time. Not even the Elite Lovers dare to put a hand to a Watcher. I will not be silenced by some meathead Lover with a temper like a firecracker.

All of these thoughts run through my mind, and I believe none of them. Instead, I hurry along nervously behind Fuschious's bulk. It's too much to hope that Akela will step out of a doorway to save me this time.

He knows. He knows it was me out in the trees last night. I'm sure of it.

Footsteps echoing on the stark white floor, we march in unison down the corridor. The artificial light makes everything shine with uncomfortable brilliance. After a few minutes walking through the classroom wing, we reach a door I've never gone through before.

My hackles rise. Fuschious waves his ID, the door swings open, and we enter a corridor of grey concrete. I have never been allowed into the Love Squad wing until this moment. I am at Fuschious's mercy, wherever he wants to take me.

The corridor opens onto another atrium, shaped like our assembly atrium but decorated in harsher fashion. I stare at the stark surroundings. Thick black beams arch overhead, meeting harsh concrete at the ceiling. A few older Apprentices wander past us, giving Fuschious a smart salute as we pass. They are wearing the standard Elite uniform, but they march like Love Squad soldiers.

We reach another bank of elevators, which look as if they've been carved into the concrete with jackhammers. My nerves zing with wild abandon. We ascend for a few moments, and then Fuschious curtly waves me out in front of him.

The first thing that hits me is the sound of grunts. Then comes the smell: stale sweat and liniment. In a large indoor gym stand dozens of circular arenas, the fighting floors elevated and hemmed in by netting walls.

Around the edge of the room, stadium seats rise up to the high roof. Small groups of Apprentices gather around the arenas, eyes focused on pairs of fighters. Clad in not much at all, the fighters grapple, kick, and punch each other. The lights are dim, save for spotlights aimed down on the writhing pairs. Their comrades shout encouragement, claps and cheers apparently announcing when points are scored.

As Fuschious weaves around the spectators, the stench of body odor and sweat is almost unbearable. I want to pinch my nose shut, but I dare not show the smallest sign of weakness. I have no idea why Fuschious is leading me through this part of the Love Squad training center, but he obviously has a purpose.

That purpose becomes clear as we approach an arena near the far end of the room. Halfway up the stadium seats, leaning back in a plastic chair and looking eminently relaxed, is Crucible. He surveys the fights with a look of smug satisfaction, not appearing to register our presence until we are standing below him at the base of the bleachers.

"Apprentice Flick. Welcome." Crucible's smile widens so that I can see his perfect white teeth. Deep pools of shadow ring his eyes, and his cheeks are sunken hollows. In this dim light, the shadows in his face are so prominent he could be mistaken for a living skeleton.

"Love abounds and abides, Executive Lover," I say, bowing my head.

"Come. Sit." The words are spoken with lightness, but there's no option for refusal. He pats the chair beside him. "I have been waiting for you."

25

Watchers do not make mistakes, so Watchers do not fall under suspicion. If an individual is found to be engaging in suspicious activities, they are not—nor have they ever truly been—a Watcher.
(Elite Watcher Training Manual, 51st edition, Appendix C)

I PERCH ON THE EDGE OF MY SEAT WITH STIFF formality. Crucible watches the fights going on before us, his face the image of utter contentment. He stretches, letting his legs splay out beside mine. I rest my hands on my knees, willing my legs to stop trembling. Fuschious has melted back into the crowd, turning to bark orders at one of the fighting pairs before wandering around, hands clasped behind his back.

"What do you see?" Crucible gestures over to the gym. A few cages away, an Elite makes a sudden sweep, knocking out the legs of her opponent. The other Apprentice lands on his back with a heavy thud and has no time to move before the girl is descending on his abdomen with her elbow.

"I see training, Executive Lover." I look at the grid of fight cages laid out across the room and catch sight of Sif in the distance. Standing on the floor, hands curled around the arena's safety netting, she is yelling at the fighters. I catch sight of Zin two cages away from her. "I see Love Squad fight training."

Crucible makes a dissatisfied sound. "Think like a Watcher. What do you see?" he asks again.

Right now it would be good to be able to read his mind, since I have no idea what he wants me to say. So I keep looking.

I start forward when I spot Hodge in one of the rings to my right. A trickle of blood runs down the scarred side of his face. But he has his opponent pinned to the mat and doesn't look like he'll let him up anytime soon. Unlike some of the other fighters, he's not punching the one who is down. It's almost as if he's just trying to incapacitate, rather than damage. His muscles strain with effort, and sweat glistens on his bare chest. I look away, cheeks burning, and focus on the task Crucible has given me to do.

Hodge's face is not the only bloody visage. More than one Apprentice attempts to fight with eyes nearly swollen shut, or blood marring their faces. A few fighters nurse injured limbs or hop gingerly on one good leg. Some dance eagerly around the edge of the ring, bouncing on the balls of their feet while they wait for their opponents to get back up with slow, painful rolls.

"No one is tapping out," I say under my breath.

"Speak up," Crucible snaps.

Fighters continue to circle, hunched and ready to strike again at their opponents, even the injured ones. One pair sways drunkenly in the distance, caught in an almost permanent crouch as they face each other across the ring. Both of them look too dazed to pounce.

I clear my throat. "They're not giving up."

Crucible gives a nod of acknowledgement. "You may make a Watcher, after all," he says wryly. "But can you tell me why, Apprentice Flick?"

"Elites focus on the goal, not the game, Executive Lover," I spout one of the Elite Axioms with ease.

"Maybe," he says. He stretches his arms above his head and returns to his relaxed spectating. "But not in this case."

I purse my lips. It's Triumph season. I thought these people would be resting up after a big night, not beating each other to a pulp. But Crucible is toying with me, like a predator playing with its lunch. I just have to wait it out and let him say what he wants to say.

"They are my Apprentices," Crucible states. He darts a glance at me. "You have no ideas?"

"I am content for you to tell me, Executive Lover," I respond.

Crucible snorts. After a few more moments of silent observation, he speaks again. "They are fighting because I told them to. No more. No less."

His dark eyes turn to me, and somehow he is enjoying this so-called conversation immensely.

"Oh, I could give you plausible-sounding reasons, of course. I could tell you Love Squad soldiers can't be touched by the temptations of Triumph revelry, or some such garbage. Or something about how we're training them to be resolute in the face of hate, blah, blah, blah," he says. "But the truth of the matter is far more simple. If I command them to do something, they do it."

I feel like a trapped fly who's watching the spider dance toward it across the web.

He stares out at the matches. "Would you do the same? Fight. Like this."

I swallow. "I live to serve the Collective, Executive Lover."

His renewed silence only increases the viselike grip fear has on my heart. Seconds tick away. Then he exhales slowly, as if my words have physically deflated him.

"Your companion has left us." His eyes are fixed on a point somewhere in the distance.

"My . . . what?" I say stupidly, looking around in bewilderment as if there might be someone standing beside me.

He turns to me. "I regret to inform you that your Watcher companion absconded from the Elite Academy last night."

It takes a second for the words to register, and then my heart sinks. Wil left the Academy? My hands are still on my knees, and I dig my fingernails into my legs. Crucible knows. They all know. I'm done.

"Nothing to say?" Crucible's expression is still relaxed, but his eyes narrow at me.

"I . . . I apologize, Executive Lover. I am . . . I am shocked."

"You do not ask why, though. Which means you have some insight into this situation."

My mind races. "At best I can only guess, Executive Lover."

"You are one of his closest peers. Your guesses are more than educated."

"He . . . I . . . we had different schedules, Executive Lover, I—"

"Apprentice Flick," Crucible interrupts, irritated. "I may be old, but I am not an imbecile. Your prevaricating does you no favors. Do I need to spell out for you the surveillance footage we have? Surveillance that shows you and the fugitive leaving the building *together* last night? At the very least, you were the last person to see him on the premises."

"How did he get out?" I ask, desperately hoping Wil didn't go through some secret bunker exit. That would be the perfect way to sell us all out in some kind of final, defiant gesture. An Apprentice vanishing from the center of the complex would be as good as standing on the obstacle course with a banner that read, Look Over Here!

"He was seen leaving through the front entrance after midnight," Crucible informs me. "Without a visitor permit."

"Oh."

"So you will tell me what your conversation was about."

"Yes, Executive Lover. I'm sorry. I just can't believe it. He . . ." I scramble for some explanation that won't get us all killed. Do I alert him to the Triumph plot? They must already know if that warehouse guy was arrested. But I can't do that, or all of the Sirens will be implicated by Wil's presence there. The Love

Collective doesn't care if an illegal meeting is to plan treason or to sing innocuous songs. Either reason will get us on the Haters' Pavilion Show.

I replay the memory in my head, seeking some kind of way out.

"He asked me to . . . to be with him," I say. It's not the whole truth, but enough to be plausible. "He had this weird idea, and I didn't like it, and it upset him."

I turn in time to see a hungry look on Crucible's face that leaves my skin crawling. But I can see the explanation is working. I decide to run with it.

"A weird idea?" Crucible's lips are moist. A nauseous wave threatens to unleash itself. The hungry look in his eyes grows. "Do tell."

I drop my gaze. "It was conduct unbecoming a Watcher, Executive Lover," I say simply. I hate myself for telling him that much, but denying everything is completely useless at this point. "I needed to get back to the Watcher room to do my duty, and I told him so."

Crucible's face droops in disappointment. He was clearly hoping for some extra juicy details. But right now I would much rather be a disappointment than a traitor.

"You were in a blind spot on the system, which we are going to remedy." His words chill me. If I ever get out of here, first thing I will do is get word out to the Sirens.

"Did he tell you where he was going?" Crucible's eyes flick to my face, and then return to the fight in front of us.

I shake my head. "No. I am sorry, Executive Lover. I had no idea he was going to leave the Academy."

"What did you do after your conversation?" Crucible sits up straight and turns his body to better fix me in his stare. He examines every corner of my face with a withering look. I can't look into his eyes for more than half a second.

"I went for a jog and came back to do some Watcher work.

I thought he'd come back to the Watcher Dorm, not leave the Academy."

Crucible's order is curt. "Find him."

My mouth goes dry. "Yes, Executive Lover." I have no idea how to find Wil. Even if I knew where to begin the search, I'd hesitate before flagging his whereabouts. "Sir? What if I can't? He gave me no clues."

"One of you is most certainly a Hater. Whether both of you are Haters is entirely up to you." Crucible isn't even looking at me now but somehow that unnerves me all the more.

"I live to serve the Collective, Executive Lover," I stumble over the words. "I will find him."

"I will believe that when I see it." With that, Crucible waves out at the crowd. A dozen Lovers emerge from the spectators, whistling to signal the end of the bouts. Fuschious strolls over to us, and stands waiting at the bottom of the stairs.

After giving Crucible a loyal salute, I leave. On my way down the stairs, I cast a quick glance toward Hodge's arena, but he's already gone from the ring. Over on the other side, Sif is in the middle of a huddle. She laughs at a joke I can't hear and shows no sign that she's noticed me at all. Nobody seems to be disturbed by this morning's fight drill. Just another typical day in Elite training.

But I feel as if my world is crumbling. Crucible's conversation replays itself over and over, and I wonder how on earth I am going to manage his mission. I have a nasty feeling that I've just been strapped into an overcar that's programmed to hurtle off a cliff. That feeling only grows on the long walk back to my Watcher Dorm. Knowing I'm being watched, I race to my private spot on my bunk, logging into the Siren app only long enough to type a few panicked words: COVER BLOWN. BUNKER NO LONGER SAFE. STAY AWAY. The last three words are hard to type, since my hands tremble with fear: WIL DESERTED. TRAITOR.

26

The Supreme Executive are our final authority on all matters of the Watch. We may do our job only as they have defined it. Our position is entirely at their command, and we change our code according to their whim and desire. This is as it should be. For they are the Supreme Lovers, and we are merely their eyes. Should they desire us to turn our gaze in a particular direction, it is our honor to do so.
   (Elite Watcher Training Manual, 51st edition, page 8)

THUMP THUMP THUMP THUMP.

"Die, Haterman, Die!"

Thump thump thump thump.

"Die, Haterman, Die!"

On the Triumph main stage, a DJ throws up one hand, the other clamping a headset to his ear. The chant continues, intermingling with the pounding beats until they form one uninterrupted wall of noise. Lights glare down on a million faces, every one fervent and intense, fists raised in the air.

I flick the vision off and let the insulated silence close in on me for a few minutes, just to try and reset the overstimulation in my brain. Triumph carnival is always awash with noise and light. Too many people. Too many things to see. Too many memories replaying over and over, until I feel like I'm stuck in a crowded room with a thousand infotab streams playing at once.

It's been twenty-four hours, and I am no closer to finding Wil. I have searched deserted streets and busy city squares. I've soared above industrial districts and roads leading out into the countryside. The Triumph festival is a bust. But I have no idea where else to go.

Weary beyond belief, I collapse onto the plush carpeted floor, soaking in silence. "Where are you hiding?" I ask the air.

At this point I'm pretty sure I've got more chance of becoming Supreme Lover Midgate than I ever have of finding my dorm mate. The weight still presses down on me.

"I can't do it," I whisper.

Alone in the darkness, I begin to discern a presence. It's not a fearsome one. The Muse caresses my heart with a care that is quiet yet certain. Solid and strong like a suit of armor that prevents me from melting into a helpless puddle on the floor. My mind wants to disintegrate into a thousand pieces, but it's as if a set of kind and gentle hands holds me together.

"Can you help me?" I'm not sure if I've actually spoken aloud.

Like floodgates opening after rain, I let words flow, keeping them behind my closed lips, hidden from prying ears. *I can't find him, Lyric. He is nowhere that I can see. But what happens if I do? If I find him, he'll expose us all. If I don't find him, I'll be the one in trouble. I have no idea how to get out of this. I need to protect the Sirens, but instead I feel like I'm going to end up betraying them. Please, can you help me?*

There is no answer. Only the invisible armor holding me together.

After another minute or two, a soft, lilting melody tugs at my thoughts, but I am too stressed to bring the lyrics to mind. I try and bring them back, but the words become like soap—slippery until they wash away.

"Why can't I think?" Frustrated at myself, I leave the

darkness and go to the lounge. Perhaps some distraction will help me relax.

With a couple of voice commands I bring up the entertainment system. Every menu is Triumph-themed. The last thing I want right now is to go back to that thumping, mind-numbing noise factory. So I flick the system to the streaming channel. A banner for *Elite Heroes* spreads across the middle of the screen.

Elite Lover Team Six. I haven't seen them for ages. For years they were my hope, lonely as I was in the Nursery Dorms. It was *Elite Heroes* that made me want to be where I am today. If I knew back then what Elite Academy was really like, would I have wanted to be here as badly? Would I have been content to live a life in service of the Collective, doing some grunt work in a factory somewhere instead?

I scroll through the menu and find the last episode I remember watching. It was one of the few times I earned enough Love Points to gain some app minutes in Nursery Dorm. Beside that old episode sits another little thumbnail.

"Why not for old times' sake?" I say to no one in particular. Then I command the system, "Play episode #358."

The episode explodes onscreen with a sudden blare of trumpets. A second later, the episode title flashes in bold white letters: "Spy Caper." The scene opens on Elite Lover Team Six headquarters, where Elite Lover Hu is slowly building a house of cards on his desk. When Elite Lover Nissa marches in, Hu's so startled he knocks the whole thing over. It still amuses me, even now.

"We've got a problem," Nissa says.

"Yes, boss," Hu responds, trying to scrape the cards into a neat pile and managing to spill half the pack on the floor.

"A spy was discovered trying to infiltrate the Hall's security system."

Hu shakes his head, still trying to scrape cards off his desk. "These Haters never learn, do they Elite Lover Nissa?"

"Nope," Nissa says with a grim smile. "But that's why we stay in business."

They laugh.

Nissa leans forward across the console table. "Bring up the algorithm."

Bringing his hand, still full of cards, up to his forehead, Elite Lover Hu salutes, spilling even more cards on the floor. "Yes, boss."

Fingers in a flurry, Hu stares intently at his console table for a second, then bobs back up again to look at his commander. "Done."

"Send it to the vidscreen."

"Done."

Elite Lover Nissa clasps her hand behind her back and stares at the screen in front of them. "Command: search," she says, and a soothing announcer's voice croons in reply. "Command accepted."

Something in my memory pokes me for attention. Something about the algorithm . . . I snap the vision off, mind suddenly awhirl with inspiration.

I snatch up my VR headset and boot up the Watcher simulation system. Since there are no waiting tasks set for me by Crucible, I land in a blank white room. With a few swipes of my gloved hands, the menu springs up in the virtual space in front of my eyes.

While the choices scroll past, I scour my memories for the only time I've ever seen the algorithm at work. In the Hall of Love, there was a Watcher using it.

I can picture it now: *The Watcher sits at the console table. His fingers poised over the keyboard, ready to go. His hands fly over it then, and a series of menus flicks up and down.*

What was on the screen? Think . . . Think.

Got it.

With feverish movements, I find the nondescript utility app, imitating my memory of the Watcher as best I can. Then a login screen pops up, and I'm stumped. I've never been given a password or username for this. What do I do?

Out of curiosity, I enter my Apprentice number, but of course it doesn't work. The screen almost gloats at me when the smooth announcer's voice croons, "Access denied." I try again, but if it didn't work the first time then of course it won't now.

Disgusted, I rip off my headset and stalk away from the VR station, feeling my last, faint hope evaporate into meaninglessness. It would be so typical of Crucible to set me an impossible task, then deny me the one thing that might make my goal attainable.

SLEEP. I NEVER REALIZED HOW PRECIOUS IT was until I couldn't get any. But tonight, I suddenly want nothing except to sink into delicious, sweet oblivion. Every time I close my eyes, my eyelids reopen like they are spring loaded. My brain races faster than a highway overcar, speeding in a thousand different directions. Memories flood my consciousness. My one desire has fled behind an impossible-to-climb mountain hidden at the end of a maze built into the depths of an impenetrable fortress.

Sleep mocks me. I'm sure of it.

I don't know how long I toss and turn on my bunk. All I know is the dim light of the emergency exit sign above the door, and the near-silent hiss of the climate-control air vents above my head. My blanket is a knotted mess, tied up into a snakelike bundle by my constant rolling. The night is cool, but sweat prickles along the back of my neck.

I am stuck.

There's only one person to blame for my torment. Crucible's face glows like a ghoulish mask in my memory. His words become reverberating echoes in my head, more frightening than an infotab horror stream.

"One of you is most certainly a Hater. Whether both of you are Haters is entirely up to you."

What am I going to do?

If I report Wil, I keep my head free of a Haterman mask. For now. But the Collective's interrogation methods are too precise to keep any of us safe for long. Wil will fold. Eventually they will get to him, and he'll give all of us up: Sirens, Akela, and all.

So I can't report Wil.

But if I don't, I'll be the one under the interrogation spotlight instead. Crucible said as much. Could I step forward in Wil's place? I've done it before, back in the Filtering exam when I protected Sif.

"The Hater is me."

It won't work a second time. Back when Midgate wanted me to betray Sif, there was only myself to lose. But now, my head holds far too much information. I have the location of the underground bunker and all Akela's been trying to do. I've met hidden Sirens in the city. I've got the Song in my head—all those fragments of illegal music. Crucible would love to get his filthy claws into that kind of juicy information. So I can't just offer myself up to be arrested.

Staggering to the bathroom, I splash my face with water and stare at the hollow-eyed Apprentice in the mirror. Frizzy hair. Sallow skin from too many days indoors. Not enough sunshine. Not enough time left.

"You're a mess," I say to my reflection.

With little enthusiasm for my useless bed, I take my infotab out into the lounge, flicking on the streams to give my brain a rest for a while. The chatter becomes the background soundtrack to my dilemma.

Find Wil, and the Sirens are exposed. Refuse to find Wil and get myself arrested, and the Sirens are just as exposed. The impossibility of my situation is strangling me like a too-tight collar. It seems hopeless.

Where are you? I call silently to the Muse. *You're supposed to be helping me. Where are you now? Why can't I find a solution to this problem?*

There's no answer.

I need you, I plead. *I can't get out of this without you. I can't betray Akela or the Sirens. I have to keep the Song safe somehow, but I don't know how. Can you show me what you want me to do?*

I should have known there'd be no answer from the Muse. My little inner companion has been annoyingly quiet of late. Maybe I should just try to go back to sleep again.

Just as my eyes close, my fitness tracker vibrates. It feels heavy when I raise my wrist to look at the tiny screen. As if it's weary and weighed down, like the rest of me.

A strange notification flashes across the tracker screen: *Check message –V.* I stare at it stupidly for a moment. Then the screen returns to tell me the time: 0300.

Who's up at this hour?

I pick up the small white rectangle that is my infotab and boot it up. But there aren't any messages.

"Weird," I say, leaning back against the couch cushion and closing my eyes wearily. But a little prod at the back of my mind keeps me from drifting off.

Not those messages, the prompt says.

I yawn, stand up with great difficulty, and make the short walk back to my bunk. As soon as I'm tucked into the back of my bunk, I switch on the Siren app. There, on the message screen, sits one blinking line:

Viola: *Are you okay, Cadence?*

Surprised, I start to type.

Cadence: *What are you doing awake?*

Viola: *The Composer woke me. Told me to message you. You okay?*

I have to read Viola's words twice before I comprehend what she's saying. There's a sudden lump in my throat. The lump in my throat grows until I am clenching my teeth against a relieved sob. I send back an answer.

Cadence: *I'm in trouble. Crucible wants me to find and report Wil, but I can't. If they catch him, we're all exposed. But if I don't . . .*

Viola: *You're the one in trouble? I get it. I knew Crucible was bad news.*

Cadence: *I was just expressing my frustrations to the Composer and asking him for help because I don't know what to do anymore. Then you messaged and . . .*

My cheeks are damp with tears. But they're relieved tears. After hours in the darkness, it doesn't feel so dark anymore. There is someone here with me.

Viola: *The Composer loves you, you know.*

Cadence: *I don't know. He hasn't been speaking to me lately.*

Viola: *Just because you don't hear a voice, doesn't mean he's not there. He's with you. That's what he wanted me to tell you.*

The breath I let out is shaky. How did Viola know? All the way across the other side of the Academy in her Coding bunk room. How could she know that I was awake up here, battling this mess?

Cadence: *I need a miracle, V.*

Viola: *Well, you've got me. Is that okay for now?*

Cadence: *You have no idea.*

Relief loosens the tense knots in my muscles. The lump in my throat disappears, replaced with a warm glow of certainty: I am loved. I am not alone. The Composer just woke someone up in the middle of the night to talk to me. How is that even possible?

Another blinking line of words pops up in the message box.

Viola: *I think I know what we can do.*

I nearly laugh at the words. Of course she does. The Composer's already done one impossible thing today, so why not more?

Viola: *You there?*

Cadence: *Yes.*

Viola: *It'll take some Coding. But leave it with me. I think I can use some of our hacks to get Crucible happy and keep you safe. Meet me in the bunker tomorrow, and we'll get the plan going.*

Cadence: *But it's compromised.*

Viola: *Pfft. Coding queen, remember? I've already blinded the tree cams they tried to install.*

Cadence: *But they could be watching.*

Viola: *Use a different route. I'll take care of the rest. Just be there, ok?*

Cadence: *What time?*

Viola: *After dinner. Oh, and C?*

Cadence: *Yeah?*

Viola: *The Composer is good. He's got this. Okay?*

Cadence: *Okay.*

27

Watchers know people better than they know themselves. Their lives are open to our gaze at all times and in every circumstance. So to be a Watcher, you must learn to hear beneath a conversation. You must see behind the course of events. You must expose what a person most longs to hide from public view.
 (Elite Watcher Training Manual, 51st edition, page 33)

AT THE APPOINTED TIME, I HEAD DOWN TO MY meeting with Viola in the bunker. I hear a soft rumble of noise echoing up the staircase, but it doesn't really register until I reach the doorway of our meeting room. When I do arrive, the surprise of what I see stops me in my tracks.

All of the Sirens are here.

I stand in the doorway, gaping in wonder at the hive of activity. Most of them are sitting with their infotabs on their laps, typing and talking. A few others are gathered in small circles, conversing in low voices. I catch sight of Hodge's back. He seems to be in the middle of some kind of intense discussion that involves lots of hand waving.

"V, did you get the script I sent you?" Piccolo calls from the back corner just as I enter the room.

Viola, seated cross-legged in the middle of the floor and typing furiously on an infotab, replies over her shoulder without looking back at him. "Got it, thanks. I'm sending back a recoded version. When you've polished it up, flick it to Allegra."

Viola looks up, and when she sees me, a smile brightens her face. She sets aside her infotab and jumps to her feet. She claps her hands. "You're here! Okay, everyone. Let's get together. Briefing time."

"Cadence is here!" echoes around the room, and Hodge gives me a wave. Around him the group moves chairs and ambles back into a vague circle shape.

Allegra comes up beside me. "We've saved you a seat." She ushers me to a chair nearby. I collapse into it, still struggling to comprehend what I'm seeing. She catches sight of my confused expression and winks. "You'll see. Viola got us all on the case."

At that moment, Viola clears her throat.

"All right. We're good to go." She fixes everyone in her gaze as if challenging them to disagree. "What have we got Allegra?"

"We scouted a likely location on the western border, about a mile off the road from the military checkpoint. Only a single camera. Makes it plausible for a sudden appearance."

"Good." Viola gives a quick nod. "Hodge?"

"We've sorted the distraction protocol for Crucible's next visit."

"Signals prepped?"

"Forty-seven of them. A dozen contingency plans just in case things go pear-shaped. Keep an eye out for the silver decorations on the atrium wall. They'll tell you where the plan is going down."

Viola draws the word out slowly, intrigued. "Can't wait to see what you've organized. Piccolo?"

"The cloaking is nearly finished. But I'm struggling to get rid of a transfer glitch. There's still a troublesome halo when we impose the sim footage over the exit."

"Do you think we can get it sorted before go time?"

"I think so." Piccolo slides a slender finger across his infotab screen. "I'd love a whole week to finesse it, but as long as we don't have to go tonight, we'll be fine."

"Okay," Viola says. She turns to me. "So, Cadence, what you need to do is—"

"Whoa, wait." I'm totally lost. "Signals? Transfer glitches? What is going on?"

There is light laughter from a couple of the Sirens. Viola explains, "Well, when you mentioned what was happening, I immediately thought of the bunker cloaking protocols."

MEMORY DATE: THREE MONTHS AGO
Memory location: Secret bunker
"This tracker has a few mods to keep you safe," Akela adds.
"Mods? But why?"
Wil begins to count off reasons on his fingers.
"One: when you approach the bunker entrance, this tracker will begin a random loop. On the Watcher system, you'll look like you go for a run around the obstacle course, then back to your room for a shower and sleep. The tracker will sense you coming out of the bunker again, and come out to meet you where the cameras start coverage."

I NOD, THINKING I UNDERSTAND. THEN I realize I actually don't understand at all. I stop. "So how is that useful?"

Viola is patient with me. "How can we get Crucible to find Wil without actually finding him?"

I look from her to the ring of expectant faces around her, and then back. "I don't . . . ohhh."

Viola smiles broadly.

The pieces suddenly clatter into place. "So you're going to fake the surveillance footage to make it look like he's somewhere he isn't?"

A heap of heads nod.

"But won't they find out?"

"Not if the plan works," Hodge says with a soldier's grim confidence.

I rub nervously at my eyes, feeling a jumpy kind of anxiety. "What if Wil surfaces somewhere else?"

"I thought about that, but then something occurred to me," Viola says. She swipes at something on her infotab screen. "We only have to convince Crucible in the moment." She looks up, showing me a mock-up of a scene full of people. "He's not going to disbelieve the footage. You're only a first-year Apprentice, and he's so confident in his own technology he'll never suspect it's made up."

I try to absorb the information. I'm still uneasy. "It's risky."

"Being a Siren and breathing is risky." Fife crosses his hands behind his head, relaxed. "This just makes it fun."

Allegra pushes her infotab toward me. "We found a place on the border of the Collective where—"

"Wait. The *border*? But that's . . . that's . . . well, I don't know how far away that is, but it's a long, long—"

"It's close enough for Wil to have travelled there by now," Allegra says. "All we have to do is show him sneaking across, and Crucible will assume he's escaped our jurisdiction."

My brain is taking forever to process what I'm hearing. "But how can you hack a camera fifty miles away? That's impossible."

A twinkle comes to Viola's eyes. "It's easy when you've already broken through the security protocols."

Piccolo reaches over and pats her on the back. "Our V is

amazing, Cadence. She can do anything with an infotab and a bit of code."

Viola shrugs off the compliment, looking a little uncomfortable at the attention. "Our regular meeting hack involves at least a dozen different cameras around the obstacle course," she continues. "And they have to synchronize precisely." She waves her infotab in the air. "This is nothing."

"Does Akela know?" I ask.

Hodge and Viola share a significant look.

"If she knew . . ." Viola begins.

"She'd probably try and stop us," Hodge finishes. "It's safer for her if she has no idea."

I look from Viola to Hodge and the little group of Apprentices all smiling warmly at me right now. "Why are you doing this?"

Viola comes and kneels beside me and looks straight into my eyes. "Cadence, my dear Siren. We're family."

And just like that, weight falls from my shoulders, and I burst into tears.

ON THE DAY OF THE TRIUMPH CLOSING ceremony, a strange arrangement of silvery streamers appears on the atrium wall. The morning sun falls on the tangle of silver strands, creating soft white glints that are meaningless to anyone except a Siren:

Plan thirty-five.

My stomach lurches. Crucible is coming today, and plan thirty-five is in place—whatever plan thirty-five is.

Hodge may have thirty-five plans, but I only have one. As instructed, I casually slap my hand on my forehead, acting for all the world as if I have just forgotten something very important.

"Gah! Left it on the bench," I say with a chuckle, loud

enough that the few Apprentices passing me can hear. I hope the agitation I display simply says to the world that I'm anxious to be reunited with my lost item. I hope it doesn't say that I'm about to embark on the most dangerous plan of my life.

MEMORY DATE: FOUR DAYS AGO
Memory location: Secret bunker
"I'm not going to lie," Viola says. "This could get you Realigned. But—" She raises her hands quickly into a placating gesture, seeing the look on my face. "This is the best way to get Crucible out of your hair."
"Are you sure?" I say, feeling doubtful.
"The Composer's preparing you," she says. "You're part of a plan that's bigger than any of us understand."

BACK IN THE WATCHER DORM, I BEGIN THE arrangements that Fife jokingly dubbed "Operation Obfuscate." I make a quick visit to the bathroom to fix up my appearance. Then I grab my infotab on the way out, flicking on the Siren app and clasping the screen to my chest. But not before I send the little notification to Viola: *Ready, set, go.*

The infotab makes a small beep, and I glance at the notification. My heart nearly stops.

DON'T GO YET, it reads. NEED ONE HOUR.

What now? Hodge gave me the 'go' signal but Viola wants me to wait. What in Love's name do I do? Maybe I should run upstairs and see if Akela will help.

MEMORY DATE: FOUR DAYS AGO
Memory location: Secret bunker
"This would be easier if we could get Akela on it," Piccolo says with a grunt.

"Akela can't know," Allegra says with a certain finality. "She's already under Crucible's watch."

"But she can get Viola into the surveillance coding system without having to hack it." Piccolo looks annoyed.

Viola shakes her head. "Don't worry. It'll only take a bit longer, that's all. A small price to pay for protecting Zed's safety."

"Yeah," Fife adds. "We need her so we can get into the bunker."

"We need her for more than that, Fife." Allegra shakes her head reprovingly.

I TURN FOR THE WATCHER ROOM. IF I HAVE TO improvise, I guess I'll have to at least look convincing.

"I wonder where I should scout today," I say aloud. With a determined shove, I push the heavy soundproofed door open and walk toward the control sphere.

MEMORY DATE: FOUR DAYS AGO
Memory location: Secret bunker
Allegra crouches in front of me. "Everything has to look like a surprise. Can you pretend to be surprised?"

I do my best impression of a surprised face.

Fife lets out a long groan. "We're dooooooooooooomed!"

"You'll be okay, Cadence." Allegra pats my hand in a condescending way. "It's probably better if you don't try to oversell it anyway."

THE WATCHER SCREEN GLOWS, WAITING FOR my command.

"Triumph carnival," I say, and the vision flicks to the entrance gates of the huge park where millions of people are already strolling through the sideshows and festival stages. Tonight's the night when the Haterman effigy will be burned, and the Triumph gifts distributed before festivities are officially closed for another year. I swing between cameras, using the control sphere's zoom to make it look like I'm flying on a trapeze. A faint strand of memory grasps for my attention, reminding me of something Wil said back in the bunker, the night before he ran away.

With sickening force, the memory coalesces into fully formed thought.

"The VIP box." The familiar wave of nausea bubbles up in my stomach.

Hearing my comment as a command, the vision dutifully flicks straight to the VIP area of the Triumph carnival. Set in the only permanent buildings of the entire park, the VIP zone forms a fortress in the midst of the sea of citizenry. High white walls ring the compound, designed to prevent unclean eyes from seeing the Executive. Razor wire forms large rings along the ground outside to prevent any crazies from considering a dash into the privileged zone. Two roads lead in to the compound, blocked by multiple Squad checkpoints to make sure that only the selected few may enter the celebration area.

A tall, black-glassed observation tower sprouts in the center, high enough to give a birds-eye view of the entire festival. If I didn't already know about the party taking place inside, I could possibly mistake it for a prison.

I swing through the cameras again, searching around the utility zones behind the celebrities' party rooms. This is where Pim was serving Carell Hummer and his crew. I catch sight of a row of food trucks in the back and fly down for a closer look.

Large crews of Engine Roomers bustle in and around the area. Some carry food from portable refrigerator units into the food trucks, while others carry decorations and other equipment toward the party rooms. I trapeze around the space for a while, hunting for any faces that look suspicious. I smile when I catch sight of Pim with a small group of Elites. She's busy sweeping the footpath, but she looks so excited that it's almost as if she received the broom as a Triumph gift.

Zooming back out, I cross to the checkpoints at the western entrance just in time to see a large truck arrive at the first boom gate. It's decorated in wild colors, with images of presents and streamers and balloons painted along every surface. As the truck driver hands a bundle of documents to the checkpoint guard, black-uniformed squad members scurry around the vehicle, waving detectors over the wheels and around the front of the grill. At least two soldiers squat down on the ground to push long-handled detectors under the truck's frame. Two other squad members open the rear doors of the trailer, revealing Triumph gift boxes neatly packed all the way to the roof.

I swing to another camera so I can take a quick look at the front of the truck. Up in the cab, two workers in brown overalls lounge at the windows. I can't see their faces, but they look relaxed. The driver, a heavyset man with thick fingers, shakes with laughter at something his companion says. For some reason unknown to me, I decide to flick on the microphone.

A wall of noise floods the room, until I focus on the two men in the cab.

"You're the funniest man I ever worked with," the heavyset man booms in an out-of-town accent. "Where you get those jokes, man?"

"I try my best," his companion replies, and at the sound of the passenger's voice a vise of fear clamps itself over my heart. For a moment, I feel faint.

I zoom around the vision, but no matter which angle I use, I can't see the passenger's face. All I can see is his figure: thin, young, with hands that look too slender to manage heavy manual labor. At the side window I catch a glimpse of deep black hair that doesn't fool me for a second. Frantic, I flick from camera to camera, desperate to find some way to see the faces of the men in the cabin.

At last, the squads retreat, and the checkpoint guard waves the truck through. Temporary concrete barriers create a road for the truck to move forward, keeping the crowds safely out of the way. As he accelerates, the driver leans out to wave at the Squad around him, and his companion casts a quick glance out of the passenger door.

That glance is enough. I pounce, freezing the vision and zooming in closer until the passenger's face nearly fills the whole screen. Although a cap covers most of his head, the tight black curls that poke out around his collar look like a wig. His face has been modified, as if he's wearing a false nose and chin. Thick black glasses cover his eyes, so I can't tell if they're green. But I would know Wil's voice anywhere.

My hand hovers over the red button, the automatic reflex kicking in to report what I know is true and dangerous. But I hold back. I can't doom my Siren friends by putting Wil in the Embracement chambers. Wil is at the Triumph carnival, and he's driven something right into the monsters' lair. But if I report what I am seeing now, we are all dead.

AFTER A HEATED DEBATE IN MY HEAD, during which I alternate between prayer to the Composer and calling myself an idiot, I force myself to walk back to my bunk. I'm sure it's obvious to anyone viewing the surveillance footage that something is bothering me, but I have no idea how to cover my feelings right now. I just hope the Watchers are so busy with Triumph they don't have time to bother looking at boring, ordinary me.

The mattress is soft and warm when I lie back onto it, and I'm tempted to just close my eyes and forget the world for a few hours of unconsciousness. But I know that's not an option right now. So with infotab in hand, I go to the message app and vent my feelings to anyone who'll listen.

Cadence: *Big trouble.*

Viola: *???*

Cadence: *X at carnival, delivering "presents" to VIP sector.*

Viola: *Oh.*

Hodge: *Don't panic. We'll think of something.*

Cadence: *Like what?????*

Viola: *What do you mean by "presents"?*

Cadence: *He just turned up in a big truck, decorated like a gift-giving supply vehicle. X was planning to make a major statement, so whatever is in there is bad.*

Viola: *What kind of statement?*

Cadence: *The bring-down-the-Collective kind of statement. Like a bomb.*

Viola: *Composer help us.*

Cadence: *We need a new plan.*

I wait for a minute or two while nobody responds. A bomb is the only explanation that makes sense to me right now.

Why else would Wil the fugitive be turning up with a massive trailer to the VIP sector of the Triumph carnival, wearing facial makeup and a disguise? He's obviously so arrogantly confident his plan will succeed, he's gone ahead with it anyway.

After counting the silent blinks of the message cursor for far too long to be comfortable, a note finally pops up.

Hodge: *I got it. Run the portable play from plan eighteen, then meet me in the atrium.*

Cadence: *But how? V hasn't cracked the encryption.*

Hodge: *V, send it to her infotab. We'll wing it.*

Viola: *Sure thing.*

Cadence: *Wait. I got doubts.*

Hodge: *Don't worry. The Composer is in this.*

Cadence: *But how will we stop X?*

Hodge: *First things first. We distract Crucible. Then maybe convince Zed to send us to the VIP center. We can stop it, if we get there in time.*

Viola: *I'll modify the footage in the main system anyway, just in case.*

Cadence: *OK.*

Hodge: *Let's go.*

I stare at the messages for a while, trying to work out what is going on. A small *ding* on my infotab brings me back to reality. Viola has sent the video file.

"I hope the Composer knows what he's doing," I think to myself, shunting the file to my video player and leaving the privacy of my bunk.

28

Although Watchers see everything, we cannot foresee every unexpected circumstance. Which is why we must act swiftly on those rare occasions that surprise us. Even in the greatest crisis, Watchers should report and allow the arms of the Collective to move and defend.

Citizens must never see a crack of alarm in our actions. Our Watching must be swift. It must give the impression that nobody is outside the Love Collective's purview. It must never, ever look afraid, for Watchers know no fear. The Love Collective is a place where fear has been permanently banished.

(Elite Watcher Training Manual, 51st edition, page 232)

I'VE GIVEN UP ALL PRETENSE OF CALM NOW and sprint back to the Watcher room.

Composer, fix this, I sing silently, before I force my hands back to the control sphere once more.

"Border Crossing Alpha," I command, and the screen instantly displays a deserted highway out in the middle of nowhere. To the left of my view, a vast expanse of cracked and broken concrete lies in a ribbon across a grassy plain. To my right, the grassy plain extends halfway to the horizon before being swallowed by a dark forest. In front of me, a long white wall stretches across the concrete, as if to block all traffic. Not that I can see any traffic here. The wall is smooth, windowless, and about as tall as the Elite Academy building.

MEMORY DATE: FOUR DAYS AGO
Memory location: Secret bunker
Viola shows me her infotab again. "I found the camera location for you. This one here looks like a drone."
I blink, surprised. "They never have those in the city."
"That's because they've got every inch covered by the fixed eyes. Almost nobody lives out at the border, so they have to find something that can follow the more mobile citizens."
"How do you know this stuff?" I ask.
With a slight smile, Viola taps the side of her nose. "The less you know, the safer you are."

TAKING A CALMING BREATH, I WALK THE VISION forward, following the edge of the highway until it reaches the wall. Where the road meets the wall, a small border station nestles into unbroken concrete. The stark black box of the border crossing is a vivid contrast to the blinding white barrier, which reflects the sun with almost painful brilliance. Two Love Squad guards stand at their posts outside the doors. It must be the most boring job in the world to guard a crossing nobody ever wants to use.

How nice it would be to have a boring life.

You'd hate that, comes a little voice at the back of my mind.

"Data check." Time begins to run backward on the screen. The sun rises and sets, and clouds skip across the sky in jerky, time-lapse speed. Nothing approaches the border except the shadows cast by an errant cloud every now and then. No vehicle. No human.

"End data check." The vision flicks back to the present. I paste on a slightly exasperated expression for the benefit of the cameras.

"But he wouldn't just walk up to the exit door, now would he?" I say out loud. "Show camera schematic." A diagram pops up onscreen, displaying the location of all of the cameras nearby. I know what I'm looking for. That one little red circle several miles to the north. The camera set for no apparent reason in the middle of an ocean of trees.

Using the drone, I turn the vision in the direction I was always heading anyway. The felted green wall of trees grows taller as the drone flies toward them. Not to the height of the border wall, but still impressive.

This is the first time I remember seeing such a large amount of trees at one time. For just a moment I'm tempted to forget all about missions and fugitives and bomb plots, and just float around the serene forest, dancing the drone through shadows and the beams of light that filter through the leaf canopy. I wonder what it would feel like. What it would smell like. I'm rocked by a sudden longing to throw off my shoes and walk barefoot beneath those branches, losing myself in the wilderness far from the noisy chaos of the Triumph of Love festival.

The drone flies above the treetops, keeping clear of the branches that might grasp at its rotors. It automatically homes in on the lone red circle on the schematic diagram. Then the trees begin to thin out, revealing wide, dusty patches of earth.

MEMORY DATE: FOUR DAYS AGO
Memory location: Secret bunker

Piccolo jumps up in the middle of our conversation. "Wait a minute!" he says. "What about the drone? How are you going to synchronize the vision from the two cameras when that thing could be flying all over the place?"

"Already thought of that," Viola counters. "We use the drone to make everyone think she is searching the forest. It'd be too suspicious if she randomly appears at an isolated camera nobody knows about. Once she finds the fixed camera, she sends the drone back to the border station."

"You should know Viola by now," Allegra says to Piccolo. "She thinks of everything."

"RETURN TO BASE," I COMMAND THE DRONE, and immediately it switches direction, speeding back to its dock at the border. "Switch vision to camera in range."

Time seems to slow down. From this moment on, all of the Sirens are in Realignment territory. As if Wil hadn't already landed us right there with his foolhardy ideas.

Composer be with us through this moment.

Onscreen, a circular drain forms a small hiccup in the pristine white wall. Pooled around the outside of the drain are fallen logs and rotting timbers. A grate once barred access to this drain, but weather or flood or some other force has long since broken holes in the rusted metal.

Viola chose well. It's a perfect place to pretend to escape. I hold the control sphere more tightly. Stretching away from the wall is a dry, empty creek bed, marked with occasional darker patches where tiny puddles of mud remain. Trees rise above the camera on either side of the creek. But the creek bed ends at a grey block of concrete bearing another circle drain. High razor-wire fences encase its top, but the mouth of the drain is open.

"What's that?" I say loudly for the benefit of the surveillance. "Send data to infotab."

Quickly I snatch my infotab from the floor where I left it. Without waiting, I switch off the vision and run from the room. On the way, I tap the code on my fitness tracker sending a message to Viola: GOING NOW.

MY NERVES TUMBLE AND SURGE, FORCING my leg into a strange twitching jiggle. This isn't going to work. There's no way anyone will believe Wil is escaping when he's at this very moment in the Triumph VIP compound, trying to set off a bomb. We're doomed, and I'm just marking time until the inevitable arrest.

Reaching the atrium level, the lift doors barely open before I burst out of them. But Hodge is already waiting, looking for all the world as if he was on a casual errand somewhere.

"Oh, hi," I say as if our meeting is an accident. "What are you doing here?"

"Crucible's heading for the Academy now. I'm on escort," Hodge says, his face giving away nothing. But underneath I hear his urgency. This is our only attempt at fooling Crucible with the video. Time is short.

"Really?" I ask. "I need to talk to him. Can I go with you?"

Thankfully, Hodge appears to be a better actor than me, and he makes a show of being surprised by my request. "I guess. Sure," he replies and directs me back to the lifts.

In Hodge's calming presence, my breathing begins to slow to a saner speed. My face no longer feels like it's burning, and my hands are not quite as shaky. But the infotab still feels heavier than it should, weighing down my thoughts at the task ahead.

I have very little hope that Crucible is going to be even slightly fooled by this video.

MEMORY DATE: YESTERDAY
Memory location: Secret bunker
"Will he buy it?" Piccolo looks doubtfully at Viola.
"Composer knows. But we have to try."

WE DESCEND IN THE LIFT AND EMERGE AT the train station. A single gilded carriage hums quietly on the tracks. As my shoes clatter across the tiles, the front door of the carriage glides open, and two figures in white linen step out. Akela's eyes widen at the sight of us, but she covers well. Crucible's gaze narrows, and his steps slow.

I salute. "May you follow your dreams and find yourself in the universe, Executive Lover Crucible. I am sorry to disturb—"

"Enough of that." Crucible waves my apology away. "You obviously have something. What is it?" He nods at the small object I am carrying. Akela stands wordlessly at his shoulder, looking stern.

"Executive Lover, sir, I have found him." In the cavernous space, the echoes of my voice sound thin and reedy—too obviously nervous.

"Apprentice—" Akela begins, but she cuts herself off when Crucible speaks.

"Oh?" is all he says.

I nod emphatically. One of his eyebrows goes up a little.

I thrust the infotab toward him. "Here, Executive Lover. See for yourself."

The air around us is thick with fumes from the train carriage and tunnel beyond. I clear my throat. Crucible doesn't move. I take a timid step. He still doesn't reach out for the device, so I swipe the screen to bring up the footage Viola has prepared.

Akela cranes her neck to peer at the screen. When she sees the video, she glances sharply at me. "What is this?"

"Executive Lover Crucible gave me orders," I explain. Her frown deepens.

"Well? Play it for me," he orders.

"Yes, Executive Lover." My heart is in overdrive. To stop my hands from trembling, I reach out with my mind for the words of a Song fragment.

> Composer go before you,
> Through Lyric's loving grace.
> With help of Muse within you,
> You'll see your maker's face.

With the words on repeat in my head, I finally feel calm enough to press play on the video. Crucible leans forward, and the surveillance footage Viola has prepared for him begins to play.

The creek bed is deserted and dry, save for occasional puddles that darken the sandstone blocks. Trees on either side of the creek twitch in the breeze. The sun sits high in the sky, shortening the shadows on the ground, and illuminating the open spaces. But most of the forest remains hidden in shadow.

For a few seconds, there is nothing except trees, rocks, and gaping pipelines. Then, at the entrance to the large stormwater pipe, a figure emerges into the light, clambering unsteadily until his legs hang from the lip of the concrete tube. After a few experimental swings of his feet, the figure jumps down from the pipe's mouth, landing with bent knees on the stones below. Then he straightens, brushes at dirty stains on his grey uniform, and begins to walk toward the camera. His gait is sure, though his appearance is filthy.

Nice touch, V, I think. I risk a glance at Crucible. His eyes are drinking in the vision, completely absorbed by what's on the screen. He takes the device in both hands, gaze still entranced by the surveillance footage.

Wil's blond hair has become caked with mud. The camera slowly swivels, programmed to follow the motion of his walk. After a few minutes, he reaches the detritus piled up around the wall. Climbing over the fallen tree trunks, he clambers up to the drain and then crouches to climb in. The last we see of him is the muddy soles of his Academy shoes, which shuffle forward and then disappear into the darkness of the drain.

The vision freezes on the tunnel entrance. It's been a masterpiece. Viola and her team have worked their magic, and the rendering of Wil's figure has been perfect. If I hadn't known the truth, I would have thought it was real footage.

Crucible slaps the infotab against my chest.

"When?" Akela's face looks pale.

I clasp the infotab in both hands, trying to stop it from smashing on the floor. "I watched this segment of the wall about half an hour ago, Executive Lover."

"You're sure it's him?"

"Yes, sir. You have met Wil, sir."

"Where?"

"The camera five miles north of Border Crossing Alpha."

"Did you flag him?"

I shake my head. "He was out in the middle of nowhere. I thought—"

Crucible clicks his tongue in annoyance.

I dig my fingernails into my palms and try to think. Viola

was so confident he would believe me. But he doesn't believe me. We're doomed . . .

Take a deep breath.

I almost turn at the sound of the voice. But then I realize I'm the only one who can hear it.

Worst-case scenarios aren't going to fix the problem right now. I am going before you.

The words are forceful, but not intimidating, and enough to silence my fretful questions. I relax, letting my fingernails disengage from my palms. I may be going down, but I'm not going down alone.

Hodge quietly comes up beside me, while Crucible prowls the room.

"What is the meaning of this?" Akela asks, looking from Crucible to me. From his pacing circle, Crucible waves his hand irritably.

"Your truant." He looks up at her. "I did your job for you."

The shocked expression Akela now transmits is perfect.

"He—I mean, you found him, Apprentice?" Her eyes are wide and fearful. I'm glad Crucible is looking the other way, because Hodge makes a Siren signal, and she visibly relaxes.

Crucible stops so suddenly I take a backward step.

"Ha!" he exclaims, his face lighting up. "That kid will never know what hit him." He slaps his leg gleefully and gives a small chuckle.

"Pardon sir?" I ask, confused.

His expression changes. Crucible shows his teeth. "You've done well, my dear. Very well. Very well, indeed. How about we have a little celebration?" Rubbing his hands together, he looks at the two of us.

"Sir?" Hodge asks, startled.

"This kind of service to the Collective deserves an excursion to the VIP compound, if I'm not mistaken," Crucible says, hand on my shoulder. "Time for you to see Triumph for yourself."

My mouth drops open in shock. Beside me, Hodge makes a little strangled noise. "Uh, yes, sir. Of course, sir," he says, recovering his composure faster than I can.

"We live to serve the Collective." I bow in the appropriate way, more to cover the look on my face than anything else.

Crucible waves expansively toward the train at the platform. "No time like the present," he says. "I bet you've just been dying to see the VIP compound. Dorm Leader, take that thing, will you?" He points to my infotab. "They won't need that where I'm taking them."

Akela bows her head and obediently retrieves my infotab. I place a carefully constructed smile on my face, and clasp my hands together in front of my heart.

"Of course, Executive Lover," I say breathily, wondering what on earth just happened.

29

Composer go before you,
Through Lyric's loving grace.
With help of Muse within you,
You'll see your maker's face.

IS THIS WHAT YOU MEANT WHEN YOU SAID you were going before us?

After a smooth, quiet ride during which Crucible gives us more details about Triumph parties than I ever wanted to know, the train deposits us at another deserted station. The pristine white tiles and squeaky-clean floors tell me this station isn't used all that often. Gilded crests and accents everywhere add a note of luxury to everything, which makes me nervous. The decor of this place is far too close to the Hall of Love for my liking.

Crucible struts along, firmly in his element. This station looks as familiar to him as it is unfamiliar to me. Feeling like prey walking into the hunter's lair, I keep my eyes carefully trained on our surroundings.

At the end of the platform where a set of blindingly white stairs ascend to ground level, the dull thumps of the Triumph carnival beat reverberate through the ground. Up there somewhere are crowds and celebrations, and Wil with his murderous intentions.

"You two are in for *such* a treat." Crucible's voice is almost syrupy. "I am *so* glad you found my target. Wait until the others hear what you've done."

His words send my mind into near meltdown. The others? Is he talking about the *Executive*? What are we doing here?

Catching my frantic looks to the side, Hodge gives my back a little pat, and I look into eyes that seem to know everything I'm thinking. My thoughts slow. I'm not alone, I remind myself. Hodge twitches his head in Crucible's direction and we continue following him.

Stepping into a glass-walled elevator, we rise up through the concrete station structure. As soon as we clear the floor, a burst of sunlight nearly blinds us. It takes a few seconds for our eyes adjust to the morning light. We pass over the group of buildings that service the VIP area and ascend higher and higher, until we are looking out over a vast expanse of people, carnival attractions, stages, and laser towers. A panoramic view stretches out before us. The giant Haterman effigy rises above the center of the carnival, surrounded by open space and safety barriers. In all directions around it, the Triumph party spreads in a seething mass of people and party.

Hodge gasps, in an uncharacteristic show of emotion.

I know how he feels. I never knew so many people existed.

The crowds are like a pulsating, living carpet that surges and undulates around every spare patch of ground. Although the lights don't shine too brightly in full daylight, I can see enough to know that the night parties would be epic. I turn slowly around in the lift which curves around half of the inner concrete service column. I can see nearly all of the grounds.

Just before we move up into the observation deck, I find it. Tucked away in one corner behind the food trucks sits a brightly colored vehicle, covered in images of balloons. I poke

Hodge's arm, and when he sees what I'm focusing on, his eyes widen. Then the lift passes through the solid concrete floor, and we are emerging into the plush, cool opulence of the VIP suite itself.

A wall of glass spans half the tower, giving a full view of the Triumph stage. That view shifts slowly as the deck rotates. Wide couches are scattered across the deep burgundy-colored floor, and a small group of well-dressed people mingles between them, drinking and laughing. To one side is an expansive bar covered in mirrors and black paneling. Dim red and purple LEDs light part of the space, but leave plenty of pockets of shadow around the lounges. There's no sign of a linen uniform anywhere.

Behind the lifts, the other half of the building is divided into private rooms marked by black velvet-covered doors. As I begin to wonder how I'm going to get back downstairs, we're approached by a tottering old man wearing a glittering gold-and-green suit that looks as if it was made of jewel-encrusted scales. The man's white hair is slicked back against his skull, and his skin is stretched across his face in a way that leaves strange puckers around the corners of his mouth.

"Gordy! You're finally here!" he says loudly and staggers across the room to us. "What are you doing in those *ridiculous* clothes?" He holds his arms in the air with a slender glass of alcohol in each hand. I hang back as he pounces on Crucible, kissing the air beside the Executive Lover's cheeks in greeting.

"I am on duty right now, Edvard," Crucible says with mock seriousness, catching the man's elbow so he doesn't careen backward. The green-suited man stares uncomprehending at him, so Crucible makes an overly obvious nod in the direction of Hodge and I. "Apprentices, this is Executive Lover Edvard Munsch. The one in charge of your entertainment."

Hodge snaps a crisp salute.

I swallow back the contents of my stomach, and give a tight bow to Munsch. "May you follow your dreams and—"

"Yes, yes, whatever." Munsch gives me a look of utter contempt, then leans drunkenly toward Crucible's face. He attempts to speak in a whisper, but his volume is a near shout. "I have a bevy of beauties waiting over there for us." Munsch waves one glass at a small group of people near the observation window, all dressed in sparkling clothes that show rather a lot of skin. "All handpicked by yours truly. Why don't you ditch the riffraff here and come join the party? Or are you up to your old tricks again, eh? Eh?" Munsch elbows Crucible in the ribs. "Boring old Midgate'll have your head if she catches you sampling the Nurseries again, you know."

Hodge is completely still beside me.

A flash of annoyance passes over Crucible's face. "Edvard, it's only 1100 hours, and you're already wasted. You're talking nonsense."

"Ain't no party like a Triumph party, man!" Munsch raises a glass so swiftly the contents slosh over the side onto his hand. "Oops, how did that happen?" He stares uncomprehending at his glass for a few seconds, then looks back at Crucible with a goofy grin. "Who cares? It's Triumph, baby! Come on." He downs the contents of his glasses, then throws them away on the carpet so he can grasp Crucible's arm. "Let's get you into some decent outfit that befits an Executive Lover, and you can live it up for the last night."

Crucible's eyes devour the "bevy of beauties" on the other side of the room and heads toward one of the private rooms. He looks at us over his shoulder. "Apprentices, go and amuse yourselves for a few hours, will you? I have some business to attend to."

My skin crawls. When the door to the room closes, I let out a sigh of relief.

"Come on," Hodge's voice is strained as he touches my elbow. "We've also got some business to attend to."

I WATCH THE CROWDS OF PEOPLE EBB AND flow as the elevator descends, wondering what Wil is planning. Something spectacular, no doubt. Probably at night when the crowds are thickest and the potential for chaos at its height.

"Let's take a closer look." I give Hodge a significant nod in the direction of the truck. We head out into the bustling throng of caterers, security guards, attendants, and wannabes.

The atmosphere is festive but with a kind of weariness. Weeks-long parties must be hard to sustain. Everyone moves quickly, but there's a tiredness around their eyes. I catch a few glimpses of tense, irritable conversations and wonder how everyone has managed to survive this level of entertainment.

Hodge leads our way through the crowds, passing management buildings, security headquarters, and other serious-looking control centers. It looks like the whole festival is controlled from this single hub. If the aim is to create mayhem and fear in an unprecedented way, Wil's cohorts have chosen well.

"How could they get through?" I wonder. "Surely they'd have been picked up."

"Let's ask questions like that later," Hodge says.

We head to the outer ring of walkways that pass around the walls of the compound. The crowds are slightly thinner here, but no less purposeful. Hodge keeps up a brisk pace, but as we round a corner, he halts.

He motions for me to hang back. Curious, I peer around him.

At the far end of the rear wall of a building, sitting as quietly as if it was a sleeping creature, is the truck. It looks for all the world like a delivery vehicle waiting to be unloaded.

"That's going to kill us all," I whisper in alarm.

"Not if we get to it first," Hodge tells me. "You wait here. I'll check it out."

The thought of waiting while Hodge goes creeping around a bomb-in-disguise is too much. So when he moves, I follow. In a semi-crouch, we scoot down the deserted alley behind the building and stop at the corner as Hodge scouts ahead.

We're now only a few meters away from the truck. There's no sign of the driver or Wil, but then I can only see the cab of the truck and the small space in front of it. The rest of my view is blocked by Hodge.

He motions for me to stay quiet. Then he makes a series of Love Squad signals involving two fingers and pointing in various directions that I'm sure makes sense to anyone trained in the right cadre. I just nod as if I understand what he's saying, but it must be clear on my face that I'm baffled. Hodge looks briefly exasperated, then makes a hand signal I definitely do understand.

You stay, his hand says. I shake my head. His expression grows stern, and I get a glimpse of the intimidating Hodge that scared me back in my first days at Elite Academy. But I know him better now. I shake my head more insistently, and Hodge glares at me.

"Fine," his whisper is curt. "Just don't get us killed."

We go slowly out into the small gap between the building and the side of the truck. Behind the truck, the service crowds bustle to and fro along the path. So many people. What on earth could Wil be thinking? Hodge looks around, then straightens.

"No cameras," he observes. "They found a blind spot. Nobody would have seen them get out of here."

We hug the wall, keeping to the end of the truck furthest from the crowds. Hodge lets go of my wrist, and jumps up to peer into the cabin. When he jumps back down, his face is shining.

"They've even left the keys in the ignition." His voice is disbelieving.

I look up at the deserted window. "So they've just run away?"

"Let's take a closer look."

We squeeze around the front of the truck and come to another smallish gap between the passenger side of the truck and the wall of a service building. A single door sits in the middle of the wall.

"They must have escaped through there." Hodge checks the door handle.

"Locked?"

He nods. "Give me a sec," he says, and dives under the truck. Like an experienced mechanic, he rolls underneath, only his shoes remaining out in the open. I wait for tense minutes, until he rolls back out. "There are obvious modifications to the undercarriage." He picks himself up and dusts off his uniform. "Any Squad member should have stopped this for closer inspection."

I shake my head. "But I saw the patrol checking the underside of the truck with their detectors. They went over the whole thing."

"Which gate?"

I nod backward. "West."

Hodge's mouth tightens in a grim line. "There's no way you could think that was standard," he says pointing at the space under the truck. "There are wires and dodgy welds everywhere. And this suspension, look." He points at the set of wheels beside us. "If the entire trailer was full of Triumph gifts, the weight would be evenly distributed. But this front end is holding something really heavy. Something that's a different density to the boxes at the back. It makes no sense that the west gate patrols would see this and not even bother to stop them."

The blood drains from my face. "Which means . . ."

"Which means there are people on the inside," Hodge finishes.

We both stare at each other, speechless. The happy thumps of the Triumph carnival swirl in the air and vibrate the ground beneath us. But my mind is a messy whirl of thoughts and worries.

"Things just got complicated."

30

In the beginning was the Lyric.

A PLAN QUICKLY FORMS. HODGE DEPARTS for the VIP lounge to try and convince Crucible, and I head for the food truck area. I know at least one of my friends will be here, so there's a slim chance we can salvage the situation before disaster strikes. The sun is high in the sky now, and sweat prickles at the back of my neck.

Crowds of workers are emerging from service buildings, heading for lunch, which makes going slow and difficult. I give up attempting to be polite and just begin pushing my way through. It earns me a few insults and harsh stares, but I figure they'll forgive me when I save their lives later.

In a large courtyard near the south wall, a caravan of food trucks rises above the crowded space, offering a variety of foods I've never seen. Delicious smells float on the air, and I almost lose my mind at the enticing fare they offer.

The crowd here is so thick that I have to strain on tiptoes to see. It's impossible to push, so I skirt around the sides, heading for the rear of the trucks. Cables and pipes litter the ground behind the vehicles, carrying water and electricity to the portable kitchens. Workers move in and around the trucks, casting suspicious looks my way. I'm about to give up when I spot a familiar uniform and an even more familiar head. Pim steps down from a food truck, a large bucket of scraps straining her arms. She heads for a portable dumpster in the back.

"Pim!" I call, and she looks around but isn't seeing me. I run toward her, waving my hand above my head. Her eyes widen in surprise and delight.

"Flick! What are you doing here?"

"I'm on a tour with Crucible. Special reward for hard work." I force as much happiness into my tone as I can. Pim smiles at me ruefully.

"Half your luck," she says with envy. "I'm cleaning out kitchens all afternoon."

"Can I give you a hand?" I reach out to take hold of the bucket Pim is carrying. She lets it go with relief, and I almost fall over. "They must think you're a machine," I gasp, fighting a losing battle against gravity.

Pim laughs. "It's okay. This festival has been super fun, and I've got more than enough material now to keep teasing the Coders for months." Her face dimples.

I smile, but the urgency of our situation begins to weigh on me. "Can I ask you something?"

Pim eyes me. "You don't want to see Carell Hummer, do you? He's mine."

"No, not that." I let the bucket sit on the ground. "Do you think they'd be mad if I borrowed you for a few minutes?"

Pim looks doubtfully at the food truck and then back at me. "It's lunchtime. Can it wait?"

I shake my head.

For a second she bites her bottom lip, then with a final backward glance, she gives a little shrug. "Okay. I guess I could take a little break."

I take her away across the compound. Hopefully by now, Hodge has gotten through to Crucible, so there may not be a need for Pim to do anything. But if there's even a hint of someone on the inside, we're going to have to go over their heads. And that means something big.

The bright colors of the truck look so festive and exciting that it's no surprise that Pim claps her hands in delight when we reach it.

"Is this the Triumph presents?" her face is alive with anticipation. "What did you get me?"

She rushes ahead and strokes the side of the trailer as if it was the present. Uncomfortable, I clear my throat. But she keeps on looking all around it, her hands caressing the side with loving care.

"Pim, that truck looks suspicious," I say pointedly.

"How?" she says, wide-eyed. "It's the one with all the Triumph gifts. There's nothing suspicious about that."

I shake my head. "It only *looks* like the one with the Triumph gifts. There's an unpleasant surprise inside."

"What do you mean?" Her brow furrows. She reaches out to touch the pink and purple decoration again.

"Trust me, Pim. I'm a Watcher. I know a suspicious vehicle when I see it."

She stares at me for a second, as if trying to read my thoughts. "What's wrong with it?"

I point to the undercarriage. "It's hiding something. Can you report it on your app?"

Her hand freezes on the side of the truck, and her eyes narrow suspiciously. "Why don't *you* do that?"

I roll my eyes and look exasperated. "Because Executive Lover Crucible is expecting me upstairs half an hour ago, and I don't have my infotab. You tell them and take the Love Points for it. Report the people who brought it as Haters."

Pim stands there, looking doubtfully at the truck. "But . . . I mean . . . the presents . . ."

I gently grasp her shoulders, turning her to face me. "Pim, I'm not sure how much I can say, but there is something hidden behind the first layer of presents. There's . . ." I drop my voice. "A *bomb on that truck.*" As I say the words, Pim's eyes widen, and her face pales.

She takes an involuntary step backward. "What the Love are you talking about?" she hisses.

"Wait Pim, listen." I reach out to stop her from going any further. "Hodge and I saw something, and we need as many people as possible to report this, but quietly before it's too late. All you have to do is go to your reporting app and put in a Hater report. The Squad will take care of the rest."

Pim stares at me for a second more, then turns sideways. Taking a deep breath, she opens her mouth, and gives a high-pitched scream.

"There's a *bomb!*" Her voice reverberates off the walls of the buildings. *"A bomb in the truck!"*

I have no time to regret the stupidity of my attempt before curious people emerge from nearby doorways. Soon we are surrounded by a small crowd. My stomach lurches, and shame heats my face.

She turns to me with an impish smile. "You wanted lots of people. You got 'em," she says with a wink, and melts away before I can stop her. I am left in the center of a circle of white and blue uniforms.

"What's going on here?" a man in a pristine white linen suit asks. He scowls at me.

"Uh," I stammer, suddenly at a complete loss for words.

"What's this about a bomb?" asks a woman beside him. "Are you making trouble?"

I shake my head violently. "No! I—"

"Did you scream just now?" another man demands.

"No, it wasn't me, I . . ."

The group all start throwing questions at me all at once, their words flying through the air like a hail of projectiles. With my hands out in front of me like a shield, I back away as they close in. My back thumps against the cold steel of the trailer door.

"This is Triumph day, Apprentice," says a small woman with black spiky hair. "Who do you think you are?"

Own it.

That pushes me forward. Stepping away from the truck, I square my shoulders. "That's Watcher Apprentice, to you." I do my best impression of haughty superiority, pointing at the accuser. "I would be careful about how you address me."

The effect is instantaneous. Gasps hiss out from the crowd. People shrink back. Fear enters their eyes. A dark, selfish part of me wants to feel triumphant right now. I push it away.

"I embrace myself in penitence, Watcher Apprentice," says the spiky-haired woman, bowing her head.

"We have no time," I say impatiently. "I need you all to—"

"She needs you all to go and enjoy a good Triumph," interrupts a deep voice from the shadows beside the truck. A hand closes around the back of my neck, and something hard and sharp digs in to my back. I cannot see what it is, but the voice brings a chill of fear. "Doesn't she?" The question is directed into my ear.

I try to shift my head sideways, but the hand on my neck keeps me staring out in front. A small prick of the object at my back leaves no room for interpretation. Wil leans past my shoulder, his face an easy smile, still disfigured by the fake chin and hair. "Smile for the crowd, Flick," he hisses through his teeth. "Or I'll give them a show they won't ever forget."

I shift slightly to move away from the knife blade, but he jabs it forward and angles my body so nobody can see what he is holding. The crowd around us continues to look confused and worried.

"Our Watcher Apprentice was just testing to see how well you responded to a crisis. You passed. Well done," Wil says loudly. I open my mouth, but receive such a hard squeeze to my neck as he continues, his voice soothing and calm. "So don't worry yourselves anymore. My Watcher friend here and I have some fun Triumph things to plan for you all. You can relax and go back to your jobs."

The spiky-haired woman looks from me to Wil, confused. Then she turns away. I try to let my eyes tell my story, to shout without words that this isn't supposed to happen, but one by one, the entire crowd shuffles back to the buildings around us. I stare desperately at the man who asked the first question.

The man looks away and gives a pathetic little grimace that looks almost apologetic. "Watcher business is not my business," he says and turns his back on us. My heart sinks.

Suspicious activities are supposed to be reported, not ignored. Why isn't anyone doing anything helpful?

"You expected something different?" Wil asks, his voice lacking its earlier charm.

"Nice to see you again, too," I reply with as much sarcasm as you can muster when someone has a knife at your back.

"I would ask you what you're doing here, but we don't have time for that." Wil pulls at my neck as he places more pressure on the knife. I wince. "Come on."

Holding me across the shoulders, he pushes me toward the tight gap beside the truck. I stumble along until we reach the door of the cab.

"Where's your friend?" I ask, stalling.

Wil keeps pushing me on to the front of the vehicle. "He was sensible and got out hours ago. I, on the other hand, worried that someone might try to mess with the truck. Which turned out to be good, because here you are."

With one hand still holding the knife to my back, Wil reaches around me to open the truck door.

"Get in," he says. I open my mouth to protest, but he shoves my shoulder. "Get in," he repeats harshly.

Trembling, I climb into the passenger seat of the truck, and he follows me in. I scoot across as far as I can go, fumbling for the other door to make an escape, but he is too fast for me. He leans across and grabs my wrist. Like a stunned Hater I fall silent, cowed into submission by his weight bearing down over me. He looks strange, wearing the black curly wig and with the prosthetics on his nose. Up this close, they look obviously fake.

"Is this your plot?" I ask him, trying to buy time.

His mouth twists. "I said we had to do something big, didn't I?"

"Blow up the VIP compound? You'll never get away with this," I tell him, although I don't really believe it. If he has insiders helping him, they just might succeed.

"Ah, Cadence, my little songbird," Wil mocks. "You know very little about the ways of the world. Whereas I—"

The words are out of my mouth before I can stop them. "Whereas you are also just an Elite Apprentice, who wants to play with the big kids." Immediately, I regret it.

With a warning glare, Wil places the knife on the dash, and leans over to the glove compartment. I try an experimental kick at his leg, but I might as well be kicking against a concrete wall. Wil pulls out a small bundle of cable ties.

"You had to go and ruin it, didn't you?" he says, sticking one of the ties in his teeth and slamming my wrists onto the hard steering wheel. "You had to show up here and stick your pretty little nose into everything." With one hand restraining my arms, he begins to tie my left wrist down on the steering wheel with the first cable tie.

"I protected you," I said, feeling a hot rush of anger fill me at the injustice of it all.

"I don't need protecting," he snaps.

"Crucible made me look for you," I protest, as I try to wiggle my hands out of his grasp. In response he just tightens his grip, sending a wave of pain up my arms.

"Well, he's never going to find me after today." Wil manages to get one of the ties around my left wrist, tethering it to one side of the wheel. With one less hand to work with, it's harder to resist his attempt to tie my other hand to the wheel as well. But I twist and turn as much as I can.

"Of course not," I huff. "We made it look like you were heading through the wall."

"Ha!" Wil snorts. "That's the best thing I've heard in weeks!"

"It wasn't for you." I stare furiously out the window. All of that hard work now seems completely useless. Wil's turned up in the middle of the most-watched event in the Collective calendar, when he should be laying low and getting out of town. "It was for the others."

"Well, I'm not sure why you're so worried, anyway. These guys are the ones who killed your parents. You should be thanking me for getting rid of the disease that is the Supreme Executive."

"But the rest of the people," I plead, thinking of the crowds milling around outside the VIP compound walls. "You're going to kill ordinary citizens."

"They're just as guilty," Wil says, failing again to grab hold of my right wrist. "Whatever the Collective did, those people just lapped it up and celebrated while the Executive murdered innocent people. They wouldn't even protect you. Why should you care what happens to them?"

MEMORY DATE: CE 2273.247, (EIGHT YEARS ago)

Memory location: Nursery Dorm 492

The Nursery Apprentices recline on white beanbags, staring up at the vision screen projected onto the wall. On the Haters' Pavilion Show, the woman bows low, brought down by a rain of blows from a Squad soldier. The crowd around me erupts in cheers.

PROMPTED BY THE MEMORY, A VOICE AS clear as crystal-pure water sings through my head, and I know the voice is not my own.

> Dear friends, love comes from the Composer
> So let us love like him.
> Lyric gave his life for ours to show
> The shape of love within
> And we should also live and love
> Like Lyric's sacrifice.
> Composer's children sing as one.
> From death brought back to life.

"But that's not Lyric's way," I remind him. "If you do this, then you're no different from the Collective."

"Predictable," he replies. "Stupid and predictable."

The effect of Wil's words on my anger is like kerosene on

the glittering embers of a fire. I become like a trapped animal, kicking and lashing out with everything I have.

"I won't be a part of this." I glare at him. "I won't let you hate people like this."

"A Hater? That's rich coming from you."

The truck's cabin isn't very big, but it's large enough for me to land a few choice shoves with my boot into Wil's leg. I'm not a Love Squad Apprentice, so my fight technique isn't pretty. But I'm trying with the last ounces of my might to get myself out of this.

"Idiot." With a violent lunge he wrenches my arm back down, pinching my wrist between his fingers. I let out a cry of pain, but he just twists my hand under the central bar of the steering wheel, tying the cable tie so firmly it immediately begins cutting off the circulation.

I bite back another cry of pain. "Someone will report you."

Wil takes the knife from the dash and points it at me. "No one cares, Cadence. That's the thing. What you don't realize is that as a Watcher, you aren't a person. You're a force they fear, like a wasp that won't stop buzzing around your head. They don't want you to be there, and they wish they could swat you away, but they know that if they make one wrong move, you could bring the squads down on them." He twirls the knife in his fingers. "So nobody will report you, because nobody wants Watchers. Especially not at Triumph time."

"So you're going to kill me?" I try to keep the desperation out of my voice. "I protected you, and this is what I get?"

Wil drops the knife back onto the dash. "You brought it on yourself. But don't worry too much." He leans back and taps the back wall of the cab. "With the explosive load this baby is carrying, the end will be quick."

"How are you going to do it?"

"That would be telling." He winks. "But if you must know,

let's just say that it won't be the effigy that gets the most attention tonight. The timer is set. The end is sure."

"The Composer will stop you."

Wil's bitter laugh startles me. "The Composer is a fairy tale told by people who should know better. The best thing the Love Collective ever did was outlaw that waste of an organization."

"But you—"

Wil smirks. "Oh, I played the part well, didn't I? Even that stupid Dorm Leader didn't catch on, and she's always made such a big deal of her expertise in this area." He touches the prosthesis on his nose and grins. "People should give me more credit. I'm a fantastic actor."

Furious, I strain against the cable ties. "You're . . . you're . . ."

"You're welcome," Wil says. His smile is infuriatingly smug, and I am about to make an angry retort when the door behind him is reefed open. Two thick hands grab Wil by his shoulders and drag him out of the cab. There are sounds of a struggle, and Hodge's determined face appears in the doorway. I'm hit by relief so overwhelming my eyes tear up.

"Sorry I'm late," he says as he jumps into the cab. He looks at the cable ties, and his jaw twitches.

"Just a moment." He gets back out of the cab.

Soon he returns, backing into the cab with an unconscious Wil. With expert hands, he ties Wil's wrists together with more of the cable ties, then straps him into the passenger seat. Hodge squeezes himself into the middle space.

"We need to go," he says. "Crucible was so drunk he didn't hear a word of what I was trying to say. So we're going to have to get it out of here ourselves."

"Can you drive?"

"You don't get to the final year of Squad training without knowing how to drive a truck," he says. "But you're in the way."

"Not my choice," I say with a weak smile.

He takes Wil's knife, and gently cuts away the plastic on

the looser tie. When he sees the tie that's currently turning my hand blue, he grimaces. "I'm sorry. This might hurt."

"Just get it off." I turn my head to look out the window.

I feel a sharp line of pain when the plastic tie digs into my wrist again, then there's a click and the pressure falls away. A thin red indentation marks the place where the tie had been, but there's no blood.

"Thank you," I say with relief, massaging my wrists.

After a small adjustment of our position in the cab, I'm now between him and Wil, balancing precariously in the space between the two truck seats. Hodge places both his hands on the steering wheel, and searches around the dash.

I'm worried by his confusion. "What are you looking for?"

"The start button."

"You said you knew how to drive a truck!"

My anxiety grows as Hodge's expression tinges with red. "Well . . . we trained in VR."

"Oh, Lyric save us," I sigh, dropping my head forward.

Just then, Hodge makes a little noise of victory. With a quick turn of his wrist, he cranks the key in the ignition, and the truck thunders into life.

"Hang on," Hodge tells me, switching into reverse. "We'll head for the east gate. This might get interesting."

31

See what love the Composer has poured out on us.

AS WE HURTLE OUT OF THE VIP COMPOUND, startled Squad officers dive for the edge of the road. Hodge makes the most of our surprise appearance. He stomps on the accelerator, and the truck roars through the boom gates at the first checkpoint, splintering the aluminum barrier and sending more guards rushing for safety. But the second checkpoint isn't quite as easy. Guards swarm forward into a line across the road. They aim their dissuasion cannons at us, and a hail of smoke clouds billows in front of the windscreen, temporarily blinding us.

"We're not going to make it," I yell through clamped teeth.

Hodge's jaw sets firmly, and he leans forward, aiming the truck at the place where the boom gates were last in view. Then he yanks the radio handset off the ceiling of the truck and puts in a call to the box.

"Checkpoint Sigma, this is Squad officer #452/08418. We have an incendiary device onboard. Attempting to remove it to a safe location. Enact bomb safety protocol Echo Bravo Delta. Over."

The radio crackles back. "Copy that, Squad officer #452/08418. We need you to stop for inspection at the checkpoint. Over."

"Negative, Checkpoint Sigma," Hodge says. "Incendiary device is timed to go off in 030 minutes. We need to remove the vehicle to a safe perimeter before it explodes. Over."

"Thirty minutes?" I yelp. "That's not enough time!"

Hodge leans sideways, his eyes still fixed on the cloud of smoke obscuring our view. "I just made that up. If we stop, the traitors on the inside will get to us."

"Oh." I reply, feeling a sick, nervous fluttering in my chest. An hour ago I was a Watcher. Now I'm . . . well, out of all of the ways I can imagine this playing out, I can't imagine a single one that keeps me safe. Or not dead.

"Squad officer #452/08418," the radio voice sounds firm. "Negative on the drive-through. Stop at checkpoint for investigation. Over."

"Roger that, Checkpoint Sigma," Hodge replies. "Over." He replaces the handset and grips the steering wheel with whitened knuckles.

"They're going to arrest us." I fail to keep a note of panic out of my voice. "What are we going to do?"

Hodge grimaces. "Pray for a miracle." He shifts down a gear, and the truck engine whines and slows.

Doubt floods my thoughts. How could this be happening? This was supposed to be easy. But right now, we're hurtling toward a hostile Squad, which makes perfect sense when you think about it. A rogue truck, breaking down barriers and screaming through the middle of Triumph festival is not exactly going to get a warm welcome. As if they're going to roll out the VIP carpet and say, "Of course! Run right through the middle of us!"

"You said you were going before us, Composer," I mutter under my breath. Now would be a good time!

The truck continues to rumble on, and the cloud of smoke clears enough to reveal shadowy figures scurrying about at the next checkpoint. A line of soldiers is still stationed across the gate, but some have moved to the side of the road. Their weapons are levelled at us. I shut my eyes tightly and begin singing in my head with all my might.

The radio crackles again. "Squad officer #452/08418, we're picking up some pretty unusual readings on that vehicle. Did you say it was an incendiary device? Over?"

We're only a hundred yards away from the gate now. "Affirmative, Checkpoint Sigma. There are some heavy booby traps on the undercarriage, so defusing not an option. We need to get away from Triumph grounds and into a safe blast zone. Over."

"Any signs of remote detonation? Over."

"Negative. Best option is to remove it to a safe perimeter. Over."

"Roger that. Clearing a path for you now. Go well. Over."

I open one eye and squint at the checkpoint in front. The line of soldiers disintegrates as one by one they run to the sides of the road. Disbelieving, I watch the boom gate rise. Behind us is the Triumph festival. Ahead is the open highway that leads right through Love City.

Without a word, Hodge kicks the truck into gear, and we lurch forward.

"Ha!" I am disbelieving and yet gleeful at the open road before us.

"You sound surprised," Hodge remarks.

"We already had one impossible thing happen today, and I thought maybe there was a limit. You know . . ."

"Yeah, I know," he says, as we speed down empty lanes, surprisingly free.

THE SQUAD CALLS IN AN ESCORT, AND before long, a line of vehicles forms a parade heading west along the highway. It would probably draw more attention if the vast majority of the population weren't already at the Triumph festival. Instead, we form an eerie, ghostlike procession: the doomed and those who came to witness on a last-ditch quest to remove the truck from harm's way.

The late-afternoon sun descends slowly in the sky as we drive. Hodge's eyes are fixed on the road, fingers clamped around the wheel. My thoughts churn. I have to keep fighting the urge to leap from the moving truck.

In the rearview mirrors beside the doors, I get a good look at the flashing lights where a wall of Love Squad vehicles fans out behind us. They're a long way back, no doubt to keep them a safe distance from any explosions. My anxious feelings escalate, threatening to send me into full-blown panic. Then an unbidden memory blinks in my mind like a light being switched on.

MEMORY LOCATION: SECRET BUNKER
"Nothing the Collective can throw at us will separate us from the Composer, Cadence," Akela says softly. "Not even death."

NOT EVEN DEATH... A STRANGE, UNNATURAL peace settles over me. Akela's words scatter my anxious flutterings the way a gust of wind scatters fallen leaves from the path. Our situation is complicated, but we're not hopeless.

We're on the outskirts of the city when Wil moans. His wrists are tied, and the seatbelt is across his chest as an added restraint, but I still freak out when he begins to stir.

"Hodge," I whisper urgently.

Hodge just makes a grunting noise and continues to keep focused on the broad line of concrete that stretches out before us.

"Hodge." I lean closer to his ear this time. "What are we going to do?"

Hodge's voice is a low rumble over the truck's high-pitched whine. "It'll be okay," is all he says. "The Composer is orchestrating."

So I keep my anxious thoughts to myself and start casting side-eye glances at Wil. After another groan, his head begins move from side to side. He raises his head, and his eyelids slowly open. He stares around for a second, squinting. Then his eyes suddenly widen in panic.

"What the—?" His whole body jolts upright. "You put me in here? What in Love's name were you thinking?"

He writhes around, scratching at the passenger door with his bound hands. For a split second I just watch him. This could solve our problem. Speeding along the highway, the truck's cab is so high up that Wil could easily . . .

Save him.

The words aren't mine, and I immediately react with anger. Why should I? Wil wants to kill us all. His continued existence is a constant burden on the safety of Sirens.

I haven't finished with him yet.

The Muse's soft music washes away the rough edges of my fury.

I am the Healer of songs, it sings. *Trust in me.*

I pull Wil away from the door. He elbows me in the face. It

is only by the Composer's strength that I don't shove him out of the cab then and there. The two of us become a struggling, scrambling mass as Wil tries to get rid of me and I try to prevent him from throwing himself to his death. My selfishness keeps telling me to let him go, but I can't ignore the Muse.

"Stop it!" I grab at Wil's wrists.

Wil keeps on trying to get his hands around the door handle. "Better than being here. You guys are insane."

"What are you going to do? Did you sprout wings?"

Wil hesitates and looks at the rectangular mirror beside the window—and gets a glimpse of the entourage following us. His whole body goes still, then he slumps back into his seat with a sullen sigh.

"You're ruining everything," he mutters.

"Well, while you're here, you can tell us how much time we have before it blows up." Hodge has kept on calmly staring at the road during all this. I don't know how he does it.

Wil, on the other hand, looks more than agitated. "What does it matter?" He fidgets, his fingers trying in vain to get to the cable tie holding his wrists together. "It's not like any of us are going to survive anyway."

Silence settles over the cabin. The sun is continuing its descent toward the horizon, and it peeks below the sun shades on the windscreen, causing bright light to burn into my eyes. Hodge is taller, so it's not yet affecting him, but on this straight line westwards, it's only a matter of time.

I raise a hand above my face to shield the light. "We can't have much time, Hodge. They set fire to the Haterman at dusk."

Wil snorts in derision. "If you guys hadn't turned up, we wouldn't be having this conversation."

"The Composer knew what you were planning," I say boldly. "He wasn't going to let you ruin your life."

Wil scoffs. "The Collective is evil, and you know it. How can you just sit there and do nothing?"

"Lyric's way isn't violence."

Wil bangs his fists in frustration. "Right. They abduct us. They kill us. They imprison us and turn our brains to mush. The only language they understand is violence. We were going to cut off the head, so the rest of the body could regenerate."

Hodge darts a glance at him. "Not the greatest analogy," he remarks dryly.

I sit forward, blocking the space between the two. "The problem isn't the head, it's the heart, Wil. You don't change anything by becoming exactly like them."

"But the Supreme Executive—"

"The people don't need another Supreme Executive, Wil. They need a new song." Wil gives an exaggerated groan and turns his face away. I figure our conversation is over.

We pass another exit ramp and a few more signs telling us about locations I don't know: Love Meadows, Executive Heights, Lake Midgate, and others. A weird, distracting thought hits me: with time running out, I am going to die without having seen even a tenth of the nation I supposedly live in. It's no big deal compared to singing with the Composer. But it still would have been nice to see at least some of my homeland in person. The Collective is a big place.

"Are we just going to drive until we explode?" Wil snaps, his agitation building again.

"I think I have an idea," Hodge says, turning the truck toward the next highway exit. "Hold on."

The truck drops back a gear and chugs up the ramp, curving away from the asphalt river into a tree-lined road. A road sign we pass says, Lake Midgate, 2 Mi. The line of flashing lights follows us up the hill.

The radio crackles. "Squad officer #452/08418, state your purpose, over."

"Attempting a ditch maneuver," Hodge replies evenly.

"Incendiary device timed for lighting ceremony. We have to get it in place before sundown. Over."

"Copy that. Calling in aerial support. Over."

"Aerial support. But what about—?" I bite my lip and point at Wil.

"There's a slow spot as we go in to the park," Hodge explains. "I've seen it on a VR exercise. We make a left 100 degree turn, which gives us a quick window where the pursuit won't be able to see the passenger side. When I slow, Wil, you need to jump into the bushes for cover. The Squad's view will be blocked by the truck just long enough for you to get away."

"You're just going to let me go?" Wil asks incredulously.

"This has nothing to do with whether you deserve to be let free, because you don't." Hodge says crisply. "But Lyric's love saved us when we didn't deserve it. He wants us to love others the way he loved us. So I'm letting you go."

"Despite this." Wil nods over his shoulder at the trailer behind us.

Hodge casts a quick glance at him. "Wil, you haven't killed anyone yet, and today we are going to take the consequences for you. You aren't a murderer," he adds.

Wil fidgets again.

"You need to get to the Exodus, though," I tell him. "You can't stay in the Collective."

"Oh, I won't. If the guys I worked with found me, I'd be dead." The green eyes are staring down at his hands. I notice they're trembling.

"We're nearly here," Hodge declares. The tree-lined road curves away to the right, slowly climbing into the mountains. On the left, a large timber sign announces in flaking paint, LAKE MIDGATE: THE HAPPIEST SPLASH IN THE COLLECTIVE. The sign is large and surrounded by hedges that obviously haven't been trimmed for a long time.

"Looks like nobody's been here for years," I say.

"Nature can't compete with app goggles," Wil replies bitterly.

"Okay. Get ready to drop," Hodge says, slowing the truck down at the turnoff. "Your target is that sign. Lay low until we're gone, then make a run for the border."

Wil nods wordlessly. He gestures at the clock. "You've got eight minutes," he says. "Sorry I didn't tell you earlier."

"What?!" I yelp, jumping in my seat.

Hodge, ever the cool-headed soldier, just utters something that sounds like, "Huh."

"Sorry." Wil looks genuinely apologetic. Not that it does anything for our situation.

My hands are clammy, and it takes precious seconds to unlatch Wil's seatbelt. He makes a grab for the door.

"Are you going to get me out of this?" he asks, holding up his cable-tied hands.

"No time." I give him a little shove. I confess that I might have put more force into it than necessary. But with seven minutes left before an enormous bomb goes off, who can blame me for being a little tense?

The truck chugs around the corner, and the sign rolls into view beside the passenger door. Tall hedges form a high screen around the edge of the sandstone face. In the stone, weathered and stained lettering announces the Lake Midgate Picnic Grounds. Hodge was right. It's a perfect hiding place, as long as Wil can reach it.

Wil tenses, then releases the door handle. The truck slows while Hodge makes a pretense of accidentally grinding the gears. Suddenly, Wil leaps from the cab and disappears. As I slide into the passenger seat, I can spot his brown-shirted back duck under the bushes surrounding the sign. Then Hodge accelerates, and we are heading down the road deeper into the park.

32

> Sing for joy, children sing,
> Lyric's country is our home.
> You are known, chosen, loved,
> With the Composer as your King.

ANXIETY FLOODS MY SYSTEM, AND IT becomes harder and harder to sit still as we drive. I alternate between watching the seconds tick away on the clock and looking out the window. My legs jiggle nervously.

"We haven't got much time."

"It'll work out fine, Cadence."

Trees close in around us, shielding our view of the setting sun. Long, dark shadows stretch out on the ground, their black voids interspersed with the soft glow of late-afternoon light. Hodge careens down the narrow drive for what seems like hours instead of minutes, heading for I-don't-know-where. But I get a vague idea when we pass between two small huts and a vista opens out in front of us.

We drive into a semicircle of grass, where picnic tables and amenities blocks punctuate the space. Beyond the picnic area is a large, glassy lake that reflects the dimming golden rays of the sun. In the distance, a small pontoon wharf juts out into the middle of the water. Straight ahead, a concrete boat ramp leads down to the still, dark lake.

"Is that where we're going?" I ask, a little bewildered.

"Not the ramp," Hodge replies. "And"—he darts a glance at me—"you're going to have to jump in a second."

My heart skips. "What about you?"

"I'll be fine." Hodge's face is grimly determined. "I just need to get some height."

He slows the truck briefly, and I check the clock again. If Wil told the truth, there's less than two minutes left.

"Get out. Now," Hodge commands.

I grab the handle, but then hesitate. Panic seizes me again. "You're not going to go down with the truck, are you?"

The smile crinkles the scar on the side of his face as he looks at me. "I know what I'm doing, Cadence," he says gently. "But you need to move, or I won't have time."

I reluctantly push open the door and jump. I stumble as I land and Hodge accelerates away. I lie on the ground for a second, winded. But only for a second. Hurrying to my feet, I scurry behind a nearby amenities building. Then I watch the pink and purple truck as it screams around the side of the lake.

The truck makes a wide arc, then spins to face the wharf, swaying dangerously. The passenger door yawns open, waving wildly with the motion of the vehicle. Hodge aims it along the short wharf, and the truck hurtles along the timber. The burst of speed is short and sharp, and as it reaches the end it hits something that sends it upward in a low, heavy arc, and it plummets trailer-first into the cold, black water. When the cab hits the waves, the whole thing tilts sideways. For a few seconds it seems to float, then the water reaches a critical height, and the entire thing disappears below the waves.

A sudden thump vibrates through my bones. The water of the lake rises into a majestic white dome, and then a towering column of water explodes upward out of the center. A large cloud of white water and grey smoke radiates out from the base of the foamy white column. I turn and run as fast as I can. Every bird for hundreds of miles—or at least it sounds like that—start to caw and cry and squawk. Waves of black feathers dart up into the open air.

I risk a look over my shoulder and instantly wish I hadn't. A circular wave rolls out from the epicenter, cresting over the edge of the lake and sloshing around the picnic tables with a fizzing roar. My mind empties of all coherent thought, and I sprint past trees back at the lake. I nearly collide with a Squad car that has just arrived. The line of cars screeches to a halt. I wait, uncertain about my forward path, water lapping at my ankles. Pelting fragments of trailer clink down into the wave like metallic rain. The air smells of water and something scorched.

With a burst of agility I never knew I had, I leap up onto the hood of the Squad car, ignoring the surprised expressions on the faces of the officers inside. Waves slosh around the wheels of the car, making it lurch and sway. I watch the water swirl and eddy, then it recedes. Only when I can see the sodden grass do I risk getting back down.

"Hey!" shouts one of the squad members as I slide off the car's roof. Ignoring him, I head around the curve of the lake toward the wharf, running as hard as I can. Misty water vapor clouds the air. I dart through the grass, frantically screaming Hodge's name at the top of my lungs. The inky darkness of the lake is slowly rocking itself to sleep, until only gentle undulations flow out from the truck's final resting place.

"Hodge? Hodge!" There's no answer.

Desperation grows. I strain my eyes to see through the deepening darkness, so intent on it that I nearly run into a picnic bench. Swerving at the last second, I dash around, ignoring the scratchy sting of grazes and cuts.

"Hodge!" My voice breaks.

Car doors open and close somewhere behind me. Men

bark orders and others respond. I'm only dimly aware of their presence. My one and only desire is to find Hodge and find him alive.

"Hodge!" I scream again as the tears begin to flow. "Hodge!" I wish that somehow my eyes were night vision goggles.

Running until my legs feel like jelly, I reach the side of the lake where the wharf used to be. Half of the timber structure is gone, splintered into a thousand fragments. My feet give out on me then. Chest heaving for air, I pant and lean on my knees for support, bent double and unable to go on.

"Hodge!" I gasp, fighting to gain air. "I . . . need . . ."

In a flash, my mind unhelpfully begins to overlay memories with an imagined future. Hodge in the Sirens meeting, replaced with an empty seat where he was. Hodge smiling at me when I walk into the room, replaced with a space where his smile used to be. Hodge and I on missions for Akela, replaced with me alone.

"Hodge!" I sob.

I stumble to the water's edge, watching the night swallow the lake. Light-bellied fish float lifeless on the edge of the waves, bobbing up and down on the same water that ended their lives moments ago. He's not here. But if dead fish are here, then maybe he wasn't in the water. Which means . . .

I clamber to my feet and stagger to the line of trees ringing the picnic area. Twilight has fallen, and the shadows have become deep pools of darkness. I walk slowly into the forest, listening for the smallest sound. That's when I hear the faint call.

My heart soars. I bound in that direction, and lying against the base of a tree, one leg twisted in an unnatural kink, is Hodge. I nearly hurl myself at him, but stop myself at the last second as I remember his leg. It's a good thing too. When I get a look at his face, pain is etched so clearly that even the near darkness can't hide it.

"Oh, Hodge . . ." The tears come anew. I collapse on my knees beside him. "Are you all right?"

"Nearly wasn't." He tries to smile. "Broke my leg when I jumped. The wave dumped me here."

"I should go get help." I jump up quickly but can't keep the idiotic delight from showing on my face.

Hodge does smile then as his eyes meet mine. We look at each other until he winces.

"Wait here. Oh, sorry. Of course you can't—I mean, I'll be right back," I assure him.

I am scratched, bruised, wet, and exhausted. But as I head to the Love Squad vehicles, I am suddenly lighter than air.

WITHIN AN HOUR, A HELICOPTER ARRIVES bearing equipment, and a perimeter of lights and evidence tents are set up. Investigators and soldiers bustle around the park, metal detectors, torches, and large bags in hand. Hodge lies on a stretcher, his leg now set and the pain on his face now evaporated, thanks to the ministrations of medics. Catching sight of me, his face breaks into a goofy grin.

"You look dirty," he says, pointing at my face. I rub at my cheeks with my thumb, and muddy streaks come away. He gives a very uncharacteristic giggle.

"At least I'm in charge of my wits," I say as heat warms my cheeks. "You sound like a three-year-old."

A distant rumble turns out to be another huge black helicopter. It lands in the center of the field, much to the disgust of the Squad's commanding officer, and a series of glittering bodies steps out in hazy, wobbling fashion. I spot Executive Lover Munsch, his arm thrown heavily over the shoulder of a skeletally thin woman in a teensy gold dress. Executive Lover

Crucible emerges behind them, his linen uniform now replaced with a shining, electric-blue suit. Most of them are carrying glasses of champagne, as if they've stepped straight from the VIP party to this random, distant lake nobody ever visits.

"My dear child, you have saved us!" Crucible announces when he sees me.

Munsch totters over. "As soon as I heard what was going on, I said to Gordy that we simply must get over there right now and see what's what. Those little Haters have very nearly wiped us out."

"Who is responsible for this?" Crucible barks.

"Wil's mates." Hodge's inhibitions are gone under the pain relief. I want to clamp my hands over his mouth and stop him from talking, but the words are out in the air now.

"The little brown-clothed pudgy man. Yes. We got him," Crucible says. And that seems to be that.

I look at Executive Lover Crucible and realize how small he looks. In his Triumph costume, he's lost that imposing appearance that always had me fearful. Now he just looks like a frail old man.

He turns to me. "You did well." His voice carries a note of surprise.

"Thank you, Executive Lover, but—"

He waves my words away. "Just ask and it's yours. The finest steak, glittering jewels? Nothing is too much for the ones who saved Triumph."

I look down, keeping my face carefully still. I hadn't anticipated the question, but suddenly the answer flows out of my mouth as if I had been expecting it for months. "Executive Lover, if it is permissible with you, I'd like to switch cadres."

I look up. Crucible's face twists. "That's no fun. Ask me for a hamburger."

"I'm sorry to disappoint you, Executive Lover, but I just

think I can do better in the Coders' cadre. My one wish is to be a Coder."

"But my dear, by this action you show us that you are precisely the right person to be a Watcher." Crucible gestures at the wreckage. "You have shown the utmost loyalty to the Collective, the most supreme bravery, the most outstanding evidence of a cool head in a crisis. It would be criminal to have you anywhere else than in the Watchers."

I stand a little straighter, pushing my head high, and staring at a point somewhere past Crucible's shoulder. "Executive Lover, sir, you said you would give me anything. That is what I request."

"You'll lose your cushy apartment." He looks sulky.

"I understand that, sir."

"You'll have to go back to that old dorm room with all of those people."

"Yes, sir."

"And you have to go back to wearing the same uniform as everyone else."

"Yes, sir."

I don't say anything else. After all, what member of the Supreme Executive would want to hear that I felt sick every time that red circle hovered over someone's face? Or that after all these months, I would still rather poke my eye out with a spoon than willingly step into that Watcher booth? They want me to be a mindless loyalty machine, not a broken, guilt-ridden Apprentice who vividly remembers the faces of each and every person who's been reported at my hand.

I will never forget those people, no matter how hard I try. Until the day I die, I will carry those faces with me, and they will always haunt me. I know the Composer has healed my song, but I still feel as if their blood is on my hands.

Crucible is frowning at me in a petulant kind of anger, then his expression transforms into resignation. "Fine." He waves his hand at me dismissively. "You shall have your wish, Apprentice. But don't think that I am happy about it." He points at me. "Do you hear me?"

"I hear you, Executive Lover." It takes a bit of effort to stop myself from grinning.

MY NAME IS KERR FLICK, ELITE APPRENTICE and former Watcher. No longer the Elite of the Elite, I am now descending to the level of ordinary. I have failed the goal I set for myself when I began here. But I have discovered that failing doesn't really mean the end. Because I'm also a Siren. And Sirens know that the end is really just the best beginning of them all.

APPENDIX: CHARACTER LIST

LOVE COLLECTIVE SUPREME EXECUTIVE

SUPREME LOVER MIDGATE—the leader of the Love Collective government.

EXECUTIVE LOVER CRUCIBLE—member of the Supreme Executive. His responsibility is to oversee the Love Collective's Education system.

EXECUTIVE LOVER MUNSCH—Executive Lover in charge of the Triumph celebrations.

EXECUTIVE LOVER WORTHING—Executive Lover in charge of Propaganda.

Executive Lover Fareyn—Executive Lover in charge of the Security Sub Commissariat.

ELITE ACADEMY SIRENS

AKELA—Dorm Leader of Elite Academy and secret Siren leader. Codename: Zed.

ALLEGRA—an Elite Apprentice. Part of the underground Siren group that meets in the secret bunker.

FIFE—Elite Apprentice. Member of Siren group at Elite Academy.

VIOLA—student leader of underground Siren group at Elite Academy. Final year Apprentice in the Coding cadre.

HODGE—Cadence's former bunk room leader and another leader of the underground Siren group at Elite Academy. Third-year Apprentice in the Love Squad cadre. Hodge's Siren codename is Harper.

LOA—former Elite Academy roommate of Cadence. A second-year Apprentice in the Love Squad cadre. Siren codename is Bell.

PICCOLO—Elite Apprentice. Member of the secret Siren group that meets at Elite Academy.

WIL—member of the underground Sirens, his codename is X. Also an Apprentice Watcher who shares a dorm with Cadence.

YIP—Cadence's former dorm roommate. A second-year Apprentice in the Love Squad cadre.

ELITE ACADEMY PERSONNEL

LOVER FUSCHIOUS—instructor in the Love Squad cadre. Specialty is physical fitness and drill discipline.

LOVER KALIS—one of Cadence's former instructors. Specialty is Elite Axioms.

ELITE ACADEMY APPRENTICES

SIF—Cadence's former best friend. Despite once wanting to be in the Pleasure Tribe, she now trains in the Love Squad cadre.

CAM—Cadence's friend and former dorm roommate. Now training in the Coders cadre.

CHU—Cadence's friend and former dorm roommate. Has never gotten over his illegal relationship with Sif. Training to be a Coder with Cam.

DONA—former dorm roommate of Cadence. Now training in the Love Squad cadre.

FARR—former dorm roommate of Cadence. Now training in the Pleasure Tribe cadre.

LEE—Cadence's friend and former dorm roommate. Now in the Engine Room cadre.

ROOK AND ARAH—twins. Former dorm roommates of Cadence. Now in the Pleasure Tribe cadre.

PIM—Cadence's friend and former dorm roommate. Now training in the Engine Room cadre.

ZIN—Former dorm roommate of Cadence. Now training in the Love Squad cadre with Sif.

LOVE CITY SIRENS

MELODY—works as a cleaner in a Love City hotel. Part of Danse's Siren crew.

DANSE—leader of a Siren group in Love City.

HALL OF LOVE PERSONNEL

CZARA FLUXX—Chief Lover in the Security Sub Commissariat.

HARO ZEE—Lover working in the Security Sub Commissariat.

ACKNOWLEDGMENTS

When I began writing this book, I had no idea the kind of year we were all going to have. But I am grateful for the kindness of Steve, Lisa, Jordan, and Trissina, who were so understanding when my world flipped upside down and deadlines sailed unhappily by. This book ended up being written in many different places: Christian campsites surrounded by young adults, hospital car parks, waiting rooms, and multiple houses that weren't my own. It is only by God's grace that this made it to the end, and for that I am so, so thankful.

When I dedicated *Apprentice* to my mother, I had no idea that she wouldn't be around to see the birth of the next one. But I'm so glad she got to see how important she was to me before she went to be with her Heavenly Father. I will always miss her. Her keen eye for detail and story holes is one I have greatly appreciated over the years, as well as her cheerleading when everything else seemed hopeless. Her single-minded love for Jesus was a witness to many. For Dad, who's been a rock through this tumultuous time, I am grateful. We don't know what the future holds for us as a family, but we know we aren't alone in the middle of it.

To my family, my husband and children, I love you so, so much. To my friends and critique partners, who keep me going when I think I've written the worst things ever, thanks. For Laura, Cecily and Christine, for your inspiration when I hit a dead end was a life saver. To Lindsay, whose eagle eyes caught so many corrections in my manuscript, and who made me laugh during the edit process, I am glad you felt the same way about that character as I did. For Iola, who once again helped me to pull my socks up and make the story as good as it could be. And to Megan, who was there with God's encouragement in the darkest night, you will always be my bestie.

ABOUT THE AUTHOR

Kristen is an Australian author, who also ministers to young people as a lecturer and pastoral worker with a Christian gap year program. Although she loves those days when she gets to dream of faraway worlds and put them into writing, she feels blessed to be able to share the good news of Jesus in her everyday work.

THE LOVE COLLECTIVE IS EVERYWHERE.
IT SEES EVERYTHING.
BE NOT AFRAID.

THE COLLECTIVE UNDERGROUND SERIES

Apprentice

Elite

Flight

Available Now!

www.enclavepublishing.com

PGIL2023USA